HOLLOW POINT

THE HOLLY LIN SERIES

HOLLOW POINT

A HOLLY LIN NOVEL

ROBERT SWARTWOOD

RMS PRESS

ISBN-13: 978-1945819124
ISBN-10: 194581912X

www.robertswartwood.com

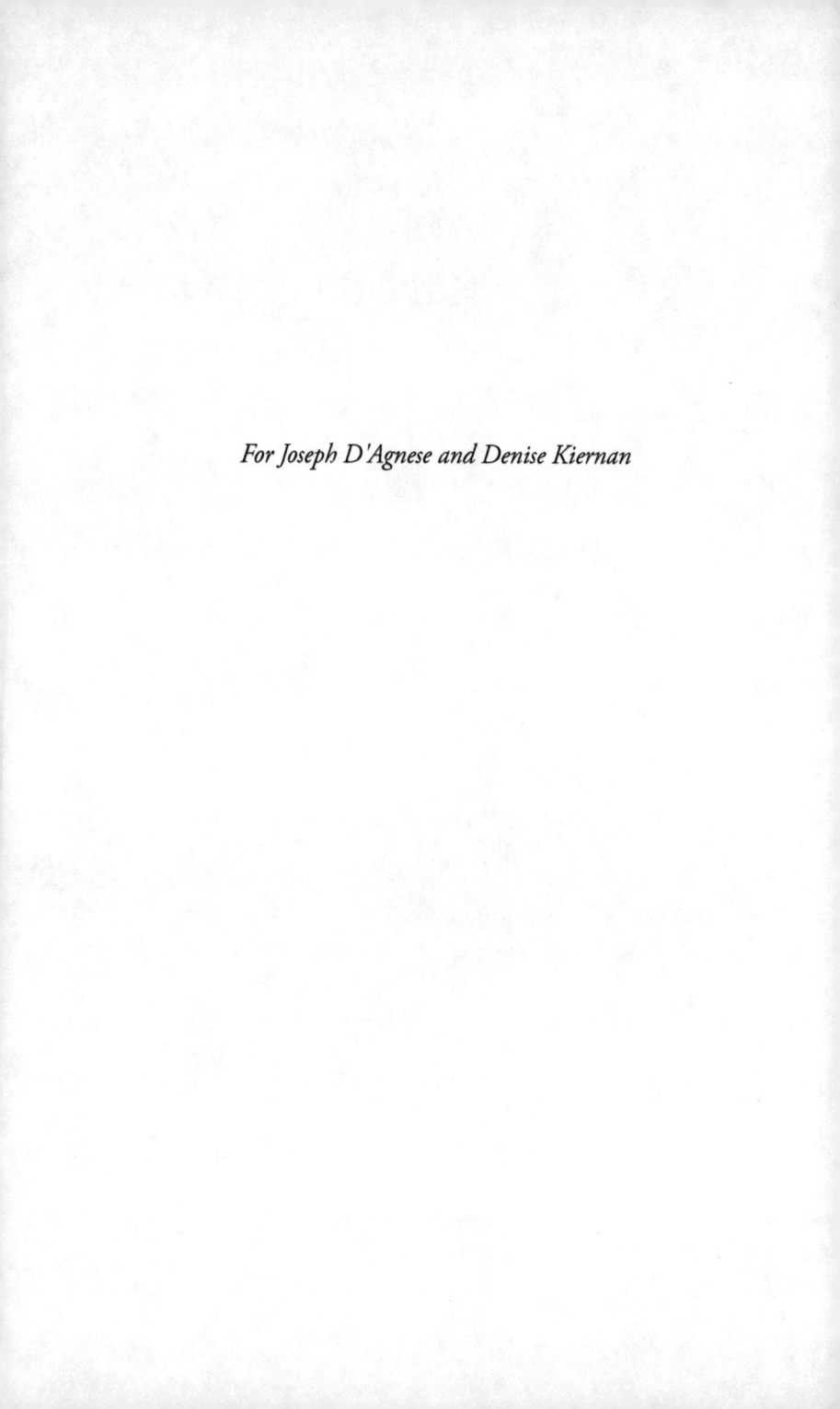

For Joseph D'Agnese and Denise Kiernan

PART I

LITTLE ANGELS

ONE

The girl is covered in blood.

That's the first thing I notice. This section of town is dark and quiet as it typically is at three o'clock in the morning. The only light streams from a few scattered streetlamps posted along the block, and as the girl passes beneath the closest one, the blood stands out even more, a sharp contrast against her light brown skin.

She barely looks sixteen, just a kid, and she wears shorts and a T-shirt and carries a duffel bag, but it's the blood that I focus on, the blood streaking her face and arms and soaking her hair and clothes.

"Please, help me, please."

She mumbles it in Spanish, her words barely intelligible, and now that she's nearly ten feet away from me, it's clear that she's limping. She's favoring her left leg, barely putting any pressure on it, and now she's less than five feet away and I can smell her, the blood, yes, but also the defecation. The girl has either pissed herself or shit herself or both, and she moves closer, still mumbling—"Please, please, help"—and she thrusts the duffel bag into my arms and then promptly falls to the ground.

Five seconds.

That's the length of time that's passed since I first heard the girl call out and turned and saw the blood.

Five seconds isn't much in the larger scheme of things, but five seconds can sometimes be an eternity. In my past life, five seconds might be a question of life and death. Countries are saved or lost in five seconds.

I haven't moved a muscle in the past five seconds, which is odd, because not too long ago I was very quick on my feet. I didn't spend too much time deliberating on different outcomes. I just made a choice and went with it and hoped for the best.

But things have changed, and I'm no longer the person I used to be. That person is long gone, dead and buried, and the person I am now—a bartender, having just closed up the bar and now headed home—doesn't deal with blood and guns and killing. For this new me, the most important thing that happens in five seconds is listening to a drink order amid loud country music and a chorus of uproarious voices and hoping I haven't fucked it up when I bring it back to the customer.

The girl's on her knees now, still mumbling in Spanish, and I take a quick moment to scan the block. It's deserted. Of course it's deserted—this area of town is usually empty during the day, the buildings long since vacated once their companies went out of business, and not once in the past year after I'd left the bar and walked home had I ever seen anybody on this block, let alone a girl covered in blood.

I realize I'm still holding the duffel bag. It was shoved into my arms so suddenly that I'd held on without much thought. Now I heft it—feels like it weighs fifteen pounds—and glance down at the girl.

"What happened? Who did this to you?"

It doesn't hit me until a second later that I asked those

questions in English, so I ask them again in Spanish, and the girl looks up at me, tears in her eyes, her voice a strangled whisper.

"Help me."

Before I can say or do anything else, the girl jumps to her feet. She pushes past me as she hurries down the block, still favoring her left leg.

The duffel bag in my arms, I turn and watch her, incredulous.

"Wait!"

She doesn't. She keeps going, faster now, and disappears into an alleyway.

I hurry after her, the thought of dropping the duffel bag not once crossing my mind, and I reach the mouth of the alleyway in time to see the girl has already made it to the other end. How she's managed to get there so fast, especially with the limp, I'm not sure, but she stands there, her back to me, looking up and down the street.

I call after her again as I chase her up the alleyway, and I'm halfway there when the girl suddenly bolts into the street—just as the front of a car slams into her and sends her flying.

TWO

The car screeches to a halt. The doors open, and two men step out. They aren't frantic like you'd expect men who just hit a girl with their car would be. Instead, they appear calm, looking up and down the street at the dark warehouses, quietly closing their doors, slowly circling to the front of the car to check on the girl.

Both of the men look to be in their late-thirties, early-forties. They wear jeans and cowboy boots. One of them has on a white short-sleeved button-down shirt tucked into his jeans, the other a blue polo. The one with the button-down shirt also wears a cowboy hat. He's the driver. He adjusts the hat as he gazes down at the girl's body.

"Well shit, there she is."

The other man says, "Yep."

"She's still alive."

"Barely."

"She doesn't have the bag, though."

"Nope."

The man with the cowboy hat crouches down beside the girl.

"Hey."

When the girl doesn't answer—she lays sprawled on the macadam, a broken mess, even more bloodied than before— the man with the cowboy hat snaps his fingers in front of her face.

"Bitch, you hear me?"

The girl still doesn't answer. Even if she wanted to, it doesn't look like she can. A hoarse wheezing comes from her mouth. Several of her ribs probably shattered on impact. Some of them probably pierced her lungs.

I'm standing around the corner of the alleyway, still holding the duffel bag, leaning out just far enough to watch these two men and the girl. My first instinct was to rush out immediately, but once those men had unhurriedly stepped out of the car, a red warning light started flashing in my head.

That red warning light starts pulsing faster when the driver walks back to the car—a piece of silver glinting on his belt— and opens his door and pulls out a black nine-millimeter.

Guns aren't rare here in Texas. Alden is a small town compared to most, maybe only a thousand residents, and almost everybody carries a gun with them wherever they go.

But very few carry suppressors.

Which this man also brings out, casually screwing it onto the barrel of his gun as he returns to the front of the car.

This entire time—maybe a minute—I've been quiet, watching the two men. This section of Alden is deserted at this time of night. People refer to it as the industrial part of town, though many of the jobs have long since packed up and left. So many of these buildings sit empty. I usually walk home after a shift because it's not far from the bar to my apartment, and besides, I like the fresh air after I work all night, try to get the cigarette smoke out of my hair and clothes as much as I can. The main thing is, there's nobody around right now. These two men—men I've never seen before—seem to know it and don't care that the girl is writhing in pain on the ground.

Part of me wants to go out there. Step out from around the corner and approach these men. I don't have a gun, don't have a knife, don't have a weapon of any kind, but somebody needs to help the girl. Somebody needs to step in before the man places a bullet in her head.

Before I can, though, the duffel bag moves.

But it's not the duffel bag—it's something *inside* the duffel bag.

The light isn't good here in the alleyway, but there's enough light that when I open the duffel bag I can easily tell what's inside.

A baby.

It looks newly born—no more than a month old—and it has a pacifier in its mouth, the only thing keeping it quiet. Its dark eyes look up at me, searching, and like that, the pacifier falls out of its mouth.

The baby's face scrunches up. It looks ready to start wailing —it even sucks in a breath—but I slip my finger into its mouth before it can. Still, it made some noise, just a tiny bit, and I hold my breath, hoping the men didn't hear.

For an instant, silence.

Then one of the men—what sounds like the passenger in the blue polo—says, "Did you hear that?"

In response, the quiet *thut thut* of two bullets from the silenced gun.

Without even looking around the corner again, I can tell the girl's now dead. Probably shot in the face to put her out of her misery. Not that she couldn't have been saved. The men could have called for an ambulance. Assuming they still wanted her alive.

The driver says, "Hear what?"

"It sounded like something came from the alley."

"I didn't hear anything. It bothers you, go check it out."

By the time the man in the blue polo steps into the alleyway, I'm no longer there. Neither is the duffel bag or the baby inside it.

A dumpster sits halfway down the alley, an abandoned dumpster that's rusting after years of disuse. I'm crouched behind it, cradling the duffel bag, my finger still in the baby's mouth.

If the man advances down the alley, he'll surely see me. In that case, I'll have to gently set the duffel bag aside, do what I can to protect the baby. The man probably has a gun, just like his partner, but that's okay. I haven't worked in a year, but I'm confident that my training will kick back in once it's needed. Two men with pistols? Easy. Then again, right now that's not my main concern. My main concern is the baby.

But the man doesn't advance much farther. He takes a couple steps forward—the dull clap of his boots echoing against the brick walls—and shines a flashlight down the alley, but that's it.

The driver calls, "Anything?"

"No."

"Then get your ass back here and help me put her body in the trunk."

"What about the bag?"

"She could've dropped it anywhere in the past couple blocks."

"We need that bag."

"What we need to do is clean up this mess. Now hurry over here and give me a hand."

The flashlight beam winks out. The man's footsteps fade away as he leaves the alley and returns to the car.

The baby's suckling on my finger so much it's starting to hurt. With my other hand, I dig around in the bag—feel a blanket, a bottle, a small container of formula, and then the pacifier.

I risk pulling out my finger just for an instant so I can replace it with the pacifier.

I wait another beat, listening to the men as they quietly work to clean up the body, and then I peek around the corner to make sure the alley is dark and empty.

Cradling the duffel bag again, I start back toward the mouth of the alleyway, hurrying as quietly as possible, intent on getting this baby as far away from the men with guns as I can.

THREE

I take the long way home.

It's only another three blocks to my apartment building, barely a five-minute walk, but instead I go a circuitous route, staying close to buildings, moving from one shadow to another. The night is quiet for the most part, just the sound of a few cars out on the highway and a dog barking in the distance.

I cradle the duffel bag as I go, rocking it slightly, trying to keep the baby quiet despite the pacifier in its mouth. The way those men were talking, they'll probably drive around once they clean up the body. The man in the cowboy hat mentioned the bag. Now that I know a baby is inside the duffel bag, I have to assume what the men really want is the baby.

I don't carry a cell phone, but even if I did, I'm not sure I would call 911. Not after seeing that piece of silver glinting on the driver's belt. A badge. Not local police—I'd recognize him —but some kind of badge that signified the man is law.

Twenty minutes later I climb the stairs to the second floor of my apartment building. The building only has two floors, and there are four apartments on the top floor. My apartment is the one on the left at the end of the hall.

I eye the apartment door across from mine for a moment before turning my key in the lock and stepping inside.

My apartment is bare and only contains the necessities. I don't have a TV or computer or phone. A pile of books—hardcovers and paperbacks borrowed from the library—are stacked beside the couch.

That's where I head once I shut the door and flick on the lights.

I gently set the duffel bag on the carpet and open it up—and at once a sour smell slaps me in the face. At some point in the past several minutes the baby has soiled itself. Which is okay, that's what babies do, but it's not like I have diapers lying around the place. Or, well, anything that I need to take care of a baby.

First things first.

I lift the baby out of the duffel bag and carry it into the bathroom. I turn both faucets to run water in the tub. I take off the diaper and discover that it's a she. I hate to keep thinking of the baby as a thing, an it, but right now I don't know what to call her.

The sour smell makes me gag, and I drop the diaper in the trashcan, but it's one of those small bathroom trashcans without a lid, so it doesn't do anything to hide the stink.

I hit the switch for the vent, as if that's going to do anything, and then cradle the baby in one hand while I test the water's temperature with my other hand to make sure it's not too hot, not too cold.

I start washing off the baby. I've never dealt with babies before, but I know you're supposed to use a special kind of soap to make sure it doesn't hurt their eyes. Still, I don't want her to smell, so I use a fresh washcloth and spritz a dollop of body wash in it and lather up the baby all the way up to her neck. She still has the pacifier in her mouth, which I'm going to need to clean at some point. My worry is what she'll do once I take it from her mouth. I figure she'll start crying, and I need to make sure that doesn't happen. My neighbors are good people, but they all know I don't have children. If they hear a baby crying, that'll create questions I don't want to begin to try to answer.

The baby has a birthmark on her back, what looks like a little starburst.

I whisper, "Star. Maybe that's what I'll call you for now. Does that sound good?"

Star doesn't answer.

Once I rinse her off, I take one of my towels and dry her and then wrap her in a new towel. I run the water in the sink and pluck the pacifier from her mouth, and at first I expect her to start crying, but she doesn't. She stares up at me, like she's fascinated by who I am and what I'm doing.

Cleaning off the pacifier the best I can, I dry it and slip it back into Star's mouth.

Okay, now what?

In my previous life I worked as a nanny, but I wasn't actually a nanny. I was an undercover bodyguard for my boss's kids. I took them places, helped them with their home-work, but I never did any actual childrearing. And when I started working with them they had moved past the diapers phase. I had seen diapers changed before, but I had never changed a diaper myself. In situations like these, one usually turns to YouTube, but again, I don't have a computer or phone.

Well, that's not true. I do have a phone—two phones, in fact. Both disposables I purchased a month after I settled into this apartment and decided to make Alden my home. I'd purchased minutes for the phones on the off chance I would ever need to use them, but to be honest, I'm not sure if those minutes have expired. And even if they haven't, who am I going to call?

Star needs actual diapers. Clothes. Food. Basically every-thing every other baby needs.

I should call the police, but I keep seeing that glint of silver on the driver's belt. For all I know, the badge is bullshit, some-thing bought off eBay to make people think he's a lawman, but I can't take that chance.

Before I head back to the couch to check out what else is in the duffel bag, I make a quick detour to my bedroom.

A three-drawer dresser stands against the wall. Cradling Star in the nook of my left arm, I open the bottom drawer, the one loaded with sweatshirts and sweatpants, and dig down for one of the two guns I have hidden underneath.

It's a SIG Sauer P320 Nitron Compact. The mag holds fifteen nine-millimeter rounds and is already loaded. All I need to do is rack the slide to put one in the chamber.

I haven't touched the gun in months. Haven't cleaned it. Haven't even looked at it. The old me would have been much more careful with weapons. Would have made sure this gun—and the Mossberg shotgun hidden in the hallway closet—was better maintained. But after a year of solitary living, of inte-grating myself into this town with my new identity, I've never once felt the need to use either weapon. My old life is far behind me.

I make sure the safety's on before I slip the gun into the waistband of my jeans.

Next I check the bedroom closet and pull out the thick wool blanket. I give it a quick sniff—musty—but it'll do.

I return to the living room and spread out the wool blanket on the floor. I fold it once, to make sure there's enough padding, and then I gently set Star down on the blanket so that she lies on her back.

My hands now free, I turn and crouch down beside the duffel bag. It still smells sour, but not as bad as before. The baby blanket is going to need to be cleaned.

I want to search the bag, but the bottle and container of formula catch my eye. I have no idea when Star was last fed, but something tells me a baby this young needs to be fed a lot.

I grab the container, scan the directions on the back. Doesn't seem too complicated.

I whisper to Star, "Stay here."

I hurry into the kitchen with the bottle and container of formula. I wash and dry the bottle, set it aside, and then follow the directions to make the formula. Return to the living room to find Star is thankfully still on the blanket. I sit on the floor, cradle her in my arm, pluck the pacifier from her mouth, and replace it with the nipple.

At first I worry she won't latch on, won't start to feed, but then she starts sucking at the nipple.

I coo to her, "Good girl, good Star," as she drinks the formula, and then I set the bottle aside, pick her up, and softly pat her on the back until she burps.

"All good for now, Star?"

She doesn't answer, and I'm not sure if I should keep going. I take a chance and put the pacifier back in her mouth, set her on the blanket.

My hands once again free, I turn to check what else is in the duffel bag.

Two other items are buried at the bottom.

A bright yellow Velcro wallet, the kind a little girl would carry, and a pinkie finger.

Before I can reach inside to pull out either item, there's a sudden knock at the door—two quick quiet raps—and a hushed voice says, "Police, open up."

FOUR

I glance at Star and hesitate, not sure I want to leave her on the floor. She lies there on her back and stares up at me as she keeps sucking on the pacifier.

Another quiet rap at the door, and I stand and move toward the door, feeling the press of the SIG against the small of my back.

I don't reach for the gun. Instead, I silently engage the security chain before opening the door the couple inches the chain allows.

Erik smiles back at me, holding up two bottles of Heineken.

"Wanna hang out?"

Hang out is code for fuck. It's something Erik and I have been doing for the past several months. Erik works as a Colton County sheriff's deputy. He lives in the apartment across the hall, was there when I first moved in, and for a couple months we would occasionally see each other, exchange smiles, but that was it. One time Erik struck up a conversation, asked me out for coffee, but I declined. Not that I wasn't interested—Erik may be a couple years younger than me, but he's hot, a tall

muscular black man with a cute smile—but dating wasn't
something I wanted at the time. Plus, as practically the only
Asian American in town, I figured going out on a date with one
of the few black guys in the area didn't seem like the best idea,
not if I wanted to stay under the radar. Fact is, dating isn't
something I'm interested in even now, but one thing led to
another, as things often do, and we started having causal sex.
No commitments. No dating. No getting to know each other.
Just pure fucking.

I look him right in the eye as I shake my head.

"Can't."

The smile fades, and for the first time he seems to notice
the security chain.

"Everything all right?"

"Everything's fine."

He pauses a beat, takes a whiff, and I can tell by his expression that some of the sourness has seeped out into the hallway.

I quietly clear my throat.

"To tell you the truth, I'm not feeling well. Think it's something I ate."

Erik forces another smile, and there's no judgment in his
dark eyes, which is another reason why I like the guy.

"Do you have any Imodium?"

"I'm not sure."

"I might have some in my apartment."

Before I can respond, he turns and disappears through his
door, comes back thirty seconds later without the beers. He
shakes his head.

"Sorry, don't have anything."

"That's okay."

"If you want, I can go pick something up."

Alden's the kind of town where nothing is open twenty-
four-seven, not even the gas station. Which means Erik would
need to drive fifteen miles to the truck stop off the highway, or

another seventy miles to the nearest Walmart. Which he would do if I asked him to—there's no doubt about it in my mind—but I shake my head.

"You're sweet, but I'll be okay. It's just been a long night, so I'm going to try to get some sleep."

Erik nods, says, "Hope you feel better. Let me know if you need anything."

"Will do."

I close the door and wait until I hear his door close across the hallway before returning to Star and the duffel bag.

I smile down at Star.

"That was Erik. He's a good guy. We agreed at the start that neither of us would fall in love with the other, but I think he broke that rule a long time ago. What can I say—must be my charm."

Star stares up at me, clearly not impressed.

I turn back to the duffel bag. Ignore the bright yellow Velcro wallet for now and focus on the pinkie finger. When the girl first approached me down the street—which was only now, what, an hour ago—I was too distracted by the blood covering her that I hadn't noticed much else. Like whether or not she had all her digits.

"Don't go anywhere, Star."

I hurry into the kitchen and check the cleaning supplies under the sink. There's a small bag of latex gloves, and I grab two of the gloves and slip them on as I return to the duffel bag.

I say to Star, "Good, you're still here."

She doesn't appear to get the joke.

I extract the pinkie finger from the duffel bag to get a closer look. The cut doesn't look clean, looks instead like it had been torn off the hand instead of sliced. Which means it was probably done by a pair of pliers. Which means the girl was probably tortured.

If the two men I saw earlier tonight had somehow caught

the girl previously, used a pair of pliers to take off her pinkie finger, what was the end game? If they were looking for the duffel bag—and presumably Star—that means neither the duffel bag nor Star were with the girl at the time. So they had been elsewhere, and then … what, the girl somehow managed to escape? Okay, that's maybe plausible. She managed to escape, ran away from the men, grabbed the duffel bag with the baby inside (or maybe Star was elsewhere beforehand and the girl put the baby inside later) and then ran through the dark streets. That part of town is usually deserted. Those buildings empty, a perfect place for bad men to do bad things to a helpless girl.

On the blanket, Star starts to fuss.

I set the pinkie finger aside, start to reach for Star, but remember the latex gloves. The small bag under the sink doesn't contain many gloves, so I don't want to waste any more than I need to.

I whisper to her.

"I know, Star, I know. I got somebody in mind to help us out, but we're going to have to wait a few more hours. First I need to clean this stuff up, okay?"

Star just watches me. Not looking happy at all.

I check the pinkie finger again, and frown. Assuming it did belong to the girl, and assuming those men in the car had torn it from her hand, and assuming she'd managed to escape, why would she have grabbed the pinkie finger to take it with her? Assuming, of course, any of my speculation is remotely close to what happened. Maybe it isn't even the girl's pinkie finger. Maybe it belongs to somebody else.

Once I'm done here, I'll put the finger in a sandwich baggie, the kind with a resealable zipper, though I'm not sure what I'll eventually do with it. A sensible person would have called the police long ago and had them deal with this mess, and while I'd like to think of myself as a sensible person, I just can't do that. Not after seeing the girl covered in blood. Not after the girl put the duffel bag—and the baby inside—in my arms. Like she was entrusting me to keep the baby safe. Then of course there's the fact that the driver who may or may not be law enforcement killed the girl.

No, I can't contact the police, at least not right now. I can't even bring Erik into this, though I'm sure he'd want to help. As far as I can tell, he's a good cop, which means he'll want to do everything by the book. Which means a moment or two after I tell him about what I witnessed, he'll call it in. Which may or may not alert the two men who killed the girl who I've come to think of as Star's mother.

I check the wallet next. The Velcro makes an irritating ripping noise. I crinkle my nose at the sound, afraid it will make Star fuss again, but Star doesn't seem to care. In fact, it looks like she's starting to fall asleep.

Inside the wallet are five one-hundred dollar bills. They're so crisp and fresh they look like they came straight from the bank. Like the only other person who touched the bills before handing them out was the bank teller.

Also inside the wallet is a business card. The background is a generic stock photo of footprints on a beach. At the top the words LITTLE ANGELS ADOPTION AGENCY with the name Leila Simmons, LSW beneath. There's an address on the card—San Angelo, about three hours away—along with a phone number and email address. On the back of the card, somebody has written out a phone number in blue ink.

LSW stands for Licensed Social Worker. Which means Leila will be my first call in the morning. Only after I do some research.

For now, though, I need to clean up this mess while Star sleeps. It's already past four o'clock, which means I'll need to wait at least another three hours before the next step.

I start to collect the pinkie finger and wallet—I plan to bag them, though again I'm not sure what will ultimately happen to them—but pause to glance back down at Star.

I pull off the latex gloves, toss them in the duffel bag, stand back up and slip the gun from the waistband of my jeans. I set the gun on the arm of the couch, and bend to gently pick up Star from the wool blanket.

Cradling her, I sit on the couch and stare down at her and do everything I possibly can not to fall asleep, too. Right now I'm running on twenty hours of no sleep, and something tells me it's going to be a long time before I close my eyes again.

FIVE

Alden used to be a large town with a population of several thousand people, but since the factories went under over a decade ago, most of those people moved away. Now there aren't many businesses in the area, and there certainly aren't any gyms. I typically get my exercise in the late mornings when I wake, running three miles around town, so I've never had any need for a gym bag. Or any other bag large enough to inconspicuously conceal Star.

Alden being the small town that it is, everybody knows everybody else. It's not like everybody is friends, but they see each other in passing, noting who is married and who is single and who is in a relationship. Noting who has children.

Everybody in town knows me as Jen Young. They know I'm single, and that I don't have children, so openly carrying one through town probably isn't the best idea.

In the end, I use a reusable cloth grocery bag. It's not as big as I'd like, but it does the trick.

I stuff the bottom with two towels—my last two clean towels—and set Star on top.

I throw on a gray sweatshirt, so the bagginess of the sweatshirt will conceal the SIG at the small of my back.

I've already stuffed the duffel and its sour shit-stained contents in a garbage bag. My first impulse is to drop the garbage bag in one of the dumpsters when I leave the apartment building, but part of me wants to hold on to it for now. It's evidence, after all, and maybe this will get to the point that the police will need to take over. In that case, I don't want to screw up the chain of evidence more than I already have.

I have a car—an '02 Honda Civic—but I don't use it much, and besides, we're only going five blocks. Not even a quarter mile.

It's just past seven o'clock and the early Saturday morning is cool and crisp, the wide sky a pale blue.

I walk holding the grocery bag in my left hand, swinging it slightly to give Star that rocking sensation. I keep my right hand free in case I have to reach for the gun. I don't expect I will, but last night I didn't expect to encounter a girl covered in blood either, so better safe than sorry.

Alden is slowly waking. As it's the weekend, most people are still home. Not much traffic is moving about. Two blocks ahead, I smell the smoker over at Benny's BBQ. The place doesn't open until noon but they're already smoking the meat.

Meredith rents a two-bedroom ranch house on High Street. The place is a dump, but it's all Meredith can afford on her salary as a waitress. She's twenty-two years old, has two kids, and is studying to become a phlebotomist. Neither of the kids' fathers are in the picture, and Meredith's mom doesn't help more than what's required. There's some resentment there for some reason, at least from what I've been able to gather. I'm not close to Meredith, but we get along fine at work. She seems like a good mother, which is the main reason I thought of her late last night while I knelt over the duffel bag. The other reason is that Meredith barely makes ends meet so she's usually desperate for extra cash.

She stands in the doorway, holding her own baby in her arms. She wipes the sleep from her eyes before she frowns at the folded wad of twenties I'm holding out to her.

"I'm confused—*how* much did you say?"

"Three hundred dollars."

"For just a couple hours of my time?"

"Yes."

"And what do you want me to do?"

Before I can answer, the pacifier falls from Star's mouth, and she starts to fuss.

Meredith's eyes immediately dart down at the grocery bag.

"Is that—"

I cut her off.

"Can I come inside?"

Before she can answer, I push my way inside, sidestepping Meredith who stands there stunned.

She says, "Is that a *baby*? Where'd you get a baby?"

Before I can say anything, a patter of footsteps charges toward us, and Meredith's other son—five-year-old Johnny—rushes up to his mom and grabs onto her leg.

"Pancakes!"

"Johnny, I told you not now."

"Pancakes!"

"Johnny, I said not now!"

There's more bite in her tone than she probably intended, and Johnny's face closes up at once. He looks almost ashen, and his bottom lip starts to tremble, and Meredith, probably sensing an oncoming tantrum, issues a heavy sigh.

"Yes, fine, pancakes. Now go watch cartoons and leave us be."

Johnny's face lights up, and he gives me a sort of triumphant smile before tearing off toward the living room.

Meredith shakes her head at me.

"Whatever you do, don't ever have kids."

But then she pauses, looking down again at the grocery bag.

"Whose baby is that, anyway?"

"I'm not sure."

"What is that supposed to mean?"

"It means I'm not sure. Look, Meredith, the less you know, the better."

The absurdity of my statement nearly causes Meredith to bark out a laugh.

"You're joking, right? You come here first thing in the morning and offer me three hundred dollars to … do what, exactly?"

"Watch Star for a couple hours."

"Star?"

"That's what I'm calling her."

"You don't know her real name?"

"Let's just say I found her last night."

"Found her where?"

"Again: the less you know, the better."

Holding her younger son, she releases a heavy breath.

"I already have two kids of my own to deal with."

"I know. And normally I wouldn't bother you, but I'm in a bind."

"What do you want me to do with her?"

"Feed her. Give her a bath. Put her in a diaper and clothes. Just keep an eye on her until I get back."

"Where are you going?"

"The less you know, Meredith."

"Shit, Jen. I don't know. This sounds shady as fuck."

"It is. But it's also worth three hundred dollars of your time."

"Three hundred dollars."

"Yes."

She stares down at the folded twenties in my hand.

"Okay. When will you be back?"

"I'm not sure exactly."

"But it'll just be a couple hours?"

"Yes."

"Is it okay with you if I call my mom to come over and give me a hand?"

"I'd prefer you don't. No offense, but your mom seems to be a gossip, and right now it's best if not many people know about this."

Meredith bites her lower lip, gazing down at the bag again.

"This isn't, like, against the law, is it?"

"No."

At least, I'm pretty sure it's not. Not as far as Meredith is concerned, anyway. She's just taking care of a baby. She doesn't know the whole story. She doesn't *need* to know.

Beyond the sound of Saturday morning cartoons from the living room, Johnny shouts, "Mommy, pancakes!"

Meredith's face tenses, and for an instant I realize I'm losing her. The money sounds good, of course, but it's another child to worry about on top of her other two children.

"Five hundred."

Her eyes go wide after I say the words, and her mouth drops open.

"*Five* hundred?"

"Yes. Three hundred now, two hundred when I get back. All you need to do is feed her and bathe her and clothe her. That's it. I'll be back in a few hours, and then you'll never see the baby again. And this whole thing will just be our little secret."

She bites her bottom lip, still clearly conflicted, but the promise of five hundred dollars is too much to pass up.

Meredith takes the grocery bag from me with her free hand, and gives me the smile she uses on the drunks at the bar when she's fishing for an extra tip.

"See ya in a few hours."

SIX

The Alden Public Library sits near the heart of town. A squat brick building with just one floor, it keeps minimal hours as not many people in town utilize the books and DVDs and free Internet.

I volunteer at the library a couple days a week, mostly helping to restock shelves. It gives me something to do during the day. Otherwise, I'd sit alone in my apartment and stare at the wall and think about things I don't want to think about.

The library keeps short hours on Saturdays—opens at nine, closes at noon—so I pull into the parking lot right at nine o'clock on the dot. Thanks to Meredith, I've had time to return to the apartment to take a shower and change into some fresh clothes. My hair is still damp as I step out of the car and make my way toward the entrance.

Despite the fact the time is now 9:01, the door is locked.

I lean close to the window in the door. The place is dark inside. Nobody around.

"Jen?"

Gloria Ruskin's voice drifts from behind me, and I turn

slightly to glance over my shoulder to watch the old woman shuffle up the walkway.

"Good morning, Gloria."

She squints at me.

"Are you feeling okay?"

"Why do you ask?"

"You're wearing a sweatshirt. It's the third week of June."

The sweatshirt, of course, is to conceal the SIG I still have pressed against the small of my back, but Gloria doesn't need to know this.

"I haven't been feeling so good the past couple days. Think I might be coming down with a cold."

Gloria's hand immediately flies to her face.

"Then stay away from me, young lady. I don't want to get sick."

"Don't worry, I promise not to sneeze on you. Is everything okay? You're usually here before nine."

I step away as Gloria approaches the door, a ring of keys in hand. She sighs as she slides a key in the lock and pulls open the door.

"Howard wasn't doing so well this morning. I thought I should maybe stay home with him, but … you know how it is."

Howard is Gloria's husband, a sweet old man who's been battling Parkinson's the past three years. Both of them are retired, children and grandchildren spread out around the country. Gloria runs the library with a sort of strict dedication that makes me envious. She's here every day, from open to close.

"If Howard isn't feeling well, why don't you take the day off? I can cover for you."

The moment I say the words I regret them, as clearly I have much bigger things to worry about. Still, Gloria is one of my favorite people in Alden, and hence so is her husband whom

I've only met once, and if Gloria needs to take care of her husband, then so be it. Besides, today the library is only open for three hours. It would give me more than enough time to do what I need to do and then close up.

Gloria waves a dismissive hand as she leads me into the library, flicking on light switches as she goes.

"That's very kind of you, Jen, but Howard will be okay."

"Are you sure?"

"Yes, yes, I'm sure."

The door behind us opens, and Mr. Tucker enters. He wears an Astros baseball cap and lifts his hand in a quick hello as he breezes toward the table of four computers.

Gloria calls over to him.

"Good morning, Frank. I haven't had a chance to turn on the computers yet. Do you mind waiting a minute?"

Mr. Tucker lifts his hand again in acknowledgment and takes what I've come to think of as Mr. Tucker's Seat at the computers. He's almost as old as Gloria's husband. A widower with no kids, he spends most of his time at the library watching YouTube videos. His favorites are cat and dog videos. Sometimes when I'm restocking books I'll hear him chuckling at one wacky video or another.

I follow Gloria into the office where she hits the button to provide power to the computers out in the main room.

Gloria says, "What brings you in this morning, anyway?"

"My Internet's acting weird at home. I was hoping to use your computer here for a couple of minutes. I'd rather not deal with Mr. Tucker out there, if at all possible."

"Certainly. Just do me one favor."

"What's that?"

"Wipe the keyboard and mouse down with a Clorox wipe once you're done."

The great thing about Gloria—she likes me so she doesn't care what I do. I'm always on time, always clean up after myself, never give her or anybody at the library attitude. Her trust in me is so high she'd probably give me her social security number if I asked for it.

As Gloria heads back out into the main room, I sit down at her desk and turn on the computer. It's an ancient PC, and takes forever to power up, the gremlins in the computer box clicking and tapping away as the screen runs through its usual nonsense before the Windows logo finally appears.

The real reason I want to use Gloria's computer is because I'd installed the Tor browser on it several months ago. Gloria doesn't know much about computers, and I made it so the browser can't easily be found. I could have done the same to one of the four computers out in the main room, but there's always the chance somebody might stumble across the program. Mr. Tucker prefers his YouTube animal videos, but maybe he's a computer genius when nobody's looking. Better to keep the program isolated.

Once the Windows logo disappears and the desktop pops up, I click the mouse several times to bring up the Tor browser. It's something that Scooter—an old friend and team member, who died saving my life—had once advised me to use what feels like a lifetime ago, but every time I use it now I think of Gabriela. It's been almost a year since she was killed by narcos. Gabriela knew being a journalist was dangerous, especially where she lived in Mexico, but that hadn't stopped her.

Tor is designed to keep websites from tracking your movements or location. Whenever I use the Internet now—and I rarely do—I use the browser.

I bring up Google and then do a search for "leila simmons" and "little angels adoption agency." The main website for Little Angels Adoption Agency is the first website listed. I scan the site, which looks legit. Real pictures of real people, not stock photos.

On the staff tab, I find Leila Simmons listed as an assistant director. She looks to be in her late-forties. Hispanic. She has a warm smile with dark eyes and curly black hair.

The phone number and email address below her picture match the same ones on the business card.

The number scrawled on the back of the business card, however, isn't anywhere on the website. Not that I expected it to be. It's probably a cell phone number. Most likely her personal cell phone number.

I close out of the website and Google Leila Simmons's name again. She has a LinkedIn account as well as a Facebook account. A few other websites mention her name, too, websites focused on adoption. One site congratulates her on winning a humanitarian award.

I close the Tor browser, wipe down the keyboard and mouse with a Clorox wipe, and head out into the main room. As expected, Mr. Tucker is chuckling at something on his computer.

Gloria stands behind the counter, checking in the books and DVDs from yesterday.

"Did you wipe everything down?"

"Yes, ma'am."

"Very good. I suggest you head home and get some sleep if you're not feeling well. Maybe make yourself some chicken noodle soup."

"Yes, ma'am. I hope Howard is feeling better."

Gloria's ever-present smile falters for a second.

"Yes, dear. So do I."

I swing by the computers to wish Mr. Tucker a good day. He lifts his hand in my direction as he continues to chuckle. When I get close enough, I see a hedgehog on the screen, balled up and floating in a tub of water.

The second I get in my car I pull out one of the disposable phones. I've already loaded this one with minutes, and as I pull out of the parking lot, I've dialed the number on the back of

the business card and listen to it ring four times before somebody answers.

"Hello?"

A soft voice. Feminine.

"Is this Leila Simmons?"

"Yes, it is."

"I found something you may be interested in."

"Who is this?"

"What I found was in a duffel bag, along with a yellow
Velcro wallet."

A long pause on the woman's end. When she speaks next,
her voice has become a low whisper.

"Is the baby okay?"

I'm not shocked by her question. Somehow I knew she
would know about the baby. Still, it's unnerving to hear her ask
it so simply.

"Yes."

"And what of Juana?"

Juana is presumably the girl I saw last night covered in
blood. The one who thrust the duffel bag—and the baby inside
it—in my arms minutes before she was struck by a car. The girl
who had five crisp one-hundred dollar bills in her wallet along
with a card for the woman I now have on the phone.

When I don't immediately answer, Leila Simmons sucks in
air and sounds like she's ready to cry. Her whisper becomes
somehow even quieter.

"She's dead, isn't she?"

SEVEN

At ten minutes to noon, Leila Simmons pulls into the parking lot of the roadside diner. She drives a forest green Volkswagen Jetta, its left rear hubcap missing. She steps out of the car wearing sunglasses, but I recognize her from the pictures on the Little Angels' website. She's a bit taller than she looked from the picture, but maybe that's because of the heels. Despite the fact it's the weekend, she'd dressed professionally, like she's about to attend a meeting. Which in a way is true. Only it's not the type of meeting the woman probably has in mind.

Leila enters the diner and looks around the place, up one row and down another, and when she doesn't see anybody wave to her she lets a waitress lead her to a booth. The waitress returns a minute later with a mug of a coffee, and Leila thanks her as she reaches for the creamers on the table.

I wait until twelve o'clock exactly before I dial Leila's personal cell phone.

By that point she's sipping at the coffee, glancing at her watch every thirty seconds, sometimes reading something on her cell phone. Leila is about to take another sip when her phone rings. She pauses, squints at the phone lying on the tabletop, sets the mug down and hesitantly holds the phone to her ear.

"Hello?"

"Change of plans."

"What are you talking about?"

"I've decided I want to meet someplace else."

"What do you—but this is where you said you wanted to meet."

"Yes, originally. Now I've changed my mind."

I'm positioned across the highway in a truck stop parking lot. Parked so I'm facing the diner across the highway. I have a good view of Leila from where I am, so I can see how frustrated she's getting, closing her eyes as her hand reaches up to pinch the bridge of her nose.

She says, almost too quietly, "I don't like games."

"Me neither. But last night I saw that girl you mentioned murdered so I don't want to take any chances."

"I'm not going to hurt you."

"You're not the one I'm worried about."

Leila drops her hand from her face, quickly looks around the diner.

"What are you saying?"

"I'm saying I want to make sure you haven't been followed. That you won't be followed when you leave there. Do you understand?"

"Yes."

"Good. Now leave a couple bucks for your coffee and head back to your car."

Her head whips around, the woman suddenly realizing that I'm watching her. First she looks around the diner again, then out through the window at the parking lot, and then across the highway at the truck stop.

"Don't worry about where I am. Just pay for the coffee and head to your car. Believe me when I say I want to get this over with just as much as you do."

Leila pulls three dollar bills from her pocket and lays them on the table as she slides out from the booth. The phone to her ear, she starts toward the exit.

"Where am I going?"

"Turn right out of the parking lot and head west."

"How far should I go?"

"I'll tell you.

"Will you call me back?"

"No. You and I are going to stay on the line until you get there."

Am I being overly paranoid? Maybe overly cautious is the better term for it. There's no reason I shouldn't be able to trust this woman, but the simple fact is I don't know anything about her other than the little I've read online this morning. Her card was found in the bag of a dead girl, along with a Velcro wallet containing five crisp one-hundred dollar bills and a pinkie finger. Oh, and a baby.

No red flags have gone off in regards to this woman yet, but that doesn't mean I still shouldn't be cautious. There's no reason to believe she has anything to do with the men who killed the girl from last night, but I still have to be certain before I allow myself to put Star in her care.

Less than a minute later Leila has pulled out onto the highway heading west. I watch the diner parking lot for a moment, then double-check the truck stop parking lot. As far as I can tell, nobody rushes to follow her. In fact, nobody even coincidently pulls out of either parking lot.

Keeping the phone against my ear, I start the engine and pull out onto the highway.

EIGHT

I don't draw this out any longer than I need to. Soon it becomes clear Leila Simmons—and by extension, me—isn't being followed. I keep watching the rearview mirror, but the cars back there look as normal as cars typically look on a weekend afternoon driving miles and miles in the middle of nowhere.

We don't speak. Leila tried asking more questions, but I kept telling her to wait, that I would talk to her when we got there, and finally she fell silent. She doesn't have the radio on in her car, and neither do I. Besides the noise of the highway whipping past beneath our tires, the only sound coming from the phone is the woman's soft breathing.

After several miles on the highway—nothing in the desert around us except buffalo grass and creosote bushes and cholla —a rest area looms ahead. It's so small and pathetic you might miss it if you blinked.

I make a split-second decision and pull off into the rest area. Leila's probably already a good half mile farther down the highway.

"Did you see the rest area you passed?"

"Yes."

"Make a U-turn and head back to it."

Leila doesn't answer, but I sense her frustration on the line between us.

"Leila, did you hear me?"

"I'm making the U-turn now."

The rest area doesn't have a bathroom. Just two weathered picnic tables and a trash bin. A slanted and rusting aluminum overhang that looks like it was built fifty years ago shadows the tables.

There aren't even any parking spots, just enough gravel for cars to temporarily park so that people can stretch their legs for a few minutes.

I'm already parked and waiting by the time the Jetta pulls into the lot. As Leila Simmons eases her car to a stop next to mine, I open my door and step out into the dry summer day. The cloudless sky above a dark blue, the only imperfection a 747 leading a puffy contrail.

I keep my door open, the P320 resting on the seat.

Leila watches me from behind the steering wheel, clearly trying to gauge the situation. She doesn't step out and instead lowers the Jetta's passenger side window.

"Where's the baby?"

"She's not here."

Despite the sunglasses on her face, I can tell her eyes dart past me at the empty car. She shakes her head, her jaw tightening.

"What is this bullshit?"

"Relax. The baby is fine. She's in good hands."

"What is this—some kind of shakedown? Do you expect me to pay you money?"

"No. Like I told you, I witnessed the girl you mentioned—"

"Juana."

"Yes, Juana. I saw two law enforcement officers murder her last night. As far as I could tell, they didn't seem like good law enforcement, either. So I want to be careful."

Leila Simmons doesn't answer for a moment. Finally she seems to make a decision. She undoes her seat belt and steps out of the car. Crosses her arms and looks around the rest area like there are a dozen people standing nearby.

"Why did you bring me all the way out here?"

"I told you—I wanted to make sure you weren't being followed."

"Who would follow me?"

"Who were the men who killed Juana last night?"

She doesn't answer at first. A slight wind picks up, blowing her curly black hair around, and she pushes a few strands from her face.

She says, "Who are you, anyway?"

"I'm just a woman who likes to mind her own business."

"Tell me what happened."

So I tell her. I tell her about how I was heading home from work last night when I heard the girl calling out behind me. How I turned and saw the blood, and how the girl placed the duffel bag in my arms before darting into an alleyway. How she was hit by a car and then murdered.

Leila takes off her sunglasses, wipes at her eyes.

"Jesus. That poor girl."

"I found your card in the duffel bag."

"Yes. I met with Juana the other day. I'd written my cell on the back of the card so that she could reach me directly at any time, day or night. I do it for all the girls."

"What girls?"

"Just"—she pauses, spreads her hands—"girls. Pregnant girls. Desperate girls."

"What aren't you telling me?"

"What do you mean?"

"I visited the Little Angels website. It looks like a legit adoption agency."

"It is a legit adoption agency."

"Sure. Then do a lot of your girls get tortured by law enforcement before being hunted down and killed?"

Her sudden paleness is amplified by the bright afternoon sun.

"What are you talking about?"

"I told you how she was covered in blood. Well, along with your business card in the duffel bag, I found a severed pinkie finger. I can't say for sure because everything happened so fast last night, but I would imagine it was Juana's."

Leila's hand goes to her mouth, and she starts shaking her head.

"No. No, no, no. No, that can't be."

"When was the last time you saw Juana?"

"I told you. The other day."

"What day?"

A shrug, the woman wiping at her eyes as she watches a tractor-trailer breeze past.

"Two days ago. I met her briefly. Many of the girls who come to us haven't given birth yet. They want to find good homes for their babies. Other girls, they've already had their babies and want to find them good homes. I have contacts all over the state who keep an eye out for certain girls—"

I cut her off.

"Illegal immigrants."

Leila pauses to wipe at her eyes again, and nods.

"Yes, *undocumented* immigrants. Most of them flee Mexico because they want to get away from the cartels and other gangs. They want their children to get an opportunity they never had. That's where Little Angels steps in. Over the years we've started helping more and more of these girls. Most times Immigration finds them and sends them back, but by then they've put their babies in our care, and we find good homes for them."

"Juana wasn't interested?"

"She was. I think. I don't know. She was nervous—I remember that. She clearly wasn't ready to trust me yet."

"Did you give her money?"

The woman's frown looks convincing.

"Money? No, of course not. We don't *pay* any of the girls for them to give up their parental rights. None of us are in this to make money. Why would you ask that?"

I hesitate, not sure I want to tell her about the cash. But then I figure what the hell, might as well lay all the cards out on the table.

"Also in the duffel bag was a wallet containing five one-hundred dollar bills. They were crisp, like they'd just come from the bank."

Leila shakes her head.

"I have no idea where that money would have come from. It most certainly didn't come from me or anybody at Little Angels."

"When I spoke to you this morning, you seemed to know Juana was dead."

"Yes."

"Why?"

"I could just tell. You know how sometimes you get a phone call, and before you even answer it, you know whoever's on the other end is going to tell you something terrible? That's the feeling I got when you called me."

"The men that killed her—any idea who they are?"

I'm expecting Leila Simmons to shake her head again, tell me no, so I'm surprised when she offers up a slight nod.

"I think I do, yes."

"Who?"

"I don't know their names. I've never actually seen them.

But I've heard stories. About two men—one of them always wears a cowboy hat—who drive around the state hunting down these girls."

The woman pauses again, wipes at another stray tear. It looks like she's on the verge of breaking out into sobs, but she manages to hold it in.

"These men—from what I can tell—they take the girls and they ... they do terrible things to them."

"Like what?"

"Use your imagination. You said you found a pinkie finger. Stuff like that barely scrapes the surface. I know for a fact that right now they have another girl."

"What are you talking about?"

"One of the girls I met with recently. Her name is Eleanora. I heard that she was taken. That these men grabbed her off the street the other day."

"How do you know this?"

"Another girl—a girl who was with Eleanora—told me. She said she had ducked into a store to use the bathroom, and when she came out the men had already shoved Eleanora into their car."

"Do you know where she was taken?"

Leila offers up another slight nod.

"I believe so. These men, they have this place out in the middle of nowhere. It's near an oil refinery. A shed. That's where they take the girls."

"How can you know this?"

"One of the girls managed to escape. She came to me, terri- fied. I told her we needed to go to the police, but she refused. The next day, she had run away. I've driven past the oil refinery but never got up the nerve to check for myself. Even though I should. I ... I should do something."

"Did you ever call the police?"

Leila lets out a desperate laugh. She looks on the verge of losing it.

"Of course I did! They claimed they would send somebody out there, but I never heard anything. When I called them back, they told me to stop wasting their time. That's when I contacted the FBI, but I never heard anything back from them, either. These men, you understand—they're ICE agents. They have a lot of pull in the state. Heck, sometimes I think some of the cops in the area are in on whatever those two are up to."

ICE stands for Immigration and Customs Enforcement. A federal agency tasked, among other things, with protecting border security. They'd been working hard on deporting undocumented citizens for years, but recently that effort had been ramped up. ICE agents going from town to town rounding up men, women, and children. It made sense to see them often in a border state. What didn't make sense was to see two of them openly murder a woman in the street.

More vehicles speed past us down the highway. A few cars, a few pickup trucks, a few tractor-trailers. I watch them for a moment before turning back to the woman.

"Okay."

She frowns at me.

"Okay?"

"I trust you. At least as much as I'm going to at this point. After what I saw last night, I wasn't taking any chances. I wanted to make sure I would be putting the baby in safe hands."

Leila nods, and slips the sunglasses back on her face.

"I understand. I will admit this has been frustrating, but I understand. Now, where is the baby?"

"Alden."

"*Alden*? That's over an hour away."

"Yes. It's where her mother was killed."

NINE

Meredith doesn't look thrilled to see me. Or maybe she does and she just has a hard time showing it through the exhaustion painted on her face.

"Where have you *been*?"

She stands with her arms crossed, her chin tilted down. Her baby sits at her feet, crying its lungs out. Past them, farther in the house, the sound of cartoons is even louder than it was this morning.

"I'm sorry. Took longer than planned."

"You *think*? You said it would only be a few hours. It's nearly two o'clock. I can barely deal with two kids at the same time by myself, but *three*?"

I don't say anything, letting her vent.

Meredith juts her jaw and blows away a loose strand of hair from in front of her face.

"My mom called and said she was going to come over, and I had to make up some excuse to keep her away. I told her I needed some stuff and that she needed to go to Walmart, and, like, I do need that stuff, but I still felt like I was lying to her, which is weird because I lie to my mom all the time, but this time it just felt, like, *really* wrong."

"Were you able to give Star a bath?"

Meredith glances down at the crying baby on the floor, and when she looks up at me again, something has changed in her eyes. They've hardened a bit, and her voice ticks down an octave.

"I want to know where you found her."

"No, you don't."

"Yes, I do. Or else I'll call the police."

Blood starts thrumming in my ears, drowning out the crying baby.

"Go ahead. When they get here I'll make sure to mention there's a chance you've got marijuana hidden somewhere inside. Probably not enough to get a conviction, but it's not going to look very good for a single mother of two, will it?"

The threat is a mistake, of course, but I can't help myself. I'm not operating on much sleep, and somehow Meredith's irritation is contagious. The angrier she gets, the angrier I get. Which isn't helping matters, I know.

Meredith's eyes grow even harder, like stone, and she opens her mouth to speak, but I shake my head and hold out my hand to silence her.

"Seven hundred dollars. That's all I have left. Give me Star, and I'll give you the cash, and we'll both forget this ever happened. Deal?"

Meredith doesn't answer at first. Her burning glare is so intense I wish I'd applied sunscreen lotion this morning. But then she sighs, blows away another loose strand of hair from in front of her face, scoops up her crying baby, and motions me inside.

"Follow me."

I step inside and let the screen door smack shut behind me as

Meredith leads me deeper into the house. Her older boy sits on the living room floor, his skinny knees pulled up to his chest, his back against the sofa, watching the TV with a wide-eyed fascination that makes me surprised he doesn't have drool falling down his chin.

Meredith says, "This way."

She directs me into the next room, where a bottom-of-the-line crib sits in the corner.

Star lies there, clothed now, asleep.

Meredith leans down to place her own child inside the crib and picks up Star, a simple swap.

She holds the baby even more tenderly than she'd held her own, smiling down at Star as she whispers.

"She's a good baby. Quiet. Didn't give me no problems."

"You bathed her?"

"Yes. And fed her. She was a dream. Her mom must be a happy camper."

She pauses, and I see the gears starting to shift again in her head, the questions that are starting to form.

I slip the bills from my pocket—the wad of twenties, as well as the five crisp one-hundred dollar bills from Juana's wallet—and place them on the table beside the crib.

"Here's the rest of the money. The three hundred from earlier this morning, plus seven hundred here, that's one thousand dollars."

I watch her, waiting to see if she'll ask any of those questions, but she eyes the money with an intense greed.

Nodding absently, still watching the money, Meredith hands me the baby.

Five minutes later I'm three blocks away, walking with the grocery bag again, Star nestled inside.

Leila Simmons is parked next to the town's only bank. By now the bank is closed, the parking lot empty except for our two cars. The flagpole is bare, but its snap hook smacks against

the metal pole in the breeze, an insistent and random *ding …*
ding … ding.

Leila steps out of the car when she spots me heading her
way. She stands there with the door open, and I can feel her
need to rush forward. But she holds back, scanning the block
as if people are watching, which so far I don't think anybody is.
It's Saturday, after all, and most people are inside or have driven
to a town that has far more to offer than Alden.

Leila Simmons doesn't ask where I've kept Star this entire
time. She doesn't ask who's been watching her, who's been
taking care of her, or why I'm currently transporting her in a
grocery bag. She simply takes the bag from me when I offer it
to her, and she immediately turns and opens the back door. A
child seat is already prepped there. Leila carefully extracts Star
from the bag, secures her in the child seat, and gently shuts the
door.

Turning to me, there isn't happiness on her face so much as
relief.

"Thank you."

"The money from the wallet—"

"Keep it. I don't know where it came from. Consider it a
reward for keeping the baby safe."

I don't want to get into how I gave the money to Meredith,
so I nod.

Leila watches me for another moment, and then she climbs
into the car. She waves just once before she pulls out onto the
road and heads north toward the highway.

I stand there in the parking lot well after I've lost sight of
her car. Still thinking about Star. Hoping that wherever she
ends up, she'll be safe.

TEN

There's a brown paper bag waiting for me outside my apartment door. On the outside of the bag is taped a small folded piece of paper.

I crouch down and inspect the piece of paper first. Lift the top half to read the note.

Hope this helps things run more smoothly.

I open the bag and glance inside. A box of Imodium A-D. Forty-eight tablets. Which is probably all the corner store had.

"Ha, ha. Very funny, you dumbass."

Erik, of course, is not here to appreciate the insult. I glance at his door, think about knocking, giving him a kiss for his trouble. When I first met Erik, he was always quiet, brooding. It felt like he took himself too seriously. But once I got to know him, especially on an intimate level, I found he could be really sweet, as well as silly. It's not the type of thing you'd expect from a guy who used to be a Marine, and maybe that's why I like him.

I decide not to knock on his door, though—he's probably

working, anyway—and instead let myself into my own apartment.

Even though the place has always felt empty, today it feels even emptier.

I have to admit, having Star here last night was a nice change of pace. Granted, the preceding events that led to her entering the apartment were not ideal, but the simple fact that there was another living body in the apartment felt nice, if only for a moment. The baby had barely been in my possession for twelve hours, but I felt like I'd grown a bond with her. Not a strong bond, no, but a bond nonetheless.

It had physically hurt having to give her to Leila Simmons, and that was why I hadn't bothered to say goodbye. Hadn't bothered to look inside the grocery bag one last time. Hadn't bothered to reach in and feel her soft skin. Even when Leila pulled her from the grocery bag and strapped her into the car, I had looked away.

I feel confident that Star is in good hands. I did as much research on Leila Simmons in as little time as possible, but I had a good sense that she was genuine when we met. After all, I'd made her drive a long distance. I couldn't blame her for feeling jerked around, but it was the only way to know she was on the level.

One of the girls I met with recently. I heard that she was taken.

Leila's words echo inside my head, unbidden.

I close my eyes.

"No."

They have this place out in the middle of nowhere.

I shake my head suddenly, as if that might dispel the words from my memory. No luck. If anything, my wanting to forget she ever said those words makes them come again, even stronger.

It's near an oil refinery. A shed.

Of course when she mentioned another girl had been taken

by the two men from last night, I heard every word and immediately wanted to ask more questions, but my focus—my entire
world at that moment—was on making sure Star would be
taken care of. Nothing else mattered.

I'd purposely not asked Leila Simmons any questions about
the girl or the location of the shed because I didn't want to get
involved. It wasn't my place. Not anymore. The person I used
to be—the one who did non-sanctioned hits for the government—would have demanded to know more about the girl and
the location of where she was being kept. Because that person
felt a need to right every wrong. To fix every slight. To correct
every injustice. There were people in the world who were helpless, who were weak, and the person I'd been felt I had no
choice but to stand up for those in need.

It had been noble, maybe, but it had also been stupid. Had
gotten me into trouble from time to time. Had even gotten
some of those close to me killed in the process.

No, I hadn't asked Leila Simmons about the girl or where
she believed the girl had been taken, because that person no
longer existed.

A yawn hits me, hard, and I glance at the clock hanging on
the wall.

Almost three o'clock.

I've been awake now for over twenty-four hours. I need
sleep, and I need a lot of it. Which means I'll have to call off
work tonight. My boss won't be happy, but he's never happy.

I still have the disposable, the one I had used to call Leila
Simmons. I dial the bar and wait through ten or twelve rings
before Brenda, one of the daytime waitresses, answers.

I ask, "Reggie in?"

Brenda recognizes my voice, asks how I'm doing, doesn't
give me the time to answer when she says to hold on a sec.

The sec takes about a minute, the phone having been
placed on a table so the music and voices can be heard in the

background, and then the phone is picked up and Reggie clears his nicotine-addled throat.

"Yeah?"

"Reggie, it's Jen. I can't come in tonight."

"Why the fuck not?"

That Reggie, he's a charmer.

"I'm not feeling so good."

"It's Saturday night. We're gonna be packed. You need to be here."

"I'm telling you, Reggie, I'm not feeling good. Best I don't come in."

"Yeah, and whatcha got?"

I think about the Imodium A-D in the paper bag, and decide with this situation the more graphic the better.

"The shits, Reggie. I got the shits."

ELEVEN

I stand in the middle of an empty street, a gun in my hand. I three-sixty the street, at first not knowing where I am or what I'm doing there, but little by little recognition starts to settle in.

The houses around me. The macadam cracked and warped in places. The dark cloudless sky.

This is a place I've been before.

This exact location.

Almost a year ago.

The heart of Culiacán sits several miles away from where I'm standing. Its lights shimmer off in the distance, but I don't hear the sounds of the city. Of course I don't. Because this is a dream.

There is complete silence. Like I'm stuck in a vacuum. Like I'm in outer space. I'm certain that if I lift the gun in my hand and fire off a round I wouldn't hear a thing.

I don't lift the gun and fire off a round. Instead, I start forward down the street. My footsteps don't make a sound. My own breathing—if one even breathes in a dream—is noiseless.

I know where I'm headed because I've walked this street before in the middle of the night, a gun in my hand.

Gabriela's house is now only two blocks away. The fearless Gabriela. Her parents died at the hands of the cartel, and so she decided to take it upon herself to stand up to the cartel. Reporting on their crimes when the national and local media refused. She had known what she was doing put her life at risk but she did it anyway, and so it was probably no surprise to her when, in the end, the narcos came for her.

Soon I'm standing on the street outside Gabriela's house. It looks exactly like it did the last time I saw it.

The garage door is closed, but the gate has been forced open.

Before, I knew it may be a trap—that narcos may be waiting for me inside—but now I have no hesitation in pushing open the gate and stepping into the yard.

Despite the cloudless night sky, the darkness is thick. I slip a penlight from my pocket, just as I did that night, and shine it at the door.

The door, too, has been forced open, the lock smashed apart. The door has been pushed closed, though, so that anybody passing by on the street would think nothing of it.

I cross my wrists—the penlight in my left hand, the gun in my right hand—and kick the door open and charge inside.

Like that night a year ago, the living room is empty.

Except it's not.

Instead of Gabriela's grandmother, Leila Simmons is propped up in the chair in the corner. Her face tilted to the side, her dead eyes open. Her throat has been sliced, and dried blood covers much of her shirt.

In real life, Gabriela's grandmother didn't have anything on her lap, so I'm surprised to see something there now.

I train the penlight's beam at Leila Simmons's lap. A duffel bag sits there.

Part of me wants to rush forward, tear the bag from her lap, look inside. The only way I'll know if Star's in there is by moving forward and opening the bag.

I don't rush forward. I shift the penlight's beam away from Leila Simmons and the duffel bag in her lap. Neither is the reason I'm here now. They're mere window dressing for whatever my subconscious wants me to see.

Because I've done this already—have gone through the house clearing the rooms one by one—I know better than to waste my time.

The penlight in one hand, the gun in the other, I head toward the door that leads into the garage.

I turn off the penlight as I open the door and flip the switch just inside. The single bulb in the ceiling blinks to life.

The cinderblock wall is the same as I remember it, as are the tools spread out around the place where Juana's dead body lies in pieces. Like Gabriela, it looks like they took their time with her.

My focus is trained so heavily on what's left of Juana that at first I'm not aware of the man in the cowboy hat standing in the corner. The badge on his belt glints in the light. A gun in his left hand, he reaches up with his right hand to tip back his hat.

"Evenin', pretty lady."

He says the words, but since this is a world of silence, I don't really hear them except inside my head.

Just as I hear his partner's words as he noiselessly steps up behind me.

"What took you so long?"

The silent voice echoing in my ears as the man presses the barrel of his gun against the back of my head and pulls the trigger.

TWELVE

I wake with a start, breathing heavily, my body covered in sweat. I reach for the gun under my pillow when I realize that it's not there, that I haven't slept with a gun under my pillow in months.

The room is dark, though the streetlamp standing outside the apartment building is just bright enough to push past the curtain and provide a scintilla of light. As my eyes adjust, I spot the P320 on the nightstand where I'd left it when I climbed into bed what must have been hours ago.

I sit up and take a deep breath, trying to slow my heartbeat and breathing. I can't remember the last time I had a dream so vivid.

Deciding to leave the gun where it is on the nightstand, I stand up from the bed and head toward the door. I left the light on out in the main living room, so it's easy to see the time on the clock hanging on the wall.

Almost 9:30. Which means I've only gotten about six hours of sleep.

I stand in the middle of my empty apartment, not sure what I should do next. Take a shower, definitely. But then what? Get something to eat, I guess, though I don't have much in the apartment, and I don't want to venture out to one of the few food joints in town because word might get back to Reggie that his all-star bartender isn't really sick. The same with calling to have food delivered. Word might get back to Reggie, too. Which means I'm stuck in my apartment for the time being. Unless I decide to get dressed and head to work. Tell Reggie it turns out it was a false alarm, I don't have the shits after all.

I mutter, "Who the hell am I kidding."

I don't bother making it a question, so maybe that's why I don't feel the need to answer myself. I can stand here for another five minutes, another ten minutes, another half hour, making excuses and plans and reasons not to go through with those plans, but in the end it won't matter what I decide to do, because I know exactly what's going to happen next. I've known since earlier today, standing in that rest area with Leila Simmons while the tractor-trailers and pickup trucks roared past us.

One of the girls I met with recently. I heard that she was taken.

The disposable still sits on the kitchen table. The disposable that I should have disposed of earlier in the day after I'd watched Leila Simmons drive away with Star. Stripped the battery from the back, dropped it in one trashcan, dismantled the rest of the phone and left pieces of them all over town. Not that I expected anything would come of it had I kept the phone—which I had, after all—but that was my mindset.

Wait, no. That wasn't my mindset, not really. Not for Jen Young, the new person I've become. That would have been Holly Lin's mindset. And Holly Lin doesn't exist anymore.

I shake my head, mutter a curse, and cross over to the kitchen table. Pick up the phone and key in Leila Simmons's number and hit the green button to complete the call.

It rings three times before she answers, her voice hesitant, hushed.

"Hello?"

"This is Jen. From earlier today."

"Yes, I remember."

"Is everything okay? You sound quiet."

"I'm at home. My husband is in the other room. What can I help you with, Jen?"

"I wanted to ask what happened to Star."

"Star?"

"Juana's baby."

"Yes, of course. Everything went well. I found an emergency foster parent to look after her tonight, and we're working on getting things situated so that she can be adopted."

"That's great."

"Yes, it is. Thank you again for reaching out to me."

I say nothing, suddenly unsure of what more I should say. While I of course wanted to learn what had become of Star, that's not the reason I called. And maybe she senses it on her end, probably standing in another room of her house, keeping her voice lowered so her husband doesn't hear. Not that she should be afraid of hiding the conversation from her husband, but in her line of work privacy is vital, and so it's probably second nature to immediately find a quiet space to answer a call.

Leila Simmons says, "Is there anything else I can help you with?"

"Actually, there is. When we spoke earlier, you mentioned one of the girls you met with recently having been taken by those men."

Her voice, already quiet, somehow becomes quieter.

"Yes, I did. I apologize. I shouldn't have said what I said. Please forgive me."

"No, it's not that. I think I might be able to help you."

A beat of hesitation on her end as she mulls this over.

"What do you mean?"

"I know a cop. A Colton County sheriff's deputy. He's a good man. He can be trusted. If you tell me where you think this girl was taken, he'll be able to help."

The silence on her end lengthens. I picture her biting her lip, looking back over her shoulder at her husband in the next room as she weighs the pros and cons. She doesn't need to know the truth—that I have no intention of telling Erik anything—but the fact that I'm presenting it as the selling point should help.

Finally she says, "I don't even know for sure she's there. Even if she was there before, she might not be there now."

"That doesn't matter. Either way, wouldn't it ease your conscience knowing for sure?"

She doesn't answer, and in my head I picture her finally sitting down, leaning forward, staring off into space as she continues to try to make up her mind.

"Leila, I understand your hesitation. But believe me, this is for the best. Either she's there or she isn't. Don't you want to know for sure?"

"But what … what if she *is* there?"

"If she is there, it's vital that she's rescued as soon as possible, don't you think?"

Keeping the phone to my ear, I move from the kitchen and into the bedroom. I flick on the light and crouch down in front of the dresser. Pull the bottom drawer out and dig down beneath the sweatshirts and sweatpants and bring up my other gun.

It's a SIG Sauer TACOPS 1911. A bit heftier than the P320 but this one has a five-inch barrel with an eight-round mag already loaded with .45 Autos.

Also buried under the clothes is a SOG Strat Ops automatic folding knife. It has a 3.5-inch steel blade that's spring-loaded to release at the touch of a button.

I toss the 1911 and the SOG on the bed as I stand back up and realize the silence has gone on much too long.

"Are you still there?"

Leila Simmons issues a hesitant whisper.

"Yes."

"I don't want to pressure you, but I don't think there's anything to debate. You said yourself these men are dangerous. Hell, I saw one of them kill Juana last night. We don't want that to happen to this other girl, do we?"

Saying *we* makes it seem more like she and I are a team, and that she can trust me. I don't want to say *you* and make it sound like I'm accusing her of anything. Right now I need her on my side if I'm going to save this girl.

When Leila Simmons speaks next, her voice has lost the hesitation.

"No, we don't."

"We want to save her, don't we?"

"Yes."

"Then tell me, Leila. Tell me where to find her."

THIRTEEN

Like in my dream, the night sky is dark and cloudless, but there's no distant shimmer of lights from a city sitting a few miles away. And while there's silence, it's a true silence, the night alive with insects making quiet noises in the blue grama and buffalo grass. A light breeze blows through the night, skimming loose dirt across the ground and making the creosote bushes shiver.

Leila said an oil refinery, but that's not quite true. It's an oil field, but it's an abandoned one. At least, it doesn't appear as if the dozen or so oil derricks are in operation anymore. They stand frozen across the landscape, looking like giant metal beasts in the dark.

I move past one of the motionless derricks toward the shed.

I'm dressed in dark jeans and a black T-shirt and sneakers. Not my preferred tactical wardrobe for a mission, but it's not like I have many other options. I especially don't like wearing my sneakers; the tread is distinct and could be matched to my shoes later if things ever got to that point, which means I'll need to dispose of them and get a new pair, which means an hour drive to the closest Walmart.

The SOG is clipped to my belt. The P320 is pressed against the small of my back, while the 1911 rests easily in my hand.

I haven't held a gun in my hand this long in almost a year. There's a familiarity to squeezing the grip—a sense of home-coming—that I'm not yet ready to accept.

The shed is larger than I'd pictured it would be. It looks to be a story and a half tall, like it could hold a truck or two or three. A large barn-style door in the front, a regular-sized door on the side. No windows.

I surveil the shed for a good fifteen minutes—crouched behind a bush—before I decide to make my move. So far I haven't seen or heard anything that's raised an alarm. If the girl's inside the shed, she hasn't moved or made any noise. Which means either she's not there or she's dead or asleep or she's been tied up to the point where she can't move.

According to Leila Simmons, the girl's name is Eleanora. She's no more than seventeen years old. She's pregnant, Leila said, or at least she was the last time Leila saw her. Which was just a few days ago. Before Eleanora disappeared. Before Leila got word that Eleanora may have been abducted by those two ICE agents, and had been taken to this shed planted here in the middle of a dead oil field.

Leila started crying when she told me this, as if the realiza-tion of how she'd failed the girl finally hit her. She told me how she was sorry that she hadn't done more, but that she was scared, and at one point I heard her husband's voice in the background, asking her what was wrong, and Leila had quickly composed herself—I pictured her wiping at her eyes as she blew her nose with a tissue—and told her husband she would be off the phone soon.

The 1911 in hand, I start toward the shed. I walk slowly, quietly, but my sneakers crunching the dirt sounds like gunshots in the silence.

I circle the shed. The only thing I find is a rusting generator on the other side, though it's doubtful the thing even works.

The door on the side is closed, its wood weathered, just like the rest of the shed. Like it was built fifty years ago and hasn't been repainted since.

There's a padlock on the large door, but there isn't one on the side door. There is a latch, where a lock would hold the door in place, but it's empty.

I push the door open and immediately step to the side, aiming the 1911 at the darkness within.

Nothing happens.

Nobody wearing a cowboy hat or blue polo steps out of the dark with a gun raised.

I pause a beat, listening to the silence inside, and soon I hear it.

A muffled noise. Like somebody trying to cry out. Only they can't because something's over their mouth.

I slip the penlight from my pocket and flick it on. Shine the beam through the doorway.

A green compact tractor sits inside, a large mower deck hooked to its back, but that's it.

That muffled noise continues, more frantic now.

I move forward, hesitantly, and sweep the penlight's beam as I step inside.

Besides the tractor, there's other equipment that means nothing to me—steel barrels and other supplies, the place rank of oil and gasoline—but then the penlight's beam focuses on the source of the muffled noise.

The girl sits on a wooden chair near the back of the shed. An entire roll of duct tape looks to have been used to hold her in place. Duct tape around her ankles and around her legs and around her middle and her shoulders, as well as over her mouth.

I make my way toward her, not hurrying but moving at a

steady speed as I sweep the penlight around the rest of the shed to ensure there are no other surprises.

When I reach her, I sweep the penlight back and see that she's most definitely pregnant. Looks to be almost eight months along.

"Eleanora?"

The girl momentarily falters from trying to shout past the duct tape. There's surprise in her dark eyes, like she didn't expect me to know her name. Then she nods, eagerly, and tries to speak through the duct tape again.

"Leila Simmons sent me. My name's Jen."

I stick the end of the penlight between my teeth to keep the beam on Eleanora's face while I use my free hand to peel the tape from her mouth.

The girl releases a half sob, tears now fleeing her eyes.

"*Gracias. Gracias. Gracias.*"

Her voice is too loud, and I take the penlight from my mouth and tell her in Spanish to be quiet.

The girl says in Spanish, "Please untie me—*please!*"

I intend to—I even bite down on the penlight again to use my free hand to unclip the SOG from my belt—but before I press the button to release the blade I pause again. Go very still. Hold my breath.

Eleanora says, "What are you doing?"

I jerk my head back and forth, the penlight's beam going left to right across her face, but the girl doesn't seem to get my meaning.

She sucks in air to ask the question again, but by then I've pressed the duct tape back over her mouth.

Her eyes go wide, and she tries to shout again through the tape.

I clip the SOG back on my belt, take the penlight from between my teeth, and lean in close to the girl to whisper.

"Quiet."

The girl goes silent, confused, and I whisper again as I flick off the penlight, shrouding us in darkness.

"Can't you hear that?"

The girl's still silent, making it even more possible to hear the approaching sound of an engine and tires crunching dirt outside.

"Somebody's coming."

FOURTEEN

The vehicle stops. Its engine shuts off. Two doors open.

I don't see the men step out—not from where I am in the shed, having shut the side door so we're enveloped in darkness —but I imagine it's the two from last night. The driver has on the same cowboy hat, the badge still displayed proudly on his belt.

A murmur of voices outside—the men conferring—and then the sound of boots scuffing the dirt as they approach the shed.

It could be the police or FBI, following up on Leila's call, but it's doubtful. It could be a nearby rancher, or the person who owns this oil field, come to check the equipment. I didn't notice any alarm system, but maybe something got tripped. Still doubtful. It seems Occam's razor applies best here—whatever is the simplest explanation is probably the right one, hence the men outside are the same ones who killed Juana last night.

One of the men jiggles the padlock on the large door, while the other shuffles over to the side door.

The one closer to the side door calls out.

"Over here."

The one playing with the padlock leaves it be and hurries over to his partner.

A moment passes, and then the door pushes open, and I can see the man in the cowboy hat from last night standing just outside. He has a gun in his hand, a flashlight in his other hand.

I'm stationed on the other side of the tractor, crouched behind the overlarge wheel, the 1911 aimed at the door. From this angle, I have a clean shot at the cowboy. A slight squeeze of the trigger, and it'll be lights out. But if I do that, I'll alert his partner, and I don't like the idea of his partner being outside while I'm trapped in here with Eleanora. Best to wait until they both enter, take the two of them out together, one after the other.

The cowboy doesn't enter. He stands at the threshold and sweeps his flashlight through the room. I have to duck when the beam comes my way, and I close my eyes for a beat, steady my breathing, my heartbeat.

That's when Eleanora can't contain herself any longer, and lets out a frightened cry.

It's mostly muffled by the duct tape, but at once the flashlight beam jerks in her direction.

The cowboy says, "Holy shit, there she is."

There's something about how he says it—almost with surprise—that makes me frown, but before I can think too much about it, the cowboy steps inside.

His partner doesn't.

He says, "Let me see if I can get that generator going."

The partner drifts away. I track him from the sound of his footsteps on the dirt outside the shed, and I consider firing at him through the wood. At least the cowboy is already inside; I could easily pivot and take him out, too. But it's still near pitch-black, and I would be aiming at the cowboy's flashlight which isn't a reliable target.

Better to wait for the lights to come on, if that's what's going to happen. For the partner to step inside so I'll have both of them in one place.

The cowboy doesn't wait for the generator. He moves forward, the flashlight beam trained on Eleanora's face.

She has her eyes closed, flinching at the bright light, and she's sobbing again, the tears falling down her face, and the cowboy murmurs as he approaches her—"Don't worry, darlin', we're gonna take real good care of you"—and the way he says it, the smarmy tone of his voice, makes me squeeze the 1911's grip so tight I'm afraid I might snap it in half.

I won't let the cowboy place one finger on Eleanora, I decide, but I can't do anything until his partner joins him in the shed.

The cowboy's close to her, his voice going even lower.

"You ever get fucked by an American? A whole hell of a lot better than those wetbacks you're used to back home."

Outside, the partner cranks the generator's starter cord— once, twice—and it's on the third time that the thing roars to life and a few dim bulbs in the shed's ceiling begin to flicker on.

The cowboy pauses, tilts his face up to the ceiling, and lets out a whistle.

"That right there—that's a sign from the good Lord Almighty. He approves of what we're about to do to you."

Eleanora keeps sobbing, but her eyes are open now, wide in terror, and it's her eyes that give me away.

They shift, just slightly, enough for the cowboy to turn to find me running at him, the 1911 in my right hand, the opened SOG in my left, and the cowboy spins and fires at me right as I fire at him. His shot goes right over my head, but I hit him in the shoulder, send him reeling to the side. I want to take him out before his partner enters the shed, but his partner's already at the door, his gun drawn, and fires at me a second later.

I twist and fire three shots at his chest. He's wearing a light green polo shirt, and three red flowers bloom just below his neck.

I turn back to the cowboy, but he's already coming at me, his gun aimed at my face.

I dip back just before he fires, readjust for a head shot, but he swats the 1911 from my grip, sends it clattering to the ground. I still have the SOG, though, and I toss it to my right hand as I step toward him, grabbing the knife with the blade pointed down and slicing him across the stomach.

The cowboy grunts and backhands me across the face.

I stumble back, the SOG still in my hand, and plan to step toward him again when I realize the distance between us—no more than five feet—isn't enough for me to reach him before he pulls the trigger.

I dive to the side, in front of the tractor, as the cowboy fires off several rounds.

I rise up on one knee, pull the P320 from the small of my back, flick off the safety.

The cowboy calls out, "You cut me, you fucking bitch!"

Using the tractor for cover, I glance over at Eleanora, her eyes wide as she watches the two of us.

The cowboy shouts again.

"Fucking *bitch!*"

"You called me that already."

"Who the fuck are you?"

I hold the SOG in my left hand a beat before tossing it toward the rear of the tractor.

The cowboy, holding his bleeding stomach with his left hand, tracks the knife with his eyes but not with his gun. He keeps that aimed toward the front of the tractor, from where he expects me to jump out. He's not a total moron, it appears, so I have to hand him that, but he's still one step behind. Because I don't go toward the tractor's front or back—I go *over*, using the metal step to jump into the seat, the P320's sight trained right on the cowboy's face.

His head snaps back an instant after I squeeze the trigger. He stands there for a second, his gun in one hand, his other hand pressed against his bleeding stomach, and then falls to the ground.

Standing tall in the open cab of the tractor, I spin to confirm both the cowboy and his partner are indeed dead, and then I drop to the ground and retrieve the SOG and the 1911 and hurry over to Eleanora.

I peel the duct tape from her mouth, cut her free from the chair, help her to her feet. Her first impulse is to hold onto me, sobbing. I step away from her, and motion at the door.

"Let's go."

Her eyes are still wide, taking in the dead bodies, and she looks at me, her face ashen, her mouth agape. But she doesn't speak, just nods her head, ready to follow me anywhere.

I scan the shed again. Focusing once more on those metal barrels. Thinking about the stench of oil and gasoline.

I tell Eleanora to go outside. She's scared, shaking, but finally she waddles toward the open side door. Once she's gone, I check both men's pockets. I find their wallets, check their IDs. Light green polo is named Samuel Mulkey, the cowboy Philip Kyer. Kyer has his badge clipped to his belt, while Mulkey has his in his pocket. Both badges look legit. Which somehow makes it even worse. There's nothing more disgusting than a corrupt cop. And here are two of them.

Both men also have cell phones. Mulkey has some nicotine gum packets, but Kyer still hasn't given up the habit. He doesn't have any cigarettes on him—those are probably in the car—but he does have a lighter. It's a fancy one, too, stainless steel with his initials engraved on the side.

It takes me five minutes before everything is set, and then I step outside into the fresh air.

Eleanora hasn't gone far. She stands there, her arms crossed, trying to keep herself warm. She's only wearing shorts and a T-shirt and sandals, not the most ideal outfit for the middle of the night in the middle of nowhere.

I take my first look at the car parked in front of the shed—the same sedan from last night—and then I take Eleanora's arm and steer her toward the field of frozen oil derricks—and my car parked in a field two miles away.

We've gone maybe two hundred yards before the fuse I've set finally catches. The shed starts to burn, and the fire hits the cluster of barrels in the corner. The ground shakes with the explosion. It's louder than I anticipated, and I'm worried it'll draw attention much quicker than planned, so I keep my hand on Eleanora's arm and whisper to her in Spanish to hurry, hurry, hurry.

FIFTEEN

Leila Simmons is already at the rest stop by the time we arrive, and the moment we park beside her, she opens her door and jumps out.

The rest stop has no exterior lights—not even a single lamp —but the half moon provides just enough light to see she's wearing sweatpants and a T-shirt. Probably the first things she managed to grab after my phone call.

Leila leans down to see the person in the passenger seat, and as soon as she confirms it's Eleanora, her eyes go wide as her hands shoot to her mouth. The next moment she rushes forward to open Eleanora's door, reaching out to touch the girl's face, like she can't believe it's truly her.

A flurry of Spanish ricochets back and forth—Leila asking Eleanora if she's all right, if she thinks the baby's okay, if she's hurt, and Eleanora doing her best to answer before Leila lobs another question—and all the while Leila helps Eleanora from my car and walks her to the Jetta.

I step out and watch them without a word.

After Leila helps Eleanora into the passenger seat, she gently shuts the door and turns to me.

"I ... I don't know what to say."

"You don't have to say anything."

"How"—she pauses, shakes her head in wonder—"how did you do this?"

"I didn't do anything."

In the dark, I note a speck of confusion on her face but it quickly morphs to understanding.

"Were ... those men there?"

I glance past her at Eleanora in the car. I figure Eleanora will probably tell her everything. Not only what happened between me and the two men, but what those men may have done to her after they abducted her. I'd tried asking Eleanora about her abduction, in case anybody else was involved, but she was exhausted once we made it back to the car, and I didn't want to put any further stress on her.

"Is she an illegal?"

Leila says nothing. Which is all the answer I need.

"Then I'm going to assume you won't report what happened to her. I would keep it that way."

Understanding flicks across her face again.

"Those men—"

I cut her off.

"Are no longer going to be a problem."

I pause, watching her in the dark, not wanting to ask the next question but knowing I have no other choice.

"Are there others?"

"Others?"

"Who were taken."

She shakes her head, a deliberate back and forth.

"Not that I know of."

My first impulse is to tell her to call if she hears of any other girls being abducted. Mulkey and Kyer can't have been the only two running this particular racket. There are no doubt others, but ... no, I can't get involved in this. I've already done more than I should. I killed two men tonight, and while I've killed several in the past, that was a different life. I'm no longer that person, and I can't risk any further exposure.

When I realize Leila Simmons is waiting for me to speak, I softly clear my throat.

"Good."

I wait another beat, and then tilt my chin at the car.

"Take care of her."

Leila Simmons nods.

"I will."

I don't tell her to call if she needs anything else. I don't tell her that the phone I'd called her on will be stripped apart and its pieces scattered along the highway. That as far as this woman is concerned she's never going to see me again. I don't tell her any of that, because I think she's smart enough to figure it out, just as she's smart enough to know she needs to be the one to leave first.

Leila doesn't say anything else. She just looks at me one last time before climbing into her car.

Eleanora twists in her seat when Leila pulls out of the rest stop, the girl raising her hand goodbye.

I don't bother returning the gesture. I don't even acknowledge her with a nod. Because I can't invest any further time in the girl or the woman. It may sound harsh, but they're strangers to me, and that's all they'll ever be.

The Jetta accelerates as it heads west, its taillights a dim red before fading completely.

I wait there for another minute, listening to the silence of the night, the distant chorus of insects calling from the desert, before I slip into my car and head back to the place I've come to think of as home.

SIXTEEN

Another brown paper bag is waiting for me outside my apartment door. This time the gift inside is big enough to tell exactly what it is. It's squat and circular, and the note on top—another folded piece of paper—simply says, *In case you run out.*

A roll of toilet paper. Hardy har har.

I consider knocking on Erik's door, playfully tossing the toilet paper at his face, but I feel sticky from sweat and smell of gasoline, and besides, I still have my weapons.

Inside my apartment, I set the toilet paper on the kitchen table next to the box of Imodium A-D, as well as the knife and the pistols. They'll need to be cleaned, which is something I'll do after my shower. It'll feel good to clean the weapons—a familiarity I've long missed—but they'll have to wait.

I head to the bathroom, stripping out of my clothes as I go, so that when I flick on the light I'm only wearing my bra and panties. I study my face in the mirror, at the place where the cowboy backhanded me. A slight bruise, but it's not too noticeable. Nothing a healthy dollop of makeup can't hide.

I slide the shower curtain back and turn on the water and

adjust the faucets until the temperature's just right, and then I step into the tub and pull the curtain shut and tilt my face down so the warm water beats at the back of my head.

Part of me hopes the shower will not only rid me of the sweat and gasoline but also my exhilaration. Tonight for the first time in a year I felt alive again. Like I had a purpose. For once my existence didn't consist of the mundane—shelving books, serving drinks—but for a couple hours I had felt like the old me.

And it wasn't only saving Eleanora—that should have been enough—but what I did to those two men. Making them pay for their crimes. Making sure they would never hurt another helpless girl.

Stop. Just stop it.

I don't want to be that person again, do I? I made the choice to walk away from everything. To tell Walter Hadden I was done—not just being a bodyguard to his two children, but to all of it. The non-sanctioned work I'd done for the government. The covert missions. The assassinations. The knowledge that with every life I took it was in service to the country and to normal Americans who went about their every day lives completely oblivious to the constant danger surrounding them.

Of course, it wasn't only Walter and the work I'd walked away from. It was the knowledge that my father—our team leader, who all my life I'd considered a hero—wasn't really dead. That he'd only faked his death. That he's out there somewhere, having aligned himself with terrorists, and part of me wants nothing more than to put a bullet through his face while another part … well, another part dreads the idea, because despite what he's become, he's still my father.

My mother never knew the truth about her husband, just as Tina, my sister, never knew the truth about her father. All they knew was he worked for the military. Not that he was an assassin for the United States government. That when the government needed full deniability and couldn't afford to risk sending in a CIA asset, they'd send my father and his team.

Besides myself, the only other person left from the team is Nova Bartkowski, who I haven't seen or talked to in a year, not since we came back from an impromptu mission in Mexico, and now that I think about Nova, where did he end up, anyway? He mentioned something about finding his father, but he didn't tell me much else. For all I know something bad may have happened to him. For all I know he may be dead.

I blink, realizing all at once I've been lost in my thoughts, still standing in the shower. How many minutes has it been? I feel the tips of my fingers, realize they've started to prune, and decide enough screwing around.

A couple minutes later I step out and dry myself off. My hair's still wet, but at least it's short now, not long like it was a year ago.

Wrapped in a towel, I walk into the kitchen and grab a bottle of water from the fridge. As I twist off the cap and start to raise the bottle to my lips, there's a soft knock at the apart-ment door, followed directly by a whisper.

"Police, open up."

I eye the two pistols and the knife on the kitchen table next to Erik's two gag gifts. I cross over to the table and collect all three weapons and place them in a drawer before heading to the door.

A quick glance through the peephole confirms Erik is standing on the other side. But he's turning away, having concluded I'm asleep or maybe mad at him, and is about to head back into his apartment.

I open the door.

He pauses, and glances at me over his shoulder.

"Oh, hello."

He says it all innocently like he's surprised to find me answering my door at three o'clock in the morning.

I say, "Don't you ever sleep?"

He turns to me, and shrugs.

"I was reading. Thought I heard you come in not too long ago. Wanted to check to see how you're feeling."

I glance down at his empty hands.

"What, no beers?"

He offers an embarrassed smile, and shrugs again.

"Figure you probably wouldn't be in the mood for a drink. Why were you out so late, anyway? I was at Reggie's earlier; they said you called out sick."

"Keeping tabs on me, are you?"

Another shrug.

"I'm merely a concerned neighbor, is all."

"Maybe I was out on a date."

"Oh. That's nice."

"Erik."

"Yes?"

"I have a confession to make."

"Okay."

I beckon him with my finger. He takes a step forward. I glance down the empty hallway, as if I expect a crowd to be watching, and then lower my voice.

"My problem from last night? It's not a problem anymore."

"Oh. Well ... that's good, right?"

"Too bad you didn't bring any beers."

His eyes light up.

"I'll be right back."

Before he can step away, though, I reach out and hook a finger on his belt, pull him toward me into the apartment.

Tilting my face up to kiss him, I murmur, "Let's skip the beers."

Erik doesn't object. He goes right with it, kissing me back, his hands grazing my body through the towel, and I jump up and wrap my legs around him as he holds me tight and walks farther into the apartment, absently reaching back to close the door.

SEVENTEEN

Light trickles in from the part in the curtain. It's not strong light—the streetlamp stands several yards away—but it's enough so that once your eyes adjust you can make out the bedroom.

We lie in my bed, Erik and I, and stare at the ceiling, both of us sweaty and spent. While we were going at it—our hands and lips exploring the familiar terrains of our bodies, my hand squeezing Erik's bicep when he entered me—it was like any other time, a recognizable rhythm, both of us already knowing what the other liked, but this was the first time we were together in my apartment, the first time Erik has ever *seen* the inside of my apartment, and now a sense of awkwardness tinges the air, Erik no doubt wanting to ask why the place is so bare, why I don't even have a TV. I've been living across the hall from him for nearly a year, and it looks like I've just moved in —or am ready to move out.

But Erik doesn't ask. He lies beside me, catching his breath, and then starts to sit up, twisting to place his bare feet on the carpet.

I don't move. Don't even tilt my head. But I watch him in

the dark, his broad shoulders rippling as he starts to stand. He thinks he's supposed to retreat to his apartment now, because that's what I always do once we finish. I've never lingered for more than a couple minutes. At first making an excuse for why I needed to leave, and then, once it became clear to Erik that I'd rather sleep alone, making no excuse at all. Just slipping out of bed, redressing, and then ghosting through his apartment to the door where I would peek out first to make sure none of our neighbors were there before darting across to my apartment.

"You don't have to go."

His shoulders twitch. Clearly he wasn't expecting me to speak.

"I have to work tomorrow."

He says it without looking at me, standing to pull on his boxer shorts.

"What time?"

He pauses and turns his head slightly to the side, so I can make out his profile in the dark.

"I go in at noon."

"What time is it now?"

He grabs his watch from the nightstand, checks the time.

"Almost three thirty."

"Good. So there's no hurry."

I pause a beat, watching him.

"But if you need to go, go."

He sits back down, the bed springs making their usual soft cries of protest. He twists, curling his left leg on the bed, and reaches out to run his finger down my arm. Even in the dark he doesn't look at me, staring instead at my arm.

"I like you a lot."

"I like you a lot."

He keeps running his finger up and down my arm, still not meeting my eyes.

"No, I mean I really like you. I think about you all the time. When you're not around, I ..."

But he trails off, shakes his head.

"Never mind."

I say, "I know."

He looks at me for the first in several minutes.

"You do?"

"Yes."

Neither of us says anything, though, nothing to further the conversation. We keep staring back at each other in the dark until Erik retracts his finger and takes a breath.

"I don't know how much longer I can keep doing this."

"I know. So let's go get a cup of coffee sometime."

"I'm being serious."

"So am I."

He appraises me, trying to study my face in the dark.

"I realized the other day, despite us doing this every so often, I don't know anything about you."

This, I want to tell him, is a good thing. The less he knows about me the better. He doesn't need to know about my past life. As for my current life, there isn't much to know. There's a backstory, but I've long since stopped thinking about the cover Atticus gave me. I eventually told myself there was never any reason to use it. I was never going to get close to anybody again.

After several seconds have passed in silence, I nod so Erik knows I heard him.

"I know. I don't know much about you either."

"To be honest with you, Jen, I want something more."

"So do I."

I'm almost as surprised as he is by the words as they slip out of my mouth.

He says, "You do?"

I reach out and grab his hand, give it a slight squeeze. But for some reason, I can't say the word. Not yet. Not until I've come to terms with the past twenty-four hours. The thrill of holding a gun in my hand again, of squeezing the trigger. I've never gotten a thrill from taking lives, though I have to admit there's sometimes been a satisfaction watching what I've thought of as evil people die. I've often questioned what kind of person that makes me. And while part of me may have felt alive tonight, another part knows that road leads to a lonely life and probably a lonely death.

Erik keeps watching me, waiting for me to say the word.

I wet my lips, try to speak, can't. Clear my throat and try again.

"Tell me something nobody else knows."

The request catches him off guard. A slight frown crosses his face.

"I can't think of anything off the top of my head."

"Did you grow up in Alden?"

"No."

"Then tell me where you grew up. Tell me about your childhood."

Erik watches me for another moment, still not sure if I'm being serious. Then he takes a deep breath, stares off at the thin line of light streaming in through the curtain, and tells me about his childhood.

About how he never knew his mom. About how his grand-mother raised him. About how just before his sixth birthday, his grandmother had a stroke and passed away. About how he then ended up in the foster care system, going from one family to another, never meshing with any of them, and about how as he got older he started acting out, being aggressive with his peers, stealing from the corner stores, the crimes at first petty but quickly escalating until he was thirteen and stole a car to go joyriding, and how then he ended up in a juvenile detention center for a year and when he was released he was sent to a place up north, to a woman named Ruby who took care of kids like him, kids who had no family, and there were other kids at Ruby's house, a few other boys who also started out with petty crimes and which had snowballed into worse things, and at first Erik was defiant with Ruby, just as he was defiant with every other adult in his life, but Ruby was patient, almost too patient, wearing him down with her patience, and she was kind too, kind but strict, making it known to Erik and the other boys in the home that she had a certain set of rules and those boys were going to abide by those rules, no ifs ands or buts about it. Of course, Erik and the other boys tested those rules, tried to push the boundaries, but Ruby had a three strike policy, and the boys quickly learned she wasn't playing and that after the third strike they were kicked out of the house, and word would often get back to the other boys still in the home how good they truly had it, how Ruby may be strict but that she actually cared, that she actually gave a damn, and this was something Erik had never experienced, not since his grand-mother passed away, somebody who gave a damn, because sure some of the other foster homes were run by good people who cared, but he never got the sense that they truly cared, that they really gave a shit. It was in Ruby's home that Erik started learning about respect, started doing better in school, started taking care of himself, and right out of graduation Erik joined the Marines because the Marines managed to get his past charges expunged, and he spent several years in the Marines before he met a girl he wanted to marry, but something happened and that girl went away, and Ruby—whom he still kept in contact with all this time—encouraged him to forget about her, to get on with his life.

"In the end, there wasn't much I wanted to do. I just ... wanted to disappear. And so I looked around for some jobs, and being a deputy here in Colton County was one of them, and guys I knew joked that being a black man in Texas wasn't the best idea, but the county was the first one to call me back and hire me, and so …"

He shrugs and looks at me for the first time since he started telling his story.

"Here I am."

I reach out, squeeze his hand.

"Thank you."

"For what?"

"Telling me that."

He shrugs, and smiles.

"Your turn."

I smile back.

"Not tonight. Later. Maybe when you buy me that cup of coffee."

"Wait"—his face all at once serious—"I thought *you* were buying me coffee."

At first I smile, and then I laugh, and it feels good because I don't remember the last time I laughed like this, a genuine, pure laugh.

I squeeze Erik's hand again, and I pull him toward me. He's stronger than me, but he lets me pull him, falling back down onto the bed so he's on his side, his head on the pillow, staring back at me.

I whisper, "Stay."

He watches me for another moment, and then he leans forward, kisses me on the lips. It's not a short kiss, and it's not a long kiss, but it's a kiss I don't think I'll ever forget. Because he doesn't say anything afterward, and neither do I. He just lies there, and so do I, and for the first time I don't think about my past life or the people I've killed or even the two men I killed tonight. All I think about is Erik, being alone with him in this bed, and it's enough to make me feel something I haven't felt in a very long time.

Safe.

EIGHTEEN

The light trickling in from the part in the curtain has changed.

It's pouring in now, the light much stronger, the sun having started to rise an hour or so ago.

I've just opened my eyes and find Erik still lying beside me in bed. I'm not sure whether or not this should surprise me. I can't remember the last time I woke up with somebody in my bed.

Erik's still asleep. Lying on his side, facing me. Snoring quietly.

Part of me wants to lean over, wake him with a kiss, but another part wants to let him sleep. He's working later today and needs all the rest he can get. Me, I'm probably going to head to work too, but that will be much later tonight. I'll need to give Reggie a call, tell him I'm feeling better. Hope that he isn't pissed and decides to fire me.

I slip out of bed, completely naked. After all, I'd answered the door last night in only my towel. It sounds sexier than it really is. If I'd known where the night would eventually lead, I would have spent a few extra minutes in the shower to shave my legs.

As I'm dressing, Erik yawns as he stirs awake.

"What time is it?"

I pull a T-shirt over my head, and glance at his watch on the nightstand.

"Almost eight o'clock."

His head still on the pillow, he squints up at me.

"Do you have any coffee?"

I don't. I don't even have a coffee maker or one of those Keurig machines, but for some reason I think that'll make me seem weird—normal adults at least have a coffee maker, right? —and so I shrug.

"Maybe. Let me check."

Yawning, he murmurs something about giving him five more minutes and turns himself over so his back is to me.

I leave him to his five minutes and head for the kitchen. I don't bother checking the fridge or cabinets. I've got almost nothing to eat or drink, and I'm not sure yet how I'll explain it to Erik.

Maybe inviting him in last night was a mistake. Instead of looping my finger on his belt and pulling him forward, I should have pressed my hand against his chest and pushed him back toward his apartment. He hadn't asked many questions last night, but he will eventually. Especially if this becomes more serious. If we do end up getting a cup of coffee. Last night, I had been so sure that was what I wanted—an actual relationship, somebody to care for, to love—but now I'm not so sure. Because I won't be able to be completely honest with him. I'll always be keeping secrets. And you can't have a solid relationship without trust, right? I'm pretty sure I once saw that on a Dr. Phil episode.

The silence in the kitchen is deeper than normal. Typically I hear my neighbor's TV. But this morning the TV's off, and so the silence is thick, and beyond the silence—somewhere outside—I can just make out a few car doors shutting.

I cross over to the window, peek out through the slit in the curtain.

The first thing that catches my eye is the red flashing lights. A second later I take in the three police cars parked out on the street, men in Kevlar vests quickly dispersing as they move into position.

By one of the cars, surrounded by a handful of cops, Sheriff Gilbert—a man I've never met, have only seen pictures of in the local newspaper—motions at the apartment building.

Points right at my window.

I step away, suddenly holding my breath. Did they see me? I don't think so. Even if they did, it doesn't matter anyway. What matters is that there isn't much time.

I close my eyes, focus on the silence.

The soft patter of boots on the macadam outside nearing the building. The men being as quiet as they can, but my ears are attuned to certain noises, like the flick of somebody undoing the safety on his pistol. Soon they'll enter through the door downstairs, start to creep up the steps.

There's only one exit from the second floor, excluding going out the window. The stairwell will be tightly covered. The men will be up here in less than a minute.

Stupid. Stupid, stupid, stupid. How could I be so stupid? Maybe at the time I didn't think I would ever be in any need to escape my apartment, but now here I am.

I hurry into the kitchen. Pull open the drawer with the pistols and the knife. I pivot toward the table, knock the Imodium A-D and toilet paper roll to the floor, and then set the weapons down. Ejecting the magazines from each pistol, setting them on the tabletop, racking the slides to cough out a round, and laying all of the pieces on the table next to the knife.

I hesitate a beat, listening to the silence.

Was that a creak down at the end of the hallway?

Maybe only thirty seconds.

I rush into the bedroom to find Erik still on his side, facing the window.

"Get up."

He grunts, mumbles something about another five minutes.

I tear open the closet door, reach up to the top and push the pillows aside and pull down the Mossberg. Even though it's not loaded—the box of shells is on the shelf—I pump it once as I turn and aim it at Erik.

As a Marine and cop, Erik knows the sound of an engaged shotgun anywhere. He's on his feet in an instant, popping up from the bed.

"What the fuck?"

I keep the shotgun aimed.

"I need you to come into the living room. Right now."

He stands there in his boxer shorts, appraising me, then starts to scan the room, looking for something he can use to defend himself.

I can't hear the men coming up the steps, but I picture them. Their hands tightly wrapped around the grips of their pistols. Following the lead man down the hallway to my apartment door. They'll be here any second. I'm not expecting a knock.

I say, "Stop fucking around. Move."

I step back to give him space.

Erik hesitates a moment, and then complies. Moving past me, out of the bedroom and into the living room. He pauses when he sees the weapons spread out on the kitchen table.

Keeping his back to me, he says, "What the fuck are you doing?"

"Trying to keep you alive. Get down on your knees and place your hands behind your head."

He turns his head, glares at me from the one eye.

"Fuck you."

I take a step forward, keep the shotgun aimed at his back.

"Do it now."

I'm worried that he won't. That he'll lunge for the knife on the kitchen table. Or one of the pistols, even though he can see the magazines have been ejected. I'm worried that he'll do something stupid when those men burst through the door, and that he'll get shot in the process. But I figure it's better the men see us immediately upon entering the apartment, not hidden back in the bedroom, where they might think we've barricaded ourselves with a cache of weapons.

Finally Erik obeys, lowering himself down onto his knees, reaching up and lacing his fingers on the back of his head.

In the hallway, the footsteps are nearing. We have maybe ten more seconds.

I lower the Mossberg and circle over to the other side of the living room, right next to the couch.

I get down on my knees, set the shotgun beside me, and lace my own fingers behind my head.

Erik stares at me, perplexed.

I whisper, "I'm sorry."

A second later, the door is kicked open.

NINETEEN

The Colton County Sheriff's Office is located roughly forty-five minutes south of Alden. That's where they take me, but they don't put me in one of the holding cells. Instead, they stick me in one of the interview rooms—a plain bright room with a metal table and two metal chairs and a security camera positioned in the corner of the ceiling—and they shackle my wrists to a ring in the top of the table and leave me for an hour or two until the door opens again and Sheriff Gilbert steps inside.

He doesn't speak as he shuts the door. Doesn't even clear his throat as he glances at the security camera. He simply steps over to the table, pulls out the chair, and sits down. He has some documents in his hands—papers, photographs—and he sets them face down on the tabletop.

I'm wearing my sneakers but no socks. A pebble must have found its way into the right sneaker because it's been bugging me the past hour, but there's nothing I can do about it. They let me keep on the sweatpants and T-shirt, though of course they searched me before cuffing me and escorting me down the hallway toward the apartment building stairs.

Sheriff Gilbert says, "Who are you?"

He's an older man in his late fifties, his white hair buzzed, his face tanned and worn. But he has kind eyes, which is maybe one of the reasons he keeps getting reelected as sheriff.

When I don't answer, he shifts in his chair, clears his throat.

"We know your real name isn't Jen Young. Well, at least we're pretty sure that's the case. Your ID looks legit, and you come up in the system, but I've got people doing research. This day and age, you can't just step out of nowhere. There's a social media footprint."

Atticus gave me this identity. He has numerous resources at his disposal, and I'm pretty confident the ID has all the bases covered, but surely something will crack if they dig hard enough.

Sheriff Gilbert clears his throat again.

"You had a Mossberg 590A1 shotgun in your possession, along with a SIG Sauer P320 Nitron Compact and a SIG TACOPS 1911, not to mention a SOG tactical knife. I respect the Second Amendment as much as the next warm-blooded American, but that sure does seem a bit excessive for a girl your age."

I doubt he'd say the same thing to a boy my age, but I don't bother taking the bait.

The man shifts in his seat again, takes a breath.

"We also found a pinkie finger in your refrigerator. It looks like a woman's. Judging by the fact it appears you have all your digits, I have to ask: whose pinkie finger is it?"

I say nothing.

Sheriff Gilbert's eyes harden.

"To what extent is my deputy involved in what happened last night?"

Shit. They're going to drag Erik into this. Not that I'm surprised, but I was hoping he might make it out of this unscathed. Despite the fact he was there when they raided my apartment, half-naked, on his knees with his hands behind his head.

I keep my gaze steady with the sheriff's when I answer.

"What happened last night?"

The kindness in the man's eyes fades.

"You know very well what happened last night. Two federal agents were murdered, and you were the one who murdered them."

"I don't know what you're talking about."

Sheriff Gilbert issues a frustrated grunt as he slides a finger under the documents and flips them over.

They're not papers, I see, but photographs, blown up to 6 x 9 so that every detail can be seen. There are three of them, and he spreads them out on the table in front of me like he's a blackjack dealer.

The sheriff taps the center photograph with his index finger.

"This is you, isn't it?"

It is, but I don't give him the satisfaction of acknowledging it. No verbal response, nothing in my eyes.

He smiles, nodding to himself as he stares down at the photograph.

"Yeah, we got photographic evidence of you murdering those men. I ain't no lawyer, but I've been doing this long enough to know you're screwed."

The center photograph shows me standing on the other side of the tractor, which means the camera must have been positioned above the side door. When the lights came on, I did a quick scan of the interior, but clearly I missed a camera hanging over the door. Unless the camera wasn't meant to be easily seen.

The other two photographs show me standing over the ICE agents, Mulkey and Kyer. In each photograph, I'm holding the 1911. In each photograph, the men are dead.

None of the photographs show Eleanora.

The sheriff leans back in his seat, crosses his arms, and takes another deep breath.

"So here's what's gonna happen next. In the next hour, U.S. Marshals will arrive to take you into their custody. They're gonna transport you down to San Antonio where there's a federal judge waiting to arraign you."

"Sheriff Gilbert."

This catches him off guard for some reason, the way I casually say his name, and he frowns at me but doesn't speak.

"Who provided you with these photographs?"

He doesn't answer. Just sits there, studying me. Clearly not sure how to proceed.

I glance down at the center photograph again, the one that clearly shows my face. It's almost too perfect. Obviously I'm being set up, but the question is by whom, and why.

"How many of these photographs did you receive?"

No answer.

"Did you receive them from the owner of the location in which these events supposedly took place?"

No answer.

"I'm sure by now you would have already spoken to the owner, so I guess my question is does he or she acknowledge having a security camera placed inside this building?"

Sheriff Gilbert still doesn't answer. He keeps watching me, his lips tight.

"Say the owner doesn't have a security camera inside this building, then how exactly were these photographs taken, and why?"

The kindness in the sheriff's eyes has long since left for vacation. His jaw has tightened, too. His chair creaks as he leans forward to start collecting the photographs.

I ask, "When do I get my phone call?"

The hardness in his eyes snaps into a glare.

"You killed two federal agents. You don't get a goddamned phone call."

I should leave it there—let the man storm out of the room to catch his breath, cool off—but I don't.

"So let me get this straight. You respect the Second Amendment, but not the Sixth? You know, it's part of the Bill of Rights that guarantees a citizen a speedy trial, a fair jury, and a—"

Sheriff Gilbert slams his fist down on the table.

"You"—pointing at me now with his free hand, his face having gone red—"you murdered two federal agents in cold blood."

I calmly keep my gaze steady with his.

"Allegedly."

His jaw tightens again. His face has gone even redder. It looks like he's ready to explode at me when there's a knock at the door.

Like somebody's just poked him with a pin, the sheriff starts to deflate. He glares at me for another moment before snatching up the photographs and pushing to his feet. He nearly tears the door off its hinges, lets it slam shut. A moment of silence outside, and then he shouts, "*What?*" before he says something else I can't make out and the door opens again. He doesn't advance toward the table, though, and stays where he is, holding the door open.

"Your lawyer is here."

His words drip with contempt.

I don't make any reaction—no smile, no frown—because I don't want to set him off any more than I already have. Plus … what lawyer? Obviously I'm entitled to one—so says the Founding Fathers who wrote the Bill of Rights—but I don't have a lawyer, or even know a lawyer. I wanted a phone call so that I could call Atticus. I wouldn't be able to speak to him, at least not right away. The only number he gave me is to a dry cleaners that doesn't exist. Atticus said to call and leave a message if I'm ever in any trouble. And this most certainly seems like trouble. Not sure what all he can do for me, anyway —the photographs Sheriff Gilbert showed me are quite damning—but at least he's somebody I can reach out to because … well, I don't have anybody else.

The sheriff lets the door slam shut. For a minute I'm left in that deep silence, and then the door opens again.

And again I don't make any reaction as I watch her enter the interview room. She's wearing a black business suit. Modest heels. Full-rim rectangle eyeglasses. Her hair isn't curly, not like it was yesterday, but long and straight.

As soon as the door closes, she moves directly to the camera in the corner, a briefcase in one hand, and leans up on her tiptoes to disconnect the power cord. Then Leila Simmons turns back to me, a small smile on her face.

"Hello, Holly."

TWENTY

She moves forward slowly, taking her time, her eyes never once leaving mine. She sets the briefcase on the table, pulls out the chair, and sits down.

"Cat got your tongue?"

When I don't answer, she frowns thoughtfully.

"Such an odd expression, isn't it? Just one of those sayings that doesn't make sense when you think about it. I looked it up once, to find out where it came from. Supposedly it goes all the way back to the Middle Ages. They say witches' cats would take a person's speech so that the sighting could not be reported to the authorities. Or something along those lines. Seriously, Holly, say something. You're starting to make me nervous."

I don't answer. Just keep staring back at her. Wondering how I could be so careless. I thought I did enough research to make sure she was legit, but apparently not.

"In case you're wondering, my name isn't Leila Simmons. But for now feel free to think of me as Leila. By the way, Eleanora is doing well. That's actually her real name. Just like Juana was really the name of the girl those two agents killed."

She pauses, shakes her head with a soft sigh.

"Such a shame what happened. But she knew what she was getting into. All the girls we take in know what they're getting into. They're desperate, you understand. They'll do anything to save their children. They'll do anything to make a better life for themselves."

Another pause, and now the small smile turns cold.

"Of course, in the end, they almost always get fucked over. But blame that on today's marketplace—it's the children who are the moneymakers, not the girls. Most of them are damaged by the time they get to us. They're no longer as ... pure as our buyers would like."

Okay, enough of this shit. I'm done staying silent.

"Give me one good reason why I shouldn't shout for the sheriff and have you arrested right this second."

The woman smiles again, and presses the buttons on the briefcase to unlatch it. She lifts the top and pulls out some photographs. Like with Sheriff Gilbert, the photographs are large, but they're not 6 x 9. These are in color, and there are three of them. She lays them out on the table in front of me. Seeing them, my heart stops.

Leila taps the tip of her fingernail on the tabletop as she speaks.

"I don't have much time, so I'm going to cut to the chase. We know who you are. We know your name is Holly Lin. That you worked covert missions for the United States government. That you spent your day keeping an eye on the children of General Walter Hadden. That your father also worked covert missions for the government, but that he went rogue a few years ago."

She keeps tapping her nail, a consistent, steady beat.

"Do your sister and mother know what you really did? Or what your father did? Do you think they wonder why you disappeared, or did you tell them why you left?"

In the center photograph is my mother. It looks like she's at the grocery store, in the produce section. Inspecting a batch of bananas.

"Your nephews are quite cute. What are their names? We know one is Matthew, but the other is …"

She lets it hang there, as if she expects me to fill in the blank, but I continue to say nothing. I stare down at the photo on the left, the one that shows the two boys playing at the park. I'm not about to tell her the other boy's name is Max.

Leila keeps tapping her fingernail on the table.

"And your sister's husband's name is Ryan. We know where he works. We know some of his coworkers. We know where he likes to have lunch during the week."

My sister and Ryan are in the third photograph. It's taken from a distance. All the photographs are taken from a distance. My family—the ones I left D.C. to save, to protect—are being watched. *Were* being watched. It all depends on how long ago these photographs were taken.

I lift my gaze to meet hers, and it takes everything I have not to launch myself across the table. Only I can't. Not with my wrists shackled. She knows this, of course, and based on the look in her eyes, it amuses her greatly.

When I speak, my voice is just above a whisper.

"What do you want?"

She lifts a finger, shakes it back and forth like a metronome, and reaches back into the briefcase. Pulls out another photograph, this one also in color.

My heart stops again. Not in fear this time, but in surprise.

Leila sets the photo on top of the others, turned so I can see it right side up.

"Does this look familiar?"

It does. Of course it does. The bedroom of a mansion overlooking the town of La Miserias. The mansion belonged to a man named Fernando Sanchez Morales. The Moraleses were the last remaining cartel family Alejandro Cortez had targeted because of what they did to his family. Morales and his men had stormed La Miserias that night out of anger because the people had risen up and defied Morales, leaving his wife and child behind only to be guarded by a few men. By the time Nova and I arrived at the mansion, those men were killed, and Morales's wife and child were cowering in the master bedroom while Alejandro Cortez stood over them.

Leila watches me stare down at the photograph.

"Morales became paranoid being locked up in his home. He wanted to make sure his family was safe, so he had security cameras installed. But he didn't want his wife to feel like she was being watched all the time, so they were tiny cameras, hidden very well."

They must have been hidden very well, but I don't remember seeing any cameras. Of course, at the time I was too focused on saving the woman's and child's lives. The possibility of hidden cameras was the last thing on my mind.

"Where did you take his body, by the way?"

She's watching me now intently, eager to learn where we buried the man known as El Diablo.

I say nothing.

With a shrug, Leila gathers the photographs and slips them back into the briefcase.

"On second thought, I don't want to know. I like the mystery. It keeps things interesting."

She closes the briefcase.

"Your friend—he's a big, handsome man. We've tried finding him, too, but with no luck. He's managed to do a better job at disappearing, it seems. You, on the other hand … you did pretty well, but social media got the better of you."

She waits a beat for a reaction, and smiles again.

"You see, the people I work for are well connected, and they have a lot of money, enough money to pay the right people to scour social media for whatever or whomever we want. We gave them your picture, and they used their facial recognition software to start digging through social media. The way it was explained to me, it's like a spider that skims the Web looking for somebody with the same dimensions as your face. For seven months they searched until they found a match. Somebody's Instagram, a photo taken at your place of employment. You were in the background, but there was enough of your face that it gave an alert. Once we learned the location of the bar, we sent people down to confirm it was you, and we've been monitoring you ever since."

"How long?"

She seems surprised I asked the question.

"What do you mean?"

"How long have you been monitoring me?"

"About two months. Don't look surprised. It's not like we had people sitting in a van outside your apartment. We just made sure to keep an eye on you until the day came that we would need your assistance."

"I'm not helping you."

"No? Come now, Holly, look at these pictures of your family. We know that Ernesto Diaz's son threatened them. That's why you killed him and his men, and why you went to Mexico to kill Ernesto."

She's right, of course. Javier Diaz did threaten my family, and because of that I did kill him and his men. I knew that once word got back to his father of what happened, his father would retaliate, and so I went to Mexico to kill him, too—and it was there that I stumbled into the war between Alejandro Cortez and Fernando Sanchez Morales.

Leila smiles again, clearly impressed with herself.

"The dots were always there. We simply needed a starting point. Don't think Javier Diaz didn't alert only his father that he planned to confront you. Others were aware. That's how we've known about your family all this time. We just weren't sure what to do with them, if anything. But like I said, we decided to keep an eye on you until we needed your assistance, and with those two ICE agents … let's call it two birds with one stone."

She laughs suddenly, a soft chuckle, and shakes her head.

"Now *that's* an expression that makes sense. There's something so simplistically barbaric about the idea of killing two things with one item, don't you think?"

I don't bother answering. I keep thinking about the photographs in the briefcase.

Leila snaps the briefcase shut, pulls it close to her.

"Obviously you aren't taking this seriously. I guess you want your family to die. So be it."

She starts to stand, but I tell her to wait, and she stands there, watching me.

I say, "What do you want?"

"Right now? I want you to know we have people watching your family. At any moment they're prepared to kill your mother and sister, even your nephews. If you don't want that to happen, you're going to do exactly what we tell you to do."

"And what is that?"

The small smile lights back on her face.

"That will come in time. For now, I want to make sure we're on the same page. And I know what you're thinking— that maybe you'll try to get them to arrest me on my way out, see the photographs in my briefcase, but I wouldn't advise that. If I don't leave here in the next five minutes, your family dies. And in terms of phone calls, I've already made them aware you don't want any phone calls. Besides, the U.S. Marshals will be here shortly. And once they take you into their custody, you won't be in any position to make phone calls."

Without another word, she heads for the door.

I watch her go, wanting to say something, wanting to lift the table and throw it at her and snap her back in half, but the afterimage of my mother and sister and my sister's family stays in my mind. As long as they're in danger, I can't make any moves against this woman or anyone else she's working with.

Leila knocks on the door to let the guard outside know that she's done. She glances at the camera in the corner by the ceiling, at the cord she'd pulled, and shrugs at me. Not her problem.

She smiles again.

"We'll be seeing you soon, Holly."

The door creaks open, and she steps out into the hallway.

TWENTY-ONE

For a solid minute, I don't move. Don't breathe. Don't even blink. I stare at the door, at the space where that woman stood, and do everything in my power not to scream.

Those photographs Leila showed me are seared into my brain. Even with my eyes open, I can still see them. My mother at the grocery store. My nephews playing in a park. My sister and her husband standing together.

Everything I did after I killed Javier Diaz was to protect them—my trip to Mexico, to take out Javier's father, and then returning to the U.S. and starting a new life in the middle of nowhere. Did I miss my family, even though they often drove me nuts? Of course. But it was my love for them that kept me strong, ensured I never gave in and contacted them.

I thought I eliminated the only link between my family and the world of killers. Apparently, I was wrong.

Finally I close my eyes, suck in a heavy breath. I need to come up with a game plan. Something to get word to Atticus. Atticus will know what to do. He'll make sure my family is safe. He'll—

The door opens again.

I expect it to be Sheriff Gilbert, or a deputy, or maybe one of the U.S. Marshals, but it's not any of them.

Erik Johnson has on jeans and gray T-shirt. He stands in the doorway. Leans in slightly to glance up at the camera, does a sort of double take when he notices the wire has been unplugged. He focuses his glare on me.

"You make me sick."

I can tell he's been practicing the line, probably running it over and over in his head. The way he would eye me down. The way he would stand there with shoulders back, his chin tilted up. He's pissed because he thinks I've been lying to him all this time, and while it's true I have been lying to him, I've been lying to him for a completely different reason. Not that it would matter to him right now, or even make sense, but that doesn't stop me from seeing him as my last chance of saving my family.

"I need your help."

This clearly surprises him, but his glare doesn't waver.

"Why the fuck would I do anything for you?"

"Don't think of it as for me. It's for my family. They're in danger."

This clearly surprises him too, and he frowns for the first time.

"What family?"

"They're not going to let me make a phone call. That woman—she's not a real lawyer. She's—"

Well, who is she? It's too complicated to get into it. I don't have time to explain how she set me up to kill those two men. Because she knew I was the kind of person who would kill them. The kind of person who wouldn't let the murder of a girl go unavenged.

Erik takes a step back, leans his head out the door to look down the hallway, then focuses his glare on me again.

"I shouldn't even be here right now. They've suspended me.

They *interrogated* me. I'm under investigation. Like I had any idea what kind of monster you are."

Obviously he's talked his fellow deputies into sneaking him in here before the U.S. Marshals take me away. So that he can tell me off. I don't blame him, and if I hadn't just had a visit from the woman I knew as Leila Simmons, I would let him vent.

I say, "Will you remember this number?"

He doesn't answer.

I recite the number Atticus gave me a year ago, the one he said to call if I'm ever in trouble or need to get hold of him. After I recite it, I say it again, slowly this time, to make sure it sinks into Erik's head.

"Nobody will answer. It'll be for a company called Scout's Dry Cleaning. Leave a message. Say Holly's family is in danger."

His face changes, clouds with confusion.

"Who the hell is Holly?"

Before I can answer, there's a sudden whistle down the hallway, one of the deputies giving him the signal that his time's up.

Erik doesn't waste time—he steps away, quietly shuts the door.

I'm left sitting there, shackled to the table, staring at empty space again, and it's another minute before the door opens and Sheriff Gilbert peers in, his face as hard and severe as his gruff voice.

"Your ride's here."

TWENTY-TWO

There are only two U.S. Marshals. Neither one speaks to me. They pat me down, one of the Marshals signs off on a form on a clipboard, and then I'm being led down a hallway toward the side entrance.

A brand-new Chevy Caprice is parked outside. It gleams under the midday sun. A few deputies stand off to the side, as well as a few state police officers, and beyond them—past a barrier of police cruisers—sits a local news affiliate van, a cameraman already set up with the reporter standing next to him. They watch me, just like everybody else, as I'm loaded into the back of the Caprice, shuffling across the seat with my ankles and wrists still shackled.

Soon the Marshals climb into the car and we begin to move.

The cameraman shifts his weight as he tracks us with his camera. I sense him from the corner of my eye, just outside the window, but I keep staring forward.

The Caprice's engine purrs as we accelerate down the street, headed for the highway.

The Marshal in the passenger seat makes a quick phone

call, says that we just left, and then sets his phone aside. Both of them have on sunglasses, and neither acknowledges me. I can't tell if the driver even glances at me in the rearview mirror.

While I've murdered two federal agents, it hasn't become a national story. At least, not yet. A news chopper doesn't follow us. The local affiliate van doesn't follow us. Nobody follows us as far as I can tell—not even a deputy's cruiser—and soon we're speeding down the empty highway, headed south, the landscape mostly desolate except for the foothills off in the distance.

The air condition is on, set to low. An uneasy silence fills the car.

Not once do I feel the need to argue my case to these Marshals. They're merely my escort. Eventually I'll be taken in front of a judge for an adjudication hearing. I'll be prosecuted on the federal level. There's a lot of damning evidence against me—the photographs, of course, as well as my weapons—and I'll be lucky if I don't end up with the death penalty.

My only hope now is that Erik moves past his sudden hatred for me and makes that phone call. All I need is for Atticus to hear that my family is in danger. At this point, I have no illusions I'll be saved. I've always known a day like this would come, anyway. All my years of killing for the government, knowing if I were ever caught the government would disavow me and that I would be on my own. I've always known that risk, and I've been okay with it just as I'm okay with it now. Those men were corrupt, and the previous night they had killed Juana, and there was no telling what they planned to do with Eleanora.

Up front, the Marshal in the passenger seat leans forward to adjust the air. He lowers his window a crack, and air whips in through the slit.

He says, "I could use a cigarette."

The driver, keeping his face tilted forward, grunts in agreement.

A billboard looms ahead, only a couple hundred yards away. It's the only thing marking the landscape, one of those full-size billboards that goes right down to the ground. There isn't even an ad on it, just a message saying that the thing is for rent with a number to call.

I find myself focusing on the billboard for some reason, and it's only a moment or two before I understand the reason why.

Movement beside the billboard, what appears to be some-body stationed there, and the sun is angled in the sky just right that it glints off what I instantly realize is a scope lens.

I shout, "Look out!"

The windshield spiderwebs and half of the driver's head disappears. Blood and bits of brain tissue splatter the inside of the car.

The passenger reacts at once, pulling his gun while he leans over to grab the wheel.

That's when I hear an engine coming up behind us and glance back through the rear window. A massive pickup truck is right on our tail. Two men sit up front, both wearing balaclavas.

The pickup swerves into the next lane, inches closer, and immediately swerves back into our lane, striking the back of the Caprice.

The passenger tries to hold onto the wheel, but he can't do it with only the one hand. He drops the gun, grabs the wheel with both hands, starts to slide himself over to the driver's side so he can press his foot down on the gas.

The billboard is less than fifty yards away, coming up fast.

The sniper steps out, rifle in hand, and sights on the remaining Marshal.

The Marshal, maybe realizing that there's no escape, makes a split-second decision.

He whips the wheel toward the right, and the Caprice veers off the highway and barrels straight into the sniper.

I'm briefly aware of the sniper going under the car and the SUV parked behind the billboard as we zoom past, but the ground here is rutted, unsteady, and as the Marshal tries to veer us back onto the highway, he loses control of the wheel and the Caprice starts to spin, whipping up a dust cloud in its wake.

Even before the car has come to a complete stop, I dive for the closest door, but it's locked from the outside. I try the other door, and it's the same.

Up front, the Marshal ducks down for his gun. He punches the gas, too, and the engine roars but we don't move, and it takes the Marshal an extra second to realize the Caprice has shifted out of gear.

Before he can shove the Caprice back into drive, the pickup skids to a halt in front of us. The pickup's passenger jumps out, an M4 in his hands. He moves at an angle, so that he's not facing the car straight on but rather from the side, and fires twice through the driver's window, the Marshal raising his gun to fire back but not getting a chance to let off any rounds.

By now I've leaned back, with my feet pointed at the rear passenger window, and I kick the window as hard as I can—once, twice, three times—and it's on the fourth kick that the window finally gives way, and I jerk forward, as quickly as the shackles will let me, and despite the shards of glass sticking up from the windowsill I fling myself through the opening and hit the ground on my side, hard, a flash of pain shooting every-where, but I ignore it as I struggle to my feet and start hopping away.

Behind me, a voice shouts, "Do you want your family to die?"

I stop at once. Stare at the foothills off in the distance.

Turning around, I watch two men in balaclavas hurrying

toward me. Both carry M4s. One of them straps the rifle over his shoulder as they near.

"Don't struggle."

The man picks me up and carries me fireman-style back toward the billboard and the SUV idling beside it. The world is upside down, but I see the Caprice from the corner of my eye, and I hear the passenger inside, the Marshal still alive. One of the men in balaclavas runs up to the Caprice with a gas can and starts to douse the car. The Marshal inside shouts no no no no as he tries to crawl from the car, but the man with the gas can uses his boot to shove him back inside as he lights a road flare and tosses it into the car. The Marshal starts to scream as the Caprice goes up in flames. I want to do something, somehow help him, but before I know it we've reached the SUV and I'm upright again, the man having deposited me so my feet are back on the ground. The back door is opened and I'm pushed inside. I hear one of the other men asking what they should do with Daniel, and another man saying they can't leave him here so load him up, too. Another man leans forward, right at me, and I can't tell what's in his hand at first—the entire world feels like it's spinning, on fire, a man screaming as he burns to death —but I realize it's a needle, that they're going knock me out. I start to struggle, and another man holds me in place, and a second later there's the sting of the needle as they inject me and then a black bag is promptly pulled down over my head and all I can see is darkness.

PART II

NEVERLAND

TWENTY-THREE

The sun had set hours ago—the vast sky going from a dark blue to a lush indigo to a heavy black—and it was almost ten o'clock when Sheriff Tom Gilbert arrived home. He wasn't driving his Ford pickup but one of the cruisers. Erik figured he had come straight from the scene out on the highway and hadn't bothered to stop by the station to swap vehicles.

Erik was parked down the street, angled so he had a good view of the house, and as soon as the sheriff had pulled into the driveway, Erik exited his own vehicle and hurried up the block. When he reached the house, the old man was already on the walkway headed to the front door, his pace sluggish, his shoulders slouched.

"Sheriff Gilbert."

The sheriff paused for a beat, issued a heavy sigh, and turned to find Erik striding up his driveway. His gaze was cautious at first, but once he realized it was one of his deputies, his eyes hardened.

"Christ, Johnson, I thought you were a reporter. What the hell are you doing here?"

Erik stopped short, raised his hands to his sides to show he meant no harm.

"I wanted to talk."

Sheriff Gilbert shook his head, issued another heavy sigh.

"Nothing to discuss, son. Not until the investigation is over."

"How long will that take?"

"Off the top of my head, I'm not sure, and right now it's the least of my worries. Do yourself a favor and head home."

As the man started to turn away, Erik said, "You know I had nothing to do with any of this."

Sheriff Gilbert took another breath, nodded slowly as he regarded his deputy.

"I know, son. You were just in the wrong place at the wrong time. Honestly—"

He glanced at the house to make sure his wife wasn't watching or eavesdropping, and then dropped his voice.

"Can't say I blame you for knocking boots with the girl. She sure is a looker. But after what she did"—the sheriff shook his head—"we need to follow protocol. I mean, it don't look good we found you half-naked in her place. You understand that, don't you?"

"I do, sir."

"And then what happened later today"—another shake of the head, this time with more anger—"shit, son, you shoulda seen what was done to that car. Both men burned alive inside. Your girl nowhere in sight."

"She couldn't have done that on her own."

"Oh, I know it. Those federal investigators who came over from Dallas know it, too. They got a BOLO out for your girl. For her and whoever she's working with."

Erik chewed the inside of his mouth. It was a nervous tic he'd developed from his years in the foster care system when he became anxious. He'd come here to confess, to tell Sheriff Gilbert how he'd snuck into the station to confront Jen—or Holly, if that was her real name—and how she told him the lawyer who had come to see her wasn't a real lawyer and how her family was in danger. He hadn't called the number she gave him—he hadn't really been listening at the time, anyway, too furious after what he'd learned, and only remembered half the number—but he had sensed something in her eyes when she spoke to him, a vulnerability he had never seen from her before, not even when they were having sex.

"Sir, the lawyer—"

Sheriff Gilbert cut him off with a heavy sigh.

"Yes, I know. She's dead. They're trying to determine when she was murdered."

The sheriff noted the frown on Erik's face, and sighed again.

"Goddamn it. You didn't know? Of course you didn't know."

"The lawyer was murdered?"

"That's right. They wanted to contact her about her client going missing the way she did. She gave her ID when she arrived at the station, and all her information was logged, and when she didn't answer her phone, we sent somebody out there and—"

Sheriff Gilbert shook his head.

"Look, I can't be talking about this with you. Not while you're under investigation."

Erik took a step forward, his entire body on edge, Jen or Holly's voice still echoing in his ears.

That woman—she's not a real lawyer.

"Sir, are we sure she's even a lawyer?"

The sheriff frowned.

"What kind of question is that? Of course we're sure she's a lawyer. But the woman who came to see your girlfriend"—he shrugged—"we don't know who the fuck she is."

This stopped Erik cold. He'd thought Sheriff Gilbert meant the woman who came to see Jen or Holly had been found murdered.

"Wait. Are you saying—"

Sheriff Gilbert cut him off again.

"That the woman who came to the station was impersonating the woman we found murdered? That's right. Now look, Johnson, you really need to leave. I know you want to help, but you just can't do that right now. Not until the investigation is over. And before you ask, no, I don't know how long that'll be."

Erik nodded. This was more than he'd expected to get. He respected Sheriff Gilbert, almost saw the man as a father figure, and he hated to disappoint him.

The front door opened a crack, and Mrs. Gilbert peeked out.

"Tom?"

The sheriff said, "Be right there, dear."

He waited for his wife to shut the door before clearing his throat, which Erik knew was his prompt to leave.

But Erik couldn't leave. Not yet.

"Sir, what are the chances I'll be reinstated?"

There was no immediate answer from the sheriff. The man watched him for a beat too long, and even in the dark Erik saw the sadness in the man's eyes.

"I don't know, son. It don't look too good, especially after what happened to those Marshals today. That's four men dead now because of your girl."

Erik had to steel himself, keep his voice calm and steady.

"She's not my girl, and I had nothing to do with any of that."

"I know, son. But something like this, heads always got to roll. Especially when the papers find out you were with her this morning. It ain't gonna come from me, but it's gonna get out at some point …"

Sheriff Gilbert trailed off, shaking his head.

"Keep your chin up. Head on home and get some rest. I need to get some rest, too. Today was a long day, and something tells me tomorrow is gonna be even longer."

TWENTY-FOUR

Erik trudged up the steps to the second floor, his hands balling in and out of fists. It was a risk confronting Sheriff Gilbert like that, but he'd had no choice. He wanted to help any way he could, but he also wanted to see where things stood in terms of his job. And Erik had come away from it with the realization there was a good chance he wouldn't have his job much longer.

The sheriff hadn't said as much, but Erik was able to read between the lines. He wondered if it would be better for him to resign before he was fired. In that case, he wouldn't be able to stay in Alden.

Being a deputy was what and who he was. He couldn't see himself doing anything else. Which meant he would need to move away and try to find work in law enforcement elsewhere. Only he was pretty sure that even if he resigned, word would make it to whoever considered him elsewhere for a job of what had happened in Alden: Erik on his knees half-naked with a woman who killed two ICE agents when the police raided the apartment.

His eyes focused on the door across from his as he walked down the hallway. A notice from the police had been taped on the jamb between the door and the doorframe. The apartment wasn't a crime scene, but the police wanted to make sure nothing was disturbed in case they needed to return at a later date. As far as Erik knew, the whole place had been searched— as well as his apartment, upon his approval—but there was always the chance they would need to check back again.

Erik shut his eyes, shook his head. He needed to forget about it. Needed to think of anything else except what happened today.

But of course he couldn't do that. The more he tried to think about something else, he immediately thought about Jen or whoever the fuck she was aiming the shotgun at him and ordering him out of the bedroom.

He opened his eyes again, took a breath, and glanced once more at the door before turning to his own door, the apartment key in his hand.

He inserted the key into the lock but paused, stood staring at his door for a beat before slowly turning and taking in the door across the hallway again.

The notice from the police—it was sliced vertically, right along the doorframe. With the door closed the way it was, it looked almost perfect, like it hadn't been touched. But from this angle, it didn't look right.

Erik quietly pulled the key back out from the lock. He took a step toward the door. Got close enough to verify that, yes, the notice had been sliced.

He took another step forward.

Leaned in so that his ear was barely touching the door.

He couldn't hear anything inside, but that didn't mean much. Maybe whoever sliced the notice had entered the apartment and had already left. Or maybe they were still inside and had heard him and gone silent. Maybe somebody was standing on the other side of the door right now, looking at him through the peephole, a gun leveled at his chest.

Erik moved without thinking.

Knowing that he didn't have time to retrieve his gun from inside his apartment—not his department-issued pistol, which he'd turned in earlier today, but his personal Glock—he stepped to the side as he turned the doorknob and shoved the door open.

He stood with his shoulder against the wall, holding his breath, waiting for a gunshot or for somebody to come running through the doorway.

Nothing.

He waited another beat, listening to the silence, when he realized that the door should have been locked.

Call Sheriff Gilbert. That's what he should do. Call it in and have the proper authorities come take care of it, but he thought maybe this was a way he could redeem himself. If there was somebody in the apartment and he managed to detain them, wouldn't that mean something? At the very least, he wouldn't lose his job.

Five seconds had passed since he opened the door, and so far nothing had happened. Down the hallway, the volume on Mr. Hobbs's television was turned up louder than it should be this time of night. Erik thought about calling out—"It's the police!"—but decided to play this a different way.

Taking another breath, he stepped forward and entered the apartment, reaching out in one fluid motion to flick on the light switch—

Which did nothing.

The apartment remained dark.

Erik paused again, suddenly nervous, the confidence he'd felt only seconds ago having vanished, and he decided to retreat, hurry into his apartment to retrieve the Glock and call Sheriff Gilbert, when he sensed motion behind him.

He spun to his left and instinctively ducked, swinging his fist in an uppercut, skin brushing against heavy fabric for just an instant before the person behind him sidestepped the follow through and then Erik felt a heavy elbow snap down on the back of his neck. He stumbled away but immediately lurched back at his attacker, pushing the person into the wall, and he had the sense the person was big, tall and strong, and while Erik himself was tall and strong, this man had a good sixty pounds on him, much of it muscle, and before Erik knew it, his legs were swept out from under him and he fell hard, landing on his back, his head knocking on the floor. He tried to roll away, to scramble to his feet, but the man was on top of him, and suddenly Erik felt cold metal pressed to the side of his head as a deep voice whispered.

"Don't fucking move."

TWENTY-FIVE

Lying on his back in the dark apartment, the man's weight holding him in place and the barrel of a gun pressing against the side of his head, Erik took a moment to consider his options.

He quickly realized he had none.

Erik whispered, "Okay."

The man didn't move at first, keeping the barrel pressed against the side of Erik's head. Erik was faintly aware of soft footsteps somewhere else in the apartment, which meant the man wasn't alone. At least one other intruder. Maybe more.

The deep voice whispered again.

"Stay flat on the floor. Move a muscle, and I'll shoot you in the face."

Erik said nothing.

The man waited a beat, and then the heavy weight pressing Erik to the floor eased away as the man stood up.

Erik stayed where he was, staring at the dark ceiling. Wondering if the other intruder had a weapon. Wondering what the chances were he could manage to commandeer one of those weapons without getting shot.

The deep voice said, "Go ahead."

At first, Erik wasn't sure what to do—was the man speaking to him?—but then he heard the soft footsteps behind him again and a light came on.

It was a sort of a lamp with a blue glow, enough to illuminate the entire apartment with subtle light. Erik took in the man who had pressed the gun to his head—he was big, just as Erik had suspected, and he had a full beard, the kind that made Erik peg the man for a SEAL.

Shifting his eyes up, he saw the other man was tall but thinner. This man regarded him curiously. He looked to have a phone in his hand, but no weapon.

The SEAL leaned over Erik, keeping his gun trained on him. Now with the soft light, Erik noted the gun was an FNX-45 with a threaded barrel.

The man said, "Who the hell are you?"

Erik wet his lips but said nothing.

"We don't have time for this shit. You have a wallet?"

Erik nodded, just once.

"Give me your wallet."

For a crazy moment, Erik wondered if he was being mugged. If these two men were here to rob the place. Alden was a small town that got a few B&Es during the year, but those were mostly from stupid kids who didn't know any better.

The man said, "I'm not going to ask you again."

Erik whispered, "My left rear pants pocket."

"Go ahead and pull it out. Slowly."

Erik did, slipping his leather wallet from his pocket. Besides his driver's license and a debit card and a couple bucks of cash, there wasn't anything else in there.

The man didn't even look inside the wallet and instead tossed it to the other man. The other man opened the wallet and pulled out Erik's DL. At first, Erik wasn't sure what this man was doing before he saw the man hold his cell phone over the DL and snap a picture.

"What the hell are you doing?"

The SEAL said, "Background check."

Erik started to sit up, but the SEAL stepped forward and aimed the gun at his face.

"Let's not do anything stupid, okay, chief?"

Erik rested his head back on the carpet. Braced himself, took another deep breath. This wasn't how he wanted to die. Not by the hands of these assholes.

The SEAL said, "Well?"

He wasn't talking to Erik. The other man stepped forward and handed him the phone. The SEAL scanned the screen before he nodded and cut his gaze at Erik on the floor.

"Erik Johnson. Was raised in foster care. Entered the Marines at eighteen, stayed for five years and was honorably discharged. Now works as a Colton County sheriff's deputy in Bumfuck, Texas."

The man paused, and grinned down at Erik.

"It doesn't say Bumfuck, but let's be honest here, this town is pretty shitty."

Erik said, "Who the hell are you?"

The man ignored him.

"Deputy Johnson, don't you realize you're trespassing?"

"Fuck you. You're trespassing."

The SEAL glanced again at the phone.

"Nothing here about unoriginal comebacks, but not every background check is complete."

The SEAL handed the phone back to the other man, then crouched down beside Erik. He was close enough that if Erik tried anything the man could squeeze the trigger and place a bullet in Erik's head before Erik moved a muscle.

"What brings you here tonight, Deputy Johnson?"

Erik felt his jaw tighten.

"Fuck you."

"Didn't you see the notice on the door? Law enforcement forbids anybody to enter, which includes neighbors. And don't go telling me it's because you're law enforcement, too. I read that you were suspended today. What's up with that?"

A chill shot through Erik's veins. He wasn't surprised basic information was so easily accessible to these men, but how would they know about his suspension as it had happened *just that afternoon*?

When Erik didn't answer, the man said, "My associate and I don't have all night."

Erik wet his lips again. For a moment he didn't think he'd have a voice, but then he managed to speak.

"I was here this morning."

"You were where?"

"In this apartment."

"Why were you in this apartment?"

"I was … in bed with her."

In the soft light, Erik thought he saw something pass across the man's face.

The man said, "Go on."

"There isn't much else to say. The police raided the apartment. Took her into custody. Because I was here, they questioned me, too, and because of what she did, they suspended me."

Erik expected the man to ask more about what Jen or Holly or whatever her name was had done, but he didn't. He glanced once at the thin man and then flicked his eyes back down at Erik.

"Sucks to be you, doesn't it?"

Erik no longer had the sense that his life was in danger. Whatever these men were doing was shady, but he didn't think they would kill him.

"Can I sit up?"

The man took a step back but kept the FNX-45 trained on him.

"Be my guest."

Erik sat up, slowly, and shifted so that his back was against the wall. He didn't know what was going to happen next, but he felt the need to keep talking.

"Do you know her?"

The man's face remained expressionless.

"Do I know who?"

"Holly or whatever her name is. I saw her for a second this afternoon before the Marshals took her away. She told me her family is in danger."

Again, Erik thought he saw something pass across the man's face.

"She said the lawyer who came to see her today wasn't even a real lawyer. And then it turned out—"

Erik paused, realizing maybe his life was in danger after all, that these two men might have visited the real lawyer earlier in the day.

The SEAL tilted his head.

"And then it turned out what?"

Erik wet his lips again.

"Did you kill her?"

"Did we kill who?"

"The lawyer."

The SEAL traded a glance with the other man and frowned down at Erik.

"Chief, I can't speak for my associate over there, but I certainly didn't kill anybody today. Care to start making some sense?"

Erik had the feeling the man honestly didn't know what he was talking about, and decided to push on.

"It turns out the real lawyer was murdered this morning,

and another woman had come to the station impersonating her."

The man glanced at his associate again, and there was something severe in the look, something that told Erik there was a lot more going on than he had first thought.

The man said, "Any idea who this woman was who impersonated the lawyer?"

"None."

"Did Holly tell you anything else?"

The man said the name so easily, so naturally, Erik realized that was in fact her real name.

"She gave me a phone number to call. She said it was to some dry cleaners only it wasn't really to a dry cleaners. Said to call and leave a message saying that her family is in danger. I figured she was bullshitting me, so I—"

He stopped when he noted the expression on the man's face. This clearly meant something significant to him.

"She wasn't bullshitting me, was she?"

The man said, "Who are you?"

"What do you mean? You read my background."

"No, I mean what are you to her—a one-night stand or something more serious?"

Erik thought about it for a moment.

"Something more serious. Why?"

"Because it's clear she trusted you. She wouldn't have given you the number otherwise. Are you positive she said her family is in danger?"

"Yes."

"Anything else?"

"No."

"All right. So what's going to happen now is my associate and I are going to leave, and you're going to stay here and act like we never had this conversation."

Erik started to stand up, saw the gun still aimed at him, and stayed where he was with his back against the wall.

"Where are you going?"

"That's no concern of yours."

"If you're"—he paused, not sure how to say the rest but then decided just to go with it—"if you're going to try to save her family, I want to help."

"Fat chance, Romeo. You're staying here."

"Please"—there was a hint of desperation in his voice, something he couldn't hide—"I need to help."

The man studied his face.

"Why?"

"I just … I can't sit by and do nothing."

The thin man tapped his foot on the floor, and when he had the SEAL's attention, he tossed him the cell phone.

The SEAL scanned the screen again, and shook his head.

"No fucking way."

The thin man nodded, his expression serious.

The SEAL said, "Fine, then I'll call him and see what he says."

He held the phone to his ear and listened for a moment, then said, "No, I don't think it's a good idea," and listened some more and then said, "We don't know anything about him," and listened some more before he finally said, "Okay, fine," and then disconnected the call and tossed the phone back to the thin man.

The SEAL leveled his gaze on Erik.

"You want to help?"

Erik nodded.

"Yes, of course."

"Then you're going to do everything I tell you to do."

"What do you need me to do?"

"For starters, I need you to shut the fuck up and listen. You were suspended and are currently under investigation. Do you understand how it's going to look if you all of a sudden disappear?"

Erik nodded—it wouldn't look good at all—and the man continued.

"Holly's family lives out near Washington, D.C. That's where James and I are headed next. We didn't manage to find any clues here about where Holly may have ended up. It's like she disappeared into thin air. So the only lead we have—if you are to be believed—is that her family is in danger. There's a private jet waiting for us at an airfield sixty miles away from here. If you want to go with us to D.C., you're welcome, but again, you need to do everything I say. Got it?"

Erik looked back and forth between the thin man and the SEAL, expecting this to be some cruel joke, like the man might put a bullet in his head anyway.

"Yes."

"For the record, I think this a terrible idea. But Holly clearly trusted you, so you have that going for you. Plus, Holly's family consists of her mother and her sister's family. Which means if they are being watched, we could use as many eyes as possible. Understood?"

"Yes."

The man holstered the gun and held out his hand to help Erik up.

"The name's Nova. That's James."

The man's grip was strong. Erik got to his feet and nodded at the thin man named James before he turned his attention back to the man named Nova.

"Her name's Holly?"

"Yes."

"Who is she?"

"We can discuss that later."

Erik looked around the dark apartment, suddenly lost.

"I get going to D.C. if that's where her family is, but shouldn't we be trying to find out what happened to her?"

"Atticus is working on it right now."

"Who's Atticus?"

"That doesn't matter. What matters is we need to leave."

Erik nodded, but still felt lost.

"Holly must be in danger."

Nova said, "That's right, she is. But she should be okay."

"How can you be so sure?"

"Trust me, chief. Holly knows how to take care of herself."

TWENTY-SIX

A low, distant buzzing, like a pulsing swarm of bees.

A quiet *buzz buzz buzz* that increases by the second.

The bees are out there, somewhere in the darkness. Only— it isn't darkness, is it?

I open my eyes. Stare up at my bedroom ceiling. The buzzing is coming from my right, on the nightstand. The alarm clock.

It's only as I reach over to silence the clock that I remember the nightstand sits to the *left* of my bed, and I sit up suddenly, realizing this isn't my bedroom at all.

The room is tiny and bare, just the bed and the nightstand and a door and an open doorway. Through the open doorway is the bathroom. From where I'm sitting on the bed, I can see a toilet and sink.

The alarm clock is still buzzing, the incessant noise having built a hive between my ears, and I reach over and smack it hard enough to crack the top, but at least it does the trick and the buzzing stops.

I take another moment to scan the room, noting the chipped plaster on the walls and the small security camera in the corner of the ceiling right above the closed door. I stare at the camera for a couple seconds before I notice the tightness around my neck.

I gently probe what's around my neck—what I quickly realize is a leather collar.

My hands scramble to find the clasp, but in my panic I can't find it at first—it's like the collar has been melded to my skin—and I start tugging at it, intent on ripping it apart.

That's when a bolt of electricity shoots through my body.

I go still all at once, my muscles tightening, but my body continues to shake for the second or two it takes before the bolt of electricity stops, and then I sit there motionless, catching my breath, my thoughts momentarily scrambled.

The door opens, and a tall man with a shaved head steps inside. He holds a Glock 17 in his right hand, a small black fob in his left.

He says, "Don't mess with your collar again. That was just a warning zap. An actual zap will knock your ass out."

Your collar. I don't like the sound of that. It's one thing to think it, but an entirely other thing to hear somebody else say it.

"Where the fuck am I?"

The man's face remains expressionless, his eyes dark.

"I wouldn't worry about it. You won't be here long."

"Where am I going?"

"That's something Mr. Hayward will explain."

"Who's Mr. Hayward?"

The man steps back, waiting for somebody else to enter the room. I expect it to be this elusive Mr. Hayward, so it's a bit of a shock when a girl appears. She can't be more than eight years old, small and petite with long black hair, and she keeps her eyes cast down as she approaches me, carrying clothing in her arms.

Around her neck, too, is a collar.

The girl comes to a stop beside the bed. She doesn't look at me. I realize she's waiting for me to take the clothes, and even though her eyes are focused on the floor, I can sense the anguish in her face, the hopelessness, and it both saddens and enrages me at the same time.

I look past the girl at the man standing in the doorway, and all I want to do is spring up from the bed and charge at the man, strip him of his pistol and shoot him in the head. But I know that's not possible, at least not right now—I'll get another zap if I try to attack him, one which will put me down —so I'll have to save that plan for later.

I take the clothing—a bundle of pants, shirts, underwear and socks with a pair of brand-new sneakers on top—and smile at her.

"Thank you."

The girl barely acknowledges me. She turns away and exits the room without a sound.

The man clears his throat.

"Mr. Hayward didn't want us to change you while you were unconscious. Those will be your clothes for tonight. There isn't a camera in the bathroom, so if you'd like to take a shower you can expect privacy, but the collar won't come off, and if you do try to take it off, just remember that your family won't appreciate your insubordination."

The man pauses, waiting to see if I have any reaction to him threatening my family. I stare back at him, giving him nothing.

He says, "Any requests for dinner?"

Because I can't help but be a smart-ass, even at a time like this, I say the first thing that comes to mind.

"I'll have a rib eye steak and a lobster tail with garlic mashed potatoes and asparagus. Oh, and a big piece of chocolate cake with a glass of milk to wash it down. Fat-free milk, if you have it."

The man doesn't blink.

"I'll run it by the kitchen. You have fifteen minutes before I return. Feel free to take a shower, but make it quick. If you aren't ready in exactly fifteen minutes, the next zap you feel will be much worse. Do you understand?"

I don't answer.

The man's eyes harden, and his voice lowers.

"I get that you think you're tough. I respect that. You wouldn't be here if Mr. Hayward didn't think you were tough. But understand right now you have zero choice in the matter. You do what you're told or you suffer the consequences, plain and simple. So I'll ask it again, now that you have fourteen minutes until I return. Do you understand?"

I swallow and nod, and speak in a quiet voice.

"Yes."

The man points at the alarm clock on the nightstand.

"The time is currently eleven twenty-seven. See you in thirteen minutes."

He closes the door, and I quickly stand with the clothes in my arms and hurry toward the bathroom.

TWENTY-SEVEN

The man returns at exactly 11:40. He doesn't knock. He simply opens the door.

I'm sitting on the bed. I decided not to shower because I didn't have the time. I've changed into the clothes—all of them my size—and as soon as the door opens I stand up.

The man has the Glock holstered but keeps the black fob in his hand. This, I understand, is the trigger for my collar.

He says, "Follow me."

I follow him out into the hallway. We pass a couple closed doors, and then we come to a door that leads outside.

The sky is dark and clear, but the moon and stars are bright. Cicadas fill the night with their song.

We leave one building and head to another. I quickly scan the area. It appears like we're out in the middle of nowhere. Three large buildings are positioned in a U formation. A shed —much like the one in that oil field—sits off near the base of a hill. A few vehicles are parked around the buildings—mostly SUVs, a few pickup trucks. One green Jetta with a missing hubcap.

I spot two men walking the perimeter, both with rifles slung over their shoulders.

The man leads me to the middle building. While the other two buildings are two stories tall, this one is three stories. Looks to have maybe a dozen rooms. The man doesn't seem to worry about me trailing him. I could rush him, grab the gun from its holster, but he knows I won't. Not with the collar around my neck.

Inside, I follow the man down a polished wooden floor to a large dining room. A middle-aged bald man with wire-frame glasses sits at the head of the table. As soon as we enter, he rises to his feet and does a half bow.

"Welcome to Neverland, Ms. Lin. My name is Oliver Hayward. Pleased to make your acquaintance. Louis, please get Ms. Lin's chair."

The man pulls out the chair at the other end of the table. I sit down on the chair, because I know that's what's expected of me, and Louis pushes me forward just a bit before he moves to stand with his back against the wall.

Oliver Hayward places his elbows on the table, folds his hands, and studies me.

"I understand Louis needed to zap you earlier. It's unfortunate, but sometimes these things happen. I do hope the rest of the time you're with us Louis won't need to repeat that action. Of course, that all depends on your behavior moving forward."

A candle flickers in the middle of the table, the room dimly lit. It's almost intimate, and I start to have a bad feeling where this may be going, but then a door at the other end of the room opens and the woman I only know as Leila Simmons appears.

Hayward rises to his feet again.

"Ah, my love. Thank you for joining us. You know Ms. Lin, of course."

The woman barely acknowledges me. Her hair is curly

again, and she isn't wearing glasses. She sits down in a chair at the corner near Hayward.

"Just so you know, I already ate."

"What?"

"I had a sandwich."

"But our guest!"

She looks at me now, a quick dismissive glance, and sighs again.

"It's almost midnight. I told you I wasn't going to eat this late."

Hayward sighs himself, only his is more disappointed. He's a peculiar man, nothing at all what I expected based on Louis. Louis is the type of man who looks like he's spent a couple years in the military. Oliver Hayward, on the other hand, looks like a college professor who yet hasn't become completely jaded.

"Be that as it may, Carla"—Hayward leaning toward the woman, reaching out to hold her hand—"thank you for joining us. I know it's late, but I thought our guest could use a familiar face. It might make her feel more at home."

Carla doesn't say anything to this. She lets Hayward hold her hand while she uses her other hand to look at something on her cell phone.

The same door Carla came through opens again, and a boy enters. The boy is no more than ten years old. He carries a tray with a glass of water and two glasses of wine on top. A man with a gun holstered to his hip follows him, a black fob in his hand.

The boy pauses first beside Hayward and Carla. He tries to balance the tray with one hand, reach for the wine glasses with his other hand, but it's clear he's worried the tray may flip so he sets the tray on the table long enough to set the wine glasses in front of Hayward and Carla before picking up the tray again and walking it down the table toward me. Now with only the glass of water he's able to balance the tray without trouble, and he sets the glass down in front of me before promptly turning and heading back toward the door he entered through.

Before the boy pushes the door open, Oliver Hayward clears his throat.

"Jose."

The boy pauses and slowly turns, his face tilted down.

Hayward says, "How many times must you be told never to place your tray on the table?"

The boy doesn't answer. He keeps his face tilted down, but his body has started to shake.

"I expect an answer, Jose."

Jose wets his lips. Swallows. Answers in a soft voice.

"Too many."

"Yes, Jose. Too many times. And quite frankly, I am beginning to tire of reminding you of such a simple command."

Before Jose can answer again, his body suddenly goes rigid. His head starts to shake. And like that, he's down on the floor, writhing in pain, the tray having fallen from his fingers and his hands now balled into fists. He doesn't cry out, though he issues an anguished moaning, and I don't realize I've stood up until Hayward speaks suddenly.

"Sit down, Ms. Lin."

I don't sit down, but I don't move forward either. I just stand there and watch the boy as he continues to writhe on the floor.

Hayward ignores the boy, watching me.

"The moment you sit back down, Ms. Lin, Jose's pain will stop."

As Jose writhes on the floor, Carla sits calmly in her chair. One hand still holding Hayward's while another continues to access her cell phone. Like it's no big thing the boy is being tortured. Like it happens all the time.

I sit back down, and the man standing over Jose disengages the fob.

Jose's body stops shaking almost at once. He lies on the floor for a couple of seconds, tears in his eyes, and then he quickly gets to feet, grabs the tray, and hurries out of the room, the man following him.

I decide at that moment when I kill Oliver Hayward he'll suffer greatly.

Hayward takes his hand back from Carla, folds his hands again with his elbows on the table as he studies me.

"You don't approve of our form of conditioning. It's understandable. You were raised to believe children should have positive reinforcement, yes? That they should be encouraged to do well, and that they should be praised for when they do well so that they continue to do well. It's a nice concept in theory, but that's all it merely is, a theory. Here at Neverland, we've come to find children are best reinforced with pain. If they do something they shouldn't do, they are zapped. If they look at somebody the wrong way, they are zapped. If they say something they shouldn't, they are zapped."

Carla seems to be off in a world of her own, both hands now tapping away at her cell phone.

Hayward notices this but keeps his eyes on me as he continues.

"My love shared with me what she spoke to you about earlier. She said she went over the basics. How we've been watching you for a while. How we knew we would someday come to need your services but weren't sure when that day would come. It was Carla's idea for you to eliminate those ICE agents. For many months they've become a thorn in our side. I respect greed as much as the next person, but there comes a point when greed becomes problematic. Those men needed to be eliminated. Killing them ourselves would have been easy— we hire freelancers all the time—but when you're killing two federal agents, it's best if somebody's face is associated with the crime. Otherwise faceless killings always turn into too much drama. It is always preferable to give the authorities and news media a villain."

He looks at the woman with adoration.

"Carla sensed you were the kind of person who would not let sleeping dogs lie, so to speak. She knew if Juana approached you covered in blood, gave you a duffel bag with a baby inside, and then you witnessed Juana murdered by those ICE agents … you would not let those men's crimes go unpunished."

He shoots me a grin.

"By the way, what did you think of the pinkie finger? That was my idea. I thought it added a nice touch."

He chuckles, realizes that Carla is still staring at her phone, and quickly composes himself.

"The agents believed Juana was delivering them money. She had been instructed to throw herself in front of their car. She knew she would die that evening, Ms. Lin, and yet she still went through with it. That is what I call ultimate compliance, though I suppose the real reason is love. Juana loved her child so much she was willing to die. She believed if she went through with what we asked, we would spare her child."

Hayward pauses to pick up his wine glass.

"Juana, as it turned out, was not very smart."

He takes a sip of his wine, sets the glass back down.

"Once we knew you would go out to the shed in the oil field, we contacted the agents to let them know we had left a girl there for them to, well, play with. Both men had a fetish for pregnant girls."

I remember how Mulkey and Kyer approached the shed like they had never been there before, jiggling the lock on the main door, and how the cowboy had been surprised that the girl was in fact there.

I stare back at Hayward across the table and speak in a calm, measured voice.

"I'm guessing the men from the highway were freelancers."

"Yes."

"They killed two U.S. Marshals."

"Yes."

"Won't that cause drama, too?"

"Certainly. And I should note it is a shame one of those men was killed in the operation, but the risk comes with the job. Anyway, all of that will be associated with you. Obviously the authorities know you couldn't have taken out the Marshals yourself, but it's doesn't matter. It's another point in your timeline for this week. First the ICE agents, then the Marshals, and then …"

He pauses again, a grin now lighting on his face.

"Love, do you think I should tell her the target now or wait for later?"

Her focus glued to her phone, Carla absently reaches out to pick up her wine glass.

Hayward tries again, much more forceful this time.

"*Love.*"

She pauses, glances at him.

"What?"

"Should I tell her the target now or wait for later?"

Carla shoots me an indifferent glance before shrugging.

"I don't care."

For the first time, Hayward looks irritated.

"If you're not going to participate in our conversation, you might as well leave."

Carla doesn't need to be told twice. She immediately pushes back the chair and stands up.

"Fine. I've had a long day as it is, and as I told you, I've already eaten."

She doesn't say anything else, simply turns and walks through the door.

Hayward forces a smile at me.

"Women! What can you do?"

Before I have the chance to tell him to slap the bitch, the door opens again and Jose reappears, followed by his minder. This time his tray holds two plates. He's much more confident with the plates, and balances the tray with one hand as he sets one of the plates down in front of Hayward. Then he walks the length of the table to set the other plate down in front of me.

I'm surprised to find a thick cut of steak, along with mashed potatoes and asparagus. The steak looks charbroiled and smells amazing.

Hayward clears his throat again.

"Louis told me what you requested to eat, and so I had the chef make this specifically for you. Unfortunately, we do not currently have any lobster tail, but you probably knew that, didn't you?"

Something in his tone has changed—it's dropped an octave, taken on an edge—and I glance up from my plate to find him glaring back at me.

"You're a smart woman, Ms. Lin. You know at the very end of this you are going to die. That's why you're here. When you accomplish your mission, they are going to want somebody to blame, somebody to point to, and that person is going to be you. And obviously it does not suit our purposes for you to still be alive when that happens. In the next seventy-two hours or so, you will be dead, but as long as you do what you're told, your family will stay alive. Do you understand me?"

I don't like being threatened, and I especially don't like my family being threatened, but there's not much one can do with a shock collar around one's neck while a man stands off to the side with a Glock holstered to his belt and other armed guards roaming the property. They're smart enough not to have given me a steak knife, but there is a butter knife on the table along with a fork and a spoon, and while they may not seem like dangerous weapons, in the right hands they can be. Still, it's the knowledge that my family is in danger that keeps me from grabbing one of the utensils and making a move at Louis.

I keep my gaze steady with Hayward's when I answer.

"Yes."

Smiling, Hayward picks up his fork. He spears one of the asparagus on his plate, takes a bite, chews for a moment, and then wipes his mouth with his napkin.

"I'm glad that we understand each other, Ms. Lin. I hope you also understand I take disrespect quite seriously. My love, well, you saw how she acts. She's allowed her little tantrums. Nobody else is. Because of your flippant attitude earlier when Louis asked you what you wanted for dinner, you won't be eating that steak. Nobody will. Jose's stomach will growl when he throws it away. He hasn't eaten for two days."

I sit in my chair, motionless, and stare back at him. Conscious of the collar around my neck. Remembering Jose writhing in pain on the dining room floor. He's just a boy, and I hate to admit I'd probably end up in the same position if they turned my collar on full blast.

Hayward forks some of the mashed potatoes, chews thoughtfully, and sets his fork aside as he wipes his mouth with his napkin.

"Jose, take her plate away."

The boy lifts my plate from the table, places it on his tray, and starts back toward the door, his minder following close behind.

I watch Hayward as he cuts into his steak, stabs a piece, and chews on it for a couple seconds before pushing the plate away in disgust. He takes a sip of wine, glaring at me over the glass, and finally shakes his head.

"I was hoping we would have a nice, quiet dinner, but no,

you had to go and be obstinate. I don't think you appreciate the fact that you're a guest here at Neverland."

Hayward takes off his glasses, uses a handkerchief from his pocket to clean the lenses.

"You see, Ms. Lin, I appreciate the fact that you think you're special. I can understand why after what I know you did to the Diaz family, and how you took down El Diablo the way you did—the cartels had been trying to take him out for over a year with no luck—but the simple truth is you are only another freelancer. You're nothing special. Just yesterday two sicarios passed through here. They were brothers. Imagine that. Brothers who work together as hitmen."

Hayward puts his glasses back on as he pushes up from his chair. He starts to walk down the length of the table. Taking his time, tapping his knuckles along the tabletop as he goes.

"I'm a businessman, Ms. Lin. That's who I am. That's what I've done all my life. I was the one who founded Neverland. I created all of this. You might not understand what it is I do, and that's all right because it doesn't matter. I'm simply a man fulfilling an obligation. People much more powerful than I want something done, and I'm the one to make it happen, and the only way that happens is for you to do what you're told. If not, your family dies."

He pauses at the corner of the table, leans down so his face is only inches from mine.

"I will admit I don't know much about your background, but from what I understand you killed people for the United States government. You were basically a drone. Just another cog in the massive war machine. You're nothing special. That's what I want you to understand before this is all over. When you fulfill your duty and Louis aims his gun at your head, I want you to accept the fact that you are not special."

He pauses, turns toward Louis.

"Give me a bullet."

I hear the frown in Louis's voice.

"Sir?"

"Give me a bullet."

From the corner of my eye I watch Louis pull the Glock from its holster, rack the slide to cough out a bullet. He catches it midair and hands it to Hayward.

The man holds the bullet close to his face, like he's inspecting a priceless diamond, and then taps it on the table.

"You see this? This is all you are. You're not a *weapon*. You're simply a bullet. Louis, what kind of bullet is this?"

"Hollow point, sir."

Hayward echoes it, nodding.

"Hollow point. That's what you are, Ms. Lin. You're nothing more than a hollow point. Your whole purpose in life is to kill. You don't make decisions. Men much more powerful than you are the ones who made those decisions in the past, just as they're making those decisions now. They're the ones that load you. They're the ones that pull the trigger."

He holds the bullet up again, and smiles.

"You see, Ms. Lin, this is what we do here at Neverland. We make the children understand that they're not special. That they'll never be special. And you know what? It works, every single time. Obviously, you won't be staying here long enough for us to break you, but I still want you to understand that you're nothing. And this bullet here? I'm going to make sure Louis holds on to this bullet, just for you. So when the time comes—after you've completed your final mission—this will be the bullet that ends your life."

TWENTY-EIGHT

They had passed through a new time zone a half hour ago, give or take, so the time was now an hour earlier than it was an hour ago, or something like that. Erik had always gotten confused about time zones when he was flying against the grain —that was the term somebody in his boot camp had once used and it had stuck with him ever since—and now here he was flying on an actual private jet.

He didn't know the kind of jet and was too intimidated to ask. Besides the two pilots—who were enclosed in the cockpit —there were the two men from Holly's apartment, Nova and James.

James hadn't said a word this entire time, while Nova had said very little. After they'd left the apartment, they drove for nearly an hour before they reached the airfield and boarded the jet, and minutes later they were in the air and now they were somewhere over Tennessee or Kentucky, Erik didn't know which and again was too intimidated to ask.

He'd flown before, of course, but he never once flew in a private jet, or even thought he ever would. Private jets were for movie stars and sports stars and billionaires, not for the likes of him. It felt almost obscene, the luxury of the cabin and the large comfortable chairs.

Part of him was exhausted, but another part couldn't sleep, too wired with everything that was going on. He kept thinking of the girl whom he knew for the past year as Jen, which was apparently not her real name. This knowledge was somehow as shocking as the fact she had killed two men—the knowledge that she had been living a double life—and part of him knew he shouldn't have agreed to come along with these two strangers, though for some reason another part instinctively trusted them. The way Erik saw it, if these men had wanted to kill him, they would have done so by now.

"Can't sleep?"

The deep voice startled him. He'd been staring out the window, down at the dark landscape below, and now glanced over at the big man sitting in the chair across from him. Nova's head was tilted back but his eyes were half-open, watching Erik.

Because he couldn't think of anything else to say—and because Nova had startled him—Erik said the first thing that came to mind.

"Your boss must be loaded."

Nova shifted in his seat, and opened his eyes fully.

"He's not my boss."

Erik frowned.

"But—"

Nova hooked a thumb over his shoulder, pointing to James sleeping in the seat behind him.

"*He* works for the man. Me ... I'm simply an associate."

Erik didn't know what this meant and didn't want to ask—somehow he knew he'd still be confused—so he tilted his head at James.

"Doesn't he talk?"

Nova shook his head.

"He's mute. Has been most of his life."

"Does he communicate with sign language?"

"I would imagine so. Why, you know sign language?"

"I do, actually. I learned it when I was a kid. I haven't used it for years, so I'm sure I'm rusty, but I remember some of it."

Nova didn't say anything to this, and glanced out his own window.

Erik said, "So can you tell me anything about what's going on?"

Nova kept staring out his window.

"We're flying to D.C."

"Yeah, I get that part. And we're going to try to find the people watching Holly's family. But what happens when we find them?"

Nova stared out his window for another moment before glancing at Erik again.

"Look, you appear to be a smart guy, so I'm sure you get the sense I'm not really on board with having you here."

Erik nodded but said nothing. He had certainly gotten that impression.

"If it were up to me, we would've left you back in that piece of shit town, probably tied up in the apartment so you couldn't contact any of your fellow deputies. But obviously the powers that be had other ideas. Atticus isn't my boss, but he's a man I've come to trust. Every time I've needed help, he's provided it."

Erik studied Nova sitting across from him, trying to decide who the man worked for.

"Are you CIA?"

Nova smiled, and shook his head.

Erik said, "FBI?"

Nova snorted, made a face, but still said nothing.

"I'm guessing you're not NSA, and you don't strike me as working for another country."

Nova said, "I'm an American boy, through and through."

"So who do you work for?"

"I told you, chief. I don't work for anybody. I'm just here to help out a friend."

"Holly."

"That's right."

"But shouldn't we, you know, try to figure out what happened to her, too?"

"Atticus is working on it. The moment she was taken into custody, he was alerted. That's how he contacted me. I was out in the middle of nowhere, had been staying at a cabin by a stream to do some fly-fishing. Atticus gave me a call, said James would meet me, and several hours later we ended up in Alden."

"And I walked in while you were searching Holly's apartment."

Nova shrugged.

"We were wrapping up by the time you walked in, but yeah, basically."

"Did you mean what you said before?"

"I guess it depends on what I said."

"That Holly can take care of herself."

Nova nodded, almost thoughtfully, and tilted his head so that he stared out his window again. Erik thought he might say something else, but he didn't.

"So what are we going to do once we land?"

Nova glanced back at him, took a deep breath.

"Once we land there will be some cars waiting, and weapons, and comms. We're going to have to split up right away. Holly's mom lives across town, and her sister's husband works during the week. Summer just started, so her nephews won't be in school, but there's no telling where they might go during the day."

"I don't get why we can't call the police."

"And tell them what? We don't have any proof her family is

even in any danger. We're doing this based on your word only. And no offense, but as far as I'm concerned, your word is worthless. Hell, you could be part of the group that abducted Holly for all we know. Playing us for fools."

Erik said nothing, too shocked to say anything at all.

Nova shifted in his seat to give Erik his full attention. His hands didn't move—they stayed where they were on the chair's armrests—but Erik was all too conscious of the fact the man still had the FNX-45 on him.

"Tell me the truth, Erik. You playing us for fools?"

Erik didn't bother shaking his head. He kept his gaze steady with Nova's as he answered.

"No."

"You sure?"

"Yes."

Nova nodded slowly, and glanced back out his window.

"I certainly hope that's the case. I hope we don't get to D.C. and find out we're wasting our time."

"What happens if and when we find the people watching Holly's family?"

Nova kept staring out his window.

"Nothing."

This wasn't at all what Erik had expected to hear.

"What do you mean, nothing?"

"I mean it exactly as I said it."

"But that's insane. If we find the men, why don't we just—"

Erik cut himself off, suddenly seeing it.

Nova glanced at him again, and nodded.

"That's right. The moment we take them out, Holly's life is over. Right now the people who took her want something from her, and they're using her family as leverage."

"Say we do find these people. Say we manage to get one of them alone and force him to tell us where to find her."

"Say we do. An operation like this is a house of cards. Take one card away, the whole thing comes down. That's why we first need to confirm the surveillance is real, and then we wait."

Erik shook his head, feeling more frustrated now than he'd felt all day.

"But what are we waiting for?"

"For Holly to do what she does best."

"And what's that?"

His head still tilted back, Nova shifted again in his seat to get comfortable and closed his eyes.

"Survive."

TWENTY-NINE

The alarm on the nightstand goes off at seven o'clock on the dot, and a second later the door opens and Louis stands there, dressed in a fresh shirt and slacks, the Glock still holstered to his hip.

"You want a shower?"

It's an odd question—like, of course I want a shower—but I don't answer him, just keep lying in bed with my head tilted up to look at him.

His expression doesn't change.

"You want a fucking shower or not?"

I nod, rising a bit on my elbows.

He tosses something at me. It's small and plops down near the end of the bed. It's a key, which will unlock the clasp on the collar.

Louis says, "Need to recharge the collar anyway. You've got five minutes."

I stand as I grab the key and start fiddling with the clasp and only pause when Louis speaks again.

"Oh, and Holly?"

He reaches toward something in the hallway with his left

hand as he unsnaps his gun from the holster and draws it, both hands seeming to work in concert, and then Jose fills the doorway with him, the boy still not looking at me, keeping his gaze tilted down at the floor, and Louis presses the barrel of his gun against Jose's temple just hard enough for the boy to flinch.

"Any funny business and the boy gets one in the head."

Louis, like his boss Hayward, finds power in making these kinds of threats, and I decide not to acknowledge it, moving straight for the bathroom and reaching into the small shower and turning on the water.

I started the countdown as soon as Louis said five minutes, and four minutes and forty-six seconds later I shut off the water and grab the towel and start drying off. When I step back out of the bathroom, wrapped in the towel, a fresh pile of clothes has been set on the bed, and a plate of scrambled eggs and bacon and toast sits on the nightstand.

Louis doesn't appear to have moved, and neither does Jose.

I say to Louis, "I was out in less than five minutes."

His expression still doesn't change.

"Yes."

I gesture at Jose.

"Well, let him go."

Louis doesn't move at first—just stands there with his gun pressed against the boy's head—but then finally he relaxes his grip on Jose.

"Put the collar on."

I'm confused at first—does he mean the collar I left in the bathroom?—but then I spot a new collar on the bed next to the pile of clothes. This collar looks to be just like the other one —it snaps together, though it can't be unsnapped without a key —and it fits snugly around my throat.

Louis says, "Where's the key?"

I tilt my chin at the bathroom.

He doesn't like this response, and presses the Glock's barrel against Jose's head again.

I quickly retrieve the key and the other collar from the bathroom and slowly approach Louis. I hold out both items—the collar in one hand, the key in the other—and still without looking at me Jose reaches out and takes the items.

Louis says, "Take four steps back."

I take four steps back, my calves brushing up against the bed behind me.

Louis waits a beat and then moves the Glock away from Jose's head.

Holstering the gun, Louis pushes Jose down the hallway, and I can hear the boy's soft footsteps rapidly retreat.

I decide when I kill Louis, he, like his boss, will suffer greatly.

Louis doesn't move from the doorway.

I say, "This isn't a striptease. Mind giving me some privacy?"

Louis points up at the camera in the corner. Of course. In Neverland, privacy doesn't exist.

I ask, "So what's on the docket for today?"

Louis keeps watching me with his blank expression.

"Ten minutes to get dressed and to eat. Don't be a second late. Or else the boy will suffer for your insolence."

Before I can say anything, he shuts the door.

I stand there for a beat, watching the space he occupied a moment ago, and then I shift my gaze up to the camera in the ceiling.

My first impulse is to give it the finger, but I think about the collar around my neck and the zap I'd felt last night. I could handle another one of those, but then I think about how Jose or maybe another child—that girl from last night—might get zapped for the gesture instead.

I haven't been here long and already I've become conditioned. I can't even begin to imagine what these children go through on a daily basis.

As I turn away and drop the towel and start to get dressed, I decide that when I kill everybody at this place—the guards and freelancers and anybody else who's had a hand in hurting these children—they'll all suffer greatly.

THIRTY

Louis leads me outside into the morning sunlight. The sky is clear, only a haze of clouds on the horizon, and it's much easier to scan the area.

Besides the three buildings and the shed sitting several hundred yards away against the rise of a hill, there isn't much else. Everything is sort of tucked in at the bottom of the hill, like we're in half a bowl.

Last night there were guards roaming the grounds, but today they're gone.

"This way."

The man's voice is flat, indifferent, and he walks ahead of me with no fear whatsoever, the fob in his hand, the Glock 17 in its holster.

We head out into an open field. Four men wait beside a folding table and chair. I peg them as the same freelancers who had abducted me from the Marshals. They each wear sunglasses, Beretta nine-millimeters holstered to their hips. Earplugs hang from strings around their necks. They don't speak as we approach, and as we near, I notice the sniper rifle laid out on the table, along with a box of ammunition and a pair of earplugs and binoculars.

Louis stops beside the table and crosses his arms.

"We didn't know which was your dominant hand, so we got you a Nemesis Valkyrie. Are you familiar with it?"

I nod, staring down at the ambidextrous bolt-action sniper rifle. The weapon has already been assembled and sits upright on its bipod.

Louis says, "We opted for the twenty-inch barrel. Supplied you with more than enough 6.5 Creedmoor to show us whether or not you can complete this mission."

I nod again and step closer to the table. Each of the free-lancers draws his Beretta as I reach for the rifle.

I raise an eyebrow at them.

"Relax, boys. How else am I supposed to fire this thing if I don't touch it?"

The men don't answer. They don't aim their pistols at me, though, and just keep them at their sides. Ready for anything.

Louis clears his throat.

"As you can see, the rifle is not loaded. We figured you would want to do that yourself."

The Valkyrie has a ten-round magazine. I open the box and start feeding the magazine cartridges.

"What am I shooting at today?"

Louis gestures at the field.

"We've set up a dozen two-liter soda bottles, as well as a few smaller bottles, roughly one thousand feet away."

I insert the magazine and pick up the rifle, and that's when the freelancers aim their Berettas at me. They've moved in a sort of V-point position—one to my left, one to my right, two behind me—so that if I were to try to take out one the rest would easily put me down.

"Like I said, boys, relax."

The freelancers don't look relaxed.

Louis says, "They're simply doing their jobs. Now, why don't you do yours?"

Ouch.

"Where do you want me to set up?"

Louis picks up the binoculars from the table, and points at the chair.

"Use the table to rest the rifle."

I sit down on the chair and secure the plugs in my ears. Pull the rifle close to me, peer through the scope. I spot the soda bottles hiding in the grass at the other end of the field. They've been stripped of their labels and look to be filled with water.

My finger touches the trigger.

I take a deep breath, let it out. Take another breath … and squeeze the trigger as I release the breath.

One of the two-liters explodes.

Louis, now with plugs in his own ears, lowers the binoculars from his face and nods at me.

"Again."

I pull back the bolt, which spits out the spent casing, and then aim at one of the smaller bottles. Squeeze the trigger again, and another bottle disappears.

This is almost too easy.

I pull back the bolt again, ready to keep shooting, when Louis shouts.

"Wait!"

I keep my finger on the trigger but don't squeeze it. Wait a couple seconds, and when Louis remains silent, I lean back and look at him.

Hayward is headed toward us. He wears chinos and a white button-down shirt and a Panama hat. Jose and his minder follow, the boy staring at the ground as he walks.

When they reach us, Louis hands off the binoculars to his

boss. Hayward peers through the binoculars at the field and then hands the binoculars back to Louis.

"Not too bad, Ms. Lin. Of course, those are stationary targets. And there isn't any pressure, is there? You have unlimited chances to hit these targets here, while when the time comes to hit your intended target, you will only get one chance."

"Thanks for the pep talk, coach."

Hayward's face colors. He glares at me for a beat, then glances down at Jose.

"You have a soft spot for children, don't you, Ms. Lin?"

Jose stands motionless, keeping his face tilted down. It's because I remember how he writhed in pain on the floor last night that I don't say something smart to Hayward.

Instead, I ask, "Who's my target?"

Hayward merely smiles.

"All in due time, Ms. Lin. You'll be a guest here at Neverland for at least another day. You and I will get to know each other better. Plus, you'll be able to practice your target shooting. So far"—he gestures at the field—"you seem to be capable, but remember, when the real time comes, you will be under a great deal of pressure. After all, if you do not follow through and successfully eliminate the target, your family will die. Your mother and sister and brother-in-law and, most importantly, your nephews. You don't want them to die, do you?"

It's a stupid question—obviously I don't want them to die —but the man is playing with me, and because he calls the shots right now, I have no choice but to play along.

"No."

"That's right, Ms. Lin. Of course you don't want them to die. And because I feel it's in your best interest to practice under some pressure, I've brought Jose along to give you extra motivation."

I don't like the sound of where this is going.

Hayward smiles again.

"I want you to shoot one of the smaller bottles. And if you miss, Jose will suffer."

Jose, still staring down at the ground, starts to tremble.

I wet my lips and again think about how when I kill Hayward I'm going to make him suffer. Break some bones. Maybe gouge an eye. But right now that's all just a distraction. I need to focus. Need to calm my nerves.

So I turn back to the rifle. Reset the earplugs. Peer through the scope. Center on one of the smaller bottles standing in the grass. Touch my finger to the trigger. Take a breath, let it out. Take another breath—

Louis kicks the table as I pull the trigger, and the shot goes wide.

At once Jose cries out as he falls to the ground. I immediately push to my feet, but a sudden bolt of lightning courses through me, and I jerk and drop to one knee as Hayward simply stands there, his hands clasped in front of him, watching me.

A couple seconds, that's all it takes, and the lightning blinks out and all that's left is a lingering pain, a shadow pain.

Jose stops writhing on the ground, but he doesn't get up.

Hayward shakes his head at me, a disappointed father.

"Turns out you're not so great under pressure after all."

He waits for me to answer, and when I don't give him one, he turns back to the boy.

"Jose, stand up."

Jose quickly climbs to his feet.

Hayward pats the boy once on the head, then smiles at me.

"You see, when he first arrived at Neverland, Jose was a very defiant boy. He refused to listen to us, even with his collar. Typically the children we have here learn to follow directions in a short amount of time, but not Jose. He was quite a stubborn boy. But everybody has a breaking point."

"What do you do with the children?"

Hayward regards me for a long time, thinking how he wants to answer, before he sighs.

"I give them purpose, Ms. Lin. These children come from terrible places. In most instances, their mothers are searching for safety. We promise them that—we promise that safety—and then we use them whatever way we see fit. And no, before you jump to conclusions, we don't sell their children off as sex slaves."

He pauses, and grins.

"Well, most of them we don't. What happens to the children once they leave here is no business of ours after a transaction has been completed. Most of these children end up in homes where they are used merely as indentured servants. They clean. They cook. Most of them have become so conditioned to do what they're told that they no longer need the collars, but we always provide collars with each bill of sale. After all, we will sometimes have children like Jose here who are so defiant that they eventually build confidence again. It's important for us to make certain once that confidence is stripped away it never returns."

Hayward gestures at the field.

"Now, Ms. Lin, one of the smaller bottles. This time, Jose's pain won't stop until you accomplish your mission."

Jose yelps again as he drops to the ground, and I immediately turn back to the rifle.

Peer through the scope, my finger on the trigger.

But I can't focus. I don't want to prematurely fire off a round and miss the target because that will keep Jose's pain going, but I don't want to wait too long either.

Breathe in, breathe out.

Breathe in, breathe out.

I squeeze the trigger. Watch the small soda bottle explode down at the other end of the field.

"There! I did it!"

I lean back, start to stand, but the freelancers each take a step forward, their pistols aimed at my head.

Jose keeps writhing on the ground. Hayward takes the binoculars from Louis, stares through them for a beat, then lowers them.

"Yes, it appears you did."

Jose keeps writhing.

I shout, "Turn off the collar!"

Hayward's face tilts toward me, and his eyes narrow.

"Do not tell me what to do, Ms. Lin."

I prepare myself for another zap—from the corner of my eye I can see Louis's thumb on the fob—but before another spike of lightning hits, Carla appears by one of the buildings. She hurries toward us.

Hayward turns away, and as soon as he does, Jose's minder lowers the fob. Jose goes still. He's crying now, sobbing into the ground, and I want to go to him, to somehow ease his pain, but the freelancers keep their Berettas aimed at me even though the rifle sits on the table untouched.

When Carla joins us, Hayward asks, "What's wrong?"

"His schedule has changed. He'll be there tomorrow."

"*What?*"

Hayward's voice echoes across the field. His hands squeeze into fists. I'm worried that he'll take his anger out on Jose again —maybe rip the fob from the minder, zap the boy himself— but then he steps toward Carla.

"There must be some mistake."

Carla shakes her head.

"I just received the call. It's tomorrow."

Hayward turns to Louis, his jaw tight.

"What are our options?"

Louis chews his bottom lip, thinking it over.

"It's fourteen hours away, depending on traffic. If we leave now, we can make it there by midnight and get everything set up. It'll be tight but doable."

Hayward thinks it over for a moment.

"Do it. Tie her up and put her in the trunk."

Louis motions at the freelancers. One of them stays where he is, his pistol aimed at my head, while the others move forward to collect the rifle and box of ammunition.

Hayward turns to me, a forced smile on his face.

"It appears we don't have much time together after all. What a shame, because I'm told the lobster tail is being delivered later today."

He steps closers, reaches out to tap the collar around my neck.

"This will be staying on you. Louis will have the trigger. Your family is depending on your compliance. Do you understand me, Ms. Lin?"

Suddenly feeling empty, I nod.

Hayward glances at Carla before clearing his throat.

"Now that you'll be leaving here shortly, I suppose I might as well tell you your target. I believe you knew his son. You killed him last year, as a matter of fact."

Hayward grins as he sees the understanding cross my face.

"That's right, Ms. Lin. You'll be assassinating Alejandro Cortez's father. The President of Mexico."

THIRTY-ONE

Tina Davis didn't know how long she'd been unhappy with her life, but in the past several weeks that unhappiness had morphed into loathing, and every day that passed—every day where she woke to Ryan's alarm or one of the boys' voices out in the hallway—she hated her life more and more.

It wasn't always like this, of course. She'd been happy once. And she knew it had nothing to do with her sister disappearing —almost a year ago now, come to think of it—or Ryan being laid off from his six-figure job about a month after Holly left.

But it had started sometime after that, in the limbo period where Ryan searched nonstop for a job until he finally found one—only a couple months ago, a job that paid considerably less, but at least it had decent benefits, so there was that—and the unhappiness had started to settle in, and even though things were beginning to look up—or at the very least weren't looking as dire—Tina just couldn't shake the unhappiness, no matter how much she tried, until it started to snowball into that loathing and then, finally, hatred.

It wasn't like she was suicidal. Tina didn't want to *end* her life; she simply hated it. The way you hate that one coworker who constantly gets on your nerves, just small stuff at first until that stuff is all you think about, and the more you think about it, the more you wonder how anybody could put up with the person until the day finally comes when you realize what had started out as simple dislike has turned into hate.

"Mom? What time is Mrs. Holbrook picking us up?"

Tina blinked. Realized she was standing at the sink, the faucet running. Lost again in her thoughts.

Matthew tried again, his tone this time hesitant.

"Mom?"

She shut off the water and turned around. Smiled down at her two sons at the kitchen table.

They had their tablets open, propped on the table in front of them. It was the only time of day they were allowed to have their tablets at the table. At dinner it was No Tablet Time. Tina had even printed up signs with a tablet in a red circle and a slash across it, like the Ghostbusters logo. It hung on the fridge, a helpful reminder, though one time Matthew tore it down when he got detention at school and they'd taken away his tablet as a punishment.

Both boys were watching her now, worried, their plates of pancakes half-eaten. For one crazy moment, Tina considered telling them she hated her life—she even started to open her mouth—and that was when Ryan tore into the kitchen like a tornado.

"Sorry, in a rush."

His tie was draped around his neck, the first two buttons of his dress shirt open. He carried his briefcase in one hand, his cell phone in the other, and he ignored the plate she'd prepared for him as he hurried past, kissing each boy on the head, and pecked her on the cheek before pivoting away and heading for the side door.

"See you when I get home."

He didn't wait for a response, disappearing outside, and

Tina was left feeling like she'd missed something, though in truth Ryan had been doing this more and more lately, staying up late because he couldn't sleep and then getting up at the last minute and rushing out of the house.

Tina knew she couldn't blame him—the new job was running him ragged—but still she wondered how this would affect the boys later in life, whether or not they would understand and respect their father or resent him.

Matthew said, "Mom?"

She blinked again. Shifted her focus down to her son.

"Yes?"

"What time is Mrs. Holbrook picking us up?"

Stacey Holbrook, a longtime family friend, had volunteered to take the boys to the zoo today, along with her son Kyle. Stacey invited Tina along too, but Tina had declined, making up some excuse why she couldn't go—right now the reason evaded her—because she worried Stacey would sense Tina's depression, and she didn't want her friend to worry about her.

Tina glanced at the clock hanging on the wall. It was almost eight thirty.

"She should be here any minute."

That was when her phone pinged on the counter, a text message from Stacey saying she's just pulled into the driveway.

"Apparently she's already here."

The boys jumped to their feet, grabbing the tablets before they made a break for the door.

Tina said, "Tablets stay here."

Max's eyes grew wide like saucers.

"But, *Mom!*"

She tilted her chin down, gave him the look that said, *Do you really wanna try me?*

Max crinkled his nose but didn't say anything, simply set his tablet aside, as did Matthew, and they called out goodbye as they tore off toward the door, Tina following them, stepping out to wave at Stacey as the boys loaded into her minivan, and soon the van disappeared down the street and Tina stepped back inside, closing the door and taking a deep breath.

She cleaned up the kitchen and headed upstairs to take a shower. Today was Monday, aka Laundry Day, but the laundry could wait. As soon as she was dressed, she headed back down the steps, grabbed her purse and keys, and headed outside.

Her Nissan was parked in the driveway, dusty in the morning sun. She couldn't remember the last time she'd gotten it washed. If and when they needed some extra cash—and that time was coming very soon, no doubt about it—her car would probably be the first thing to go. Though, Tina had to admit with a pang of disappointment, she didn't expect them to get much for it. Maybe two thousand dollars if they were lucky.

As she backed into the street, her mind was so focused on how much she hated her life that she didn't notice the car parked at the end of the block and how it pulled away from the curb to follow her.

THIRTY-TWO

Twenty-four hours earlier Nova Bartkowski was out in the middle of nowhere, in a cabin nestled in the woods, thinking about fly-fishing.

He had never been big into fishing before, but there was something about fly-fishing that was soothing. Standing in a bubbling stream with the woods quiet around you, whipping the line back and forth, watching and waiting for a fish to strike mellowed him out, calmed him down, and made him appreciate life in a way he never did before.

Of course, that was twenty-four hours ago, and things had moved fast after he received Atticus's call. Now he was back in D.C. and following Holly's sister down the highway. He made sure to keep far enough back that she wouldn't notice, but also far enough back that whoever was tracking her wouldn't notice either.

So far, he hadn't spotted a tail, and that worried him.

They each had disposable cell phones, and each phone was logged into Signal, an encrypted communications app. They were in a group text, Nova and James and Erik and Atticus, so that way each knew each other's movements. They had comms gear too, and could easily communicate via voice, but as James couldn't talk, it was easier to shoot off a quick text.

Nova's text not too long ago: Sister left the house. Following now. Don't see a tail.

James responded: Mother still home.

Erik: Boys arrived @ zoo with what looks like friend & friend's mother. Should I follow them in?

Nova thought about it. The zoo would be packed as it was the summer, and it was a public place, so he doubted the boys would be taken. But he figured if Holly's family was in fact under surveillance and their lives were at risk, her nephews were prime targets. As was her sister. And mother. Not so much her brother-in-law. That was why they hadn't bothered to follow him to work. It was a risk, and one Nova didn't think they had any choice but to make.

He texted back: Yes. Keep us updated.

Ten minutes later, Holly's sister exited the highway. Nova followed her up the ramp and turned right at the stop sign.

He kept checking the rearview mirror, hoping to spot somebody following, but so far nothing stood out. Which again didn't make sense. Unless Holly's family wasn't under surveillance. Which meant that son of a bitch had been lying to them this entire time.

Soon it was clear where Holly's sister was headed. Nova sent James a direct message through Signal: Sister headed your way.

It was a quiet residential area. The kind with large trees and sidewalks and a blue mailbox posted at the end of the one block.

Nova paused at the stop sign and watched Tina as she parked along the curb in front of Holly's mom's house. He circled the block and then came up from the south and parked behind James.

He stepped out of the car and scanned the quiet street. It

was the kind of street that made random vehicles conspicuous. People knew what their neighbors drove, what their family and friends drove. A new vehicle might go unnoticed for a couple hours, maybe a day, but not much longer. So it wasn't the kind of place a panel van could sit all day and night. Which meant whoever was watching Holly's mom—assuming that was even the case—was doing it by other means.

Nova slid into the passenger seat and glanced at James behind the steering wheel.

"Should have brought you some coffee and donuts. My bad."

James shrugged.

Nova tilted his chin at Holly's mom's house.

"Nothing, huh?"

James shook his head.

Nova said, "I'm starting to think this is a waste of time."

James merely looked at him.

"You don't think so?"

Another shrug.

Nova said, "I'm telling you right now, if that kid lied to us I'm going to fucking kill him."

James picked up his phone and typed something on the screen. Nova's phone vibrated with an incoming direct message.

I think he's telling the truth.

"How can you be so sure? I haven't seen a tail. Have you seen a tail?"

James tapped on his phone.

How long would you advise I stay parked here? Not too long before I'll be noticed.

"Yeah, okay, I get the point. None of these are prime stakeout places. That's why I'm starting to think this whole thing is bullshit."

James shook his head as he typed out another message.

This is old school surveillance. There are other means.

"Like what?"

James seemed to carefully consider his response before tapping on the phone again.

I need to pick up some equipment. Can you wait here until I get back?

Nova didn't know James well, but he knew the man took his work seriously and there was no use questioning him. He nodded and stepped out of the car and got back into his own car as James pulled away.

THIRTY-THREE

Her mother stepped away from the coffee brewer and returned to the kitchen table, carrying two mugs.

Tina said, "I could have helped you with that."

Her mother set down the mugs and waved a dismissive hand as she sat across from her.

"I may be old, but I'm not completely useless yet."

Her mother blew at the top of the mug as she studied her daughter. Tina stared down at her own coffee.

"How's Ryan?"

Tina shrugged.

"He's okay. Working a lot."

"What about the boys?"

"They're good. Stacey Holbrook took them to the zoo today."

"I haven't seen them in a couple weeks."

Tina nodded slowly, still not looking at her mother.

"I know. It's just been … hard lately."

For the six months Ryan was unemployed, they'd had no choice but to dip into their savings, into the boys' college fund, and right now they were living paycheck to paycheck.

This, Tina knew, was where her hatred of life began.

Ever since the boys were born she had stayed at home; Ryan made more than enough that they were quite comfortable, and she used the extra time to work on her art. Her paintings, she knew, were good but not great, and it was during those months after Ryan was laid off—her husband not leaving for work in the morning as he usually did, but instead sitting at the dining room table and emailing his resume to firm after firm, calling old classmates who might know somebody who might know somebody—Tina realized she'd been fooling herself.

She fancied herself an artist, had once envisioned her work being displayed in an art gallery in New York, one of those ritzy places that would have an opening where they'd pop champagne and everybody would clap, and while she had never shared this dream with Ryan, he knew how much she loved to paint and had always encouraged her. And for a while it had been fine—again, they were quite comfortable—but now their savings were practically gone and she realized she needed to step up and find a job herself.

Only she had no idea what she could do. She'd been out of the workforce for almost twelve years. The gap in her resume would send up red flags at HR departments. And even assuming she did get called in for an interview, she worried she would say or do the wrong thing and embarrass herself.

After putting it off, she'd finally broken down and asked her mother for some money to help out. Her mother gladly wrote a check for two thousand dollars. Tina had felt tears stinging her eyes when she accepted it, promising her mother she and Ryan would pay her back in a couple months, definitely a couple months, all the while knowing it might take much longer.

Now her mother asked, "How's the job search coming?"

Tina felt ready to burst out in tears. It was one of the

reasons she kept her face tilted down, so she wouldn't have to look at her mother. Wouldn't have to see the disappointment on the woman's face. The shame.

She whispered, "Not great."

"Any interviews yet?"

Tina shook her head.

"Hey"—her mother reached across the table to touch her hand—"look at me."

Tina blinked, shifted her focus up to meet her mother's eyes. Her mother squeezed her hand and offered up an encouraging smile.

"Nobody ever said life was going to be easy. Everybody has hard moments. You and Ryan will make it through this."

Tina wet her lips, tried to speak but couldn't. She shook her head again. Looked away, stared off toward the living room, and sighed.

"It's just … I feel so worthless."

"Tina, don't."

"It's true, Mom."

Looking back at her mother, tears stinging her eyes.

"I've been a mother so long—have been a wife—I don't know what else I can be."

"You're creative. There are plenty of places who would hire someone with your artistic talent."

Tina wanted to bark out a laugh.

"I'm not talented."

"Sure, you are. You made that painting right there."

Her mother pointed off toward the piece hanging on the wall in the hallway, an abstract Tina barely remembered working on but which she'd given her mother for her birthday one year.

Tina said, "I'm not a *real* artist."

Her mother squeezed her hand again, issued a soft sigh.

"I know it's difficult, but you and Ryan will be okay. Do

you need some more money? I don't have much, but I could lend you a bit more."

It hurt her heart to hear her mother say those words. This wasn't why she came here. Not to beg for money. Not for her mother's pity.

"I think we're okay for now."

"Are you sure? My checkbook is right in the next room."

"Yes, I'm sure. I … I wanted to get out of the house. Wanted to come see how you're doing."

There was a heavy silence as they both considered the meaning of Tina's words. In the next room, the clock softly ticked. Now it was her mother who tilted her face down so she wouldn't have to look at her daughter.

Tina spoke quietly.

"It's been almost a year since Holly … since she went away."

Tina wasn't sure how else to put it. She hadn't learned that Holly decided to leave until it had already happened. Her mother had phoned her but Tina didn't believe it at the time, thinking her sister was simply being melodramatic. Holly wanted to stop working as a nanny for the Haddens—a job Tina had never thought matched Holly to begin with—and had wanted to find a different job, and then she had just disappeared.

For the longest time her mother didn't answer, staring down at her coffee, and then she sighed and took a hesitant sip. Set the mug back down, and glanced up at her daughter.

"I never told you about the day she came to see me. Well, I did tell you, but I left something out."

Tina found herself leaning forward. She had never known her mother to keep secrets from her.

"What didn't you tell me?"

Her mother looked back down at her coffee, shook her head.

"Holly had a bruise on her face that morning. I asked her what happened, asked her who hit her, but she didn't want to talk about it. She said she ... wanted to say goodbye. She said she would be leaving and might not be back. I didn't know what she meant. I thought she was just being cryptic for some reason. But now it's been almost a year, and I still haven't heard from her."

She paused, and a hopeful glint entered her eyes.

"Have you heard from your sister?"

Tina wanted nothing more than to keep the hope glowing in her mother's eyes, but she didn't want to lie to her either.

"No, Mom, I haven't."

Her mother tried to smile but it was a weak attempt.

"Your father's been gone three years. Losing him was hard, and I thought it was something I could get over, and I thought maybe I was starting to, but then Holly ..."

She paused, her eyes growing intense.

"What if something happened to her? What if she was in an accident or worse? How would we even know?"

Tina realized she had never been in a position where she needed to comfort her mother. She wasn't sure she was up for the task, but she wanted to take this burden off her mother's shoulders any way she could. She thought that if she could—if she somehow managed to make her mother feel better—that might help make her hatred of life subside.

Reaching across the table, Tina took her mother's hand in hers and gave it a soft squeeze. She forced a smile.

"It'll be okay, Mom. You know how Holly is. She's like a cat. She always lands on her feet."

THIRTY-FOUR

Eventually the car slows to a stop, and the trunk pops open. Louis stands outside, the fob in his hand, but he's not alone. Two freelancers stand behind him, their Berettas drawn.

Louis says, "Would you like to come out?"

It's hard to judge how long I've been in the trunk. At least twelve hours. The sky behind Louis has some light in it, but it's mostly dark, the sun about to set.

I sit up, slowly, my muscles having cramped from being squeezed into the trunk all this time, and the two freelancers take a step back for caution.

We're parked behind what looks to be an abandoned warehouse. The SUV idles a couple yards away. I climb out of the trunk and tilt my head back and forth on my neck, stretching the muscles, and then I stretch my arms over my head and rotate my shoulders.

Louis watches with his blank gaze.

"Did you get any rest?"

I just look back at him.

"What do you think?"

Louis steps away, toward the SUV, and returns with a bottle

of water. He hands me the bottle, and I take a long swallow, the kind that's too greedy and causes water to dribble down my chin.

"Now what?"

Louis motions toward the car.

"Now we continue on our way. The only reason we stopped was because I felt it was time for you to get out of the trunk."

What a gentleman.

My instinct is to try to sit behind the driver, but Louis knows better. He opens the rear passenger door. Once I climb in, he shuts the door and circles around to climb in beside me, and the driver—another freelancer—starts the car and gets us moving.

I'm conscious of the Beretta holstered to the driver's hip, just as I'm conscious of the Glock holstered to Louis's hip. I could easily make a move for one, wrestle it away before the other reacted, but there's the collar around my throat to take into consideration, plus the fact these assholes will kill my family if I don't do what they say.

As we drive over the gravel toward the front of the warehouse and back onto the highway, I think about how many hours I've been in the trunk, how many miles that adds up to, and what Louis said before we left. So it's no surprise when I spot one of the highway signs alerting drivers that Los Angeles is thirty-two miles away.

Louis sits slightly shifted toward me, which is smart. If I were to make a move, he's better prepared for it. Plus, he still has the fob in his hand.

He says, "You should get some rest."

"That's very thoughtful of you."

"You need to make sure you're focused enough to accomplish this mission."

"Get me a gallon of Red Bull, and I should be good to go."

Louis makes a face and glances out the back window at the

trailing SUV. The setting sun slants through the windows, casting a dark orange glow on the side of his face.

"What time is the hit, anyway?"

Louis looks at me again, considers his answer carefully, but then gives a slight shake of his head.

I frown at him.

"Hey—you want me to kill this guy, I need more intel."

"You'll get it when the time is right."

"And when is that?"

"When we get there."

"Where is there?"

Again Louis doesn't answer. He's looking annoyed. Which makes me think I might soon earn myself another zap.

"Look, aiming through a scope and pulling the trigger? That's a piece of cake. When I'm out alone in a field shooting at a stationary target. And something tells me Cortez isn't going to stand still long enough for me to get off the perfect shot. So I need to know what I'm dealing with. Where I'm going to be positioned. Where he's going to be positioned. How many people will be around him. The time of day. Where the sun is placed in the sky. Whether there'll be clouds. You know, important stuff like that."

Louis stares ahead, out at the highway and the traffic ahead of us. He doesn't look like he's going to answer, and while I'm certainly game to keep asking him questions, something tells me it isn't in my best interest to bug him too much either.

Finally he says, "You'll be in a hotel room in downtown Los Angeles."

"A hotel room."

"Yes. Seventh floor. Five blocks away from where your target will be."

"And where's that?"

"Another hotel. He'll be entering from the street."

"Why not the parking garage?"

Louis's lips curl into a thin smile.

"Someone on the inside has taken care of that. It'll be a great photo op for the president. There will be some reporters there, photographers, the local TV news. His car will pull up outside, he'll step out, wave to them, and that's when you'll shoot him."

"Where will the sun be in relation to our hotel?"

The smile fades from Louis's face, and he makes an annoyed frown.

"I'm not sure."

"It's important."

"Yes, I'm sure it is."

"If your boss wants this to happen, everything has to be in place."

Louis says nothing. Looking even more annoyed.

I say, "Can I be honest with you for a second?"

He says nothing.

"This whole thing seemed rushed. Carla said it herself when she came out into the field. What's that all about?"

The sun is almost gone from the sky, only a soft glow washing the side of Louis's face.

He clears his throat but doesn't look at me when he answers.

"There's a summit in Canada later this week. The American president, Canadian prime minister, and Mexican president will all be there. Cortez had planned to stop in Los Angeles after the summit on his way back to Mexico to meet with the governor, but plans changed at the last minute on the governor's end. So Cortez was agreeable to stopping in Los Angeles first. There's an initiative they're pushing to ensure Mexican immigrants are treated fairly if they come into the state illegally."

"Sounds like a hot-button issue."

"It is."

"Which means there'll be protestors."

"Probably."

"Which means there'll be heavier police presence than usual, even with the governor and Mexican president all in the same place."

Louis tilts his face toward me, his gaze still blank.

"If you don't do this, your family will die."

"What guarantee do I have they won't die even if I do assassinate Cortez?"

Louis doesn't answer, simply looks back out his window, which is answer enough.

Part of me didn't believe my family would be truly saved if I went through with this, but another part—a tiny naïve part—thought there might be a chance. Even for me, somebody who has cynicism running through her blood, I had hoped my family might be spared, but apparently not.

The highway crests, and Los Angeles opens up ahead of us, aglow in the failing light.

For some reason, the city of angels has never looked so bleak. As if it knows a team of fallen angels is headed its way.

THIRTY-FIVE

The evening had come on fast and strong, and the sky was darker than Nova had remembered it being in D.C. It had only been a year since he left, but something about the town felt different. Everybody was tenser. Angier. Or maybe that was just his imagination.

They had parked on a street lined with elm trees, and Nova cut through a park that was thankfully deserted this time of night. He knew he needed to be careful because police often kept their eye on parks like these at night. And if a cop were to stop him, what would he find? A big guy armed to the teeth carrying a quadcopter. They probably could have launched it from where they had parked, but Nova wanted to check out the motel across the highway first.

It was where they'd tracked the signal. Whoever was watching Holly's family was stationed in one of those rooms.

Earlier, James had returned to Holly's mother's house with some kind of high-tech RF detector. James did a quick sweep of the block, searching for any abnormal radio frequencies, and almost immediately found the source. A tiny camera was placed across the street from Holly's mother's house, positioned near the top of a telephone pole. James also determined a tracking device had been placed on Holly's mother's car.

Whether any cameras had been set up inside the house itself was difficult for James to tell, and the only way he could know for sure was to enter the premises and do a sweep. Which presented a few obstacles, the first being it didn't appear like Holly's mother was ready to leave the house any time soon, and second, assuming there *were* cameras inside and they managed to enter without the camera out front spotting them, that would alert the people watching the family, which was the last thing they wanted right now. So far the element of surprise was on their side, and Nova wanted to keep it that way.

James then took the RF detector over to Holly's sister's house and determined a camera was placed there, too—this one on a light post half a block away. Tracking devices were on the two cars in the driveway as well.

Which made sense, once Nova thought about it—set up devices to watch and track their prey, and sit back and wait for the signal to attack if need be. Otherwise, idling vehicles would go easily noticed, just as they'd determined when they first considered staking out the houses.

Nova had his earpiece in and whispered, "Let me know when."

The disposable phone vibrated with a text message from James through the Signal app.

Go.

Nova set the quadcopter on a picnic table and stood back.

"It's all set."

The propellers started spinning at once. The quadcopter lifted, hovered for a beat, and then continued higher into the air.

James was controlling the quadcopter from the car. Nova had seen the setup, an iPad with a controller. It seemed too simple, but the way James explained it via texting, the quadcopter had an infrared camera attached and would be able to sense heat signatures inside the motel. James had already determined where he believed the signals from the cameras and tracking devices went—a room on the second floor—but they wanted to make sure the room was occupied. Because if it was occupied, there was a good chance the entire team was inside.

The phone in Nova's hand vibrated with an incoming call. It was Atticus.

He said, "I see it on my end. Are you still in the park?"

Wherever Atticus was located, he was watching the same thing James saw from the iPad as the quadcopter flew over the highway toward the motel.

Despite the park being deserted, Nova still found himself whispering.

"Yes."

"Where's Erik?"

"He's keeping an eye on the sister's place."

Atticus was quiet for a beat.

"I trust him."

Nova merely grunted.

"I understand we don't know much about him, Nova. But I did a quick background check. He's clean. And Holly obviously trusted him enough to give him my number."

Nova grunted again.

"Don't be jealous, Nova."

Heat rose to Nova's face.

"What do I have to be jealous of?"

"Never mind. I—wait, I think I see something."

Across the highway, the quadcopter started to dip down toward the motel. It was one of those shady motels. Probably less than a hundred bucks a night for a room that was rarely cleaned. Obviously they wouldn't want to put themselves up in too nice of a place. The good hotels had cameras on every floor, had security, while with cheap motels like this you were lucky if the locks on the doors actually worked.

Atticus spoke quietly in Nova's ear.

"It looks to be four."

"Level of confidence?"

Before Atticus could answer, the motel room door opened. The quadcopter shot up in the air, out of view of the two men stepping out onto the walkway. They lit cigarettes and stood at the railing.

Nova realized he was holding his breath. He slowly let it out. Watching the two men smoke on the second-floor walkway. The quadcopter hovering several yards above their heads, just out of their line of sight. Nova figured the sound of traffic on the highway drowned out the quadcopter's spinning blades.

Atticus didn't speak, and neither did Nova. They waited. After another minute, both men flicked away their cigarettes and headed back into the room. A moment later, the quadcopter looped around in front of the motel door, hovered there for a beat, and then started back across the highway.

Atticus finally answered.

"Confidence level is high."

That was good enough for Nova. Wherever Atticus was, he had the technology to determine there were four people inside the room—two of which they had just seen.

Nova asked, "Any luck yet?"

The defeat in Atticus's voice was sharp.

"None so far. It's like she disappeared off the grid."

"How is that possible?"

"I don't know, Nova, but I'm searching. It would be easier if I had James here with me, too—he's much more proficient with this kind of stuff—but I believe the team is better served having him with you right now."

Nova had to agree. Especially because without James it

would only be Nova and Erik, and Nova still wasn't sure he trusted the kid.

The quadcopter floated over the trees, dipped down, and landed back on the picnic table from where it had launched.

Nova said, "I wish we could take them out right now."

Atticus sighed on his end.

"I know. But unfortunately that isn't an option at the present time. The moment you take out those men, Holly's life is over. Right now I believe it's best you don't make a move until you have no other choice. As long as Holly is still valuable to these people, they won't move on her family."

Nova picked up the quadcopter and started back through the park toward the car.

"That's not what I'm worried about right now."

Atticus was quiet for a beat.

"What are you worried about?"

"The team packing up and leaving. Maybe grabbing the cameras and tracking devices before they disappear, just to make sure there's no trace, but still they disappear. Because you know what it means if that happens."

Another sigh on Atticus's end, this one much more despondent.

"I do, Nova. It means Holly is dead. But look on the bright side."

The car was up ahead. James stepped out and went to the trunk so they could put away the quadcopter.

Nova said, "What's that?"

"They haven't packed up and left yet."

THIRTY-SIX

The alarm clock on the nightstand reads 3:37 a.m.

The hotel room has two beds. The TV sits on a dresser facing the beds, and one of the freelancers has turned it to cable news.

Louis sits at the desk, staring down at his phone.

Two of the freelancers lounge on the two separate beds, their feet up, chowing down on prepackaged sandwiches as they watch the news.

The other two freelancers—well, I don't know where they are. Once we entered downtown, I lost sight of them. We parked in the basement garage and took the elevator up to the seventh floor. Louis made me wear a scarf to hide the collar in case we ran into anybody.

I've been sequestered to the chair in the corner, my wrists zip-tied together.

The only window in the room is off to my left; it's a large window, about six feet across, and curtains conceal the outside. When we first entered the room, Louis parted the curtains enough for me to see the hotel five blocks away. The window has locks on both sides and can slide open a couple inches for fresh air. The space will be more than enough to shoot through.

Speaking of which, the Valkyrie sits in pieces in a backpack on the desk. No reason to get it out and put it together quite yet. It'll probably wait until an hour or so before President Cortez is scheduled to arrive.

Louis glances up from his phone and notices me watching him.

"You should try to get some rest. We need you focused in the morning."

I tilt my head toward the two freelancers.

"Tweedledum and Tweedledee are hogging the beds."

The freelancers ignore me; one has his cell phone out, looking at who knows what, while the other hasn't touched his phone. It's remained in his left pocket since we got here. All the phones—even Louis's—look to be disposables. These men are professionals and wouldn't bring their own personal phones with them on a job like this, but that doesn't matter as long as I can make a call with one of the phones.

Louis says, "I'm sure you can get some rest just fine in that chair."

"You want me to get a crick in my neck? That might throw me off in the morning."

The fob rests on the table. Louis absently touches it with his finger. Like that's supposed to scare me.

I force a smile.

"I'm hungry."

"We offered you a sandwich."

"I'd rather have something else as my last meal. Something that doesn't taste like shit."

Louis's finger doesn't leave the fob.

"A sandwich is your only option."

I release a heavy sigh.

"Fine. I'll take a sandwich. What's left?"

Tweedledee swings his feet off the bed and opens the small cooler on the floor. They brought along prepackaged sandwiches and bottles of water as they didn't want to deal with room service or be seen outside the hotel picking up food.

He holds up two sandwiches.

"Ham and cheese or tuna salad."

Gag me.

I ask, "Is the cheese low fat?"

He just stares back at me.

I release another heavy sigh.

"Fine, the ham and cheese."

Tweedledee drops the other sandwich back in the cooler and brings me the ham and cheese with a bottle of water.

My eyes drift down from his face to what he probably thinks is the sandwich and water, but it's really to the phone in his left pocket. His pants look to be a size too loose, probably for comfort, but it means the phone isn't tight in his pocket. Which is good.

After Tweedledee hands off the sandwich and water, he climbs back onto the bed.

Louis says, "Anything else, your highness?"

Yeah, you can shove that fob down your throat and choke on it, I think, but decide not to say out loud.

I start unwrapping the sandwich.

"Chips would be nice."

Louis's face remains expressionless.

"There are no chips."

"This place has vending machines, doesn't it?"

Louis decides he's bored with me and turns his attention back to his phone.

The two freelancers keep watching the news. Something about a recent scandal involving the president. On screen, four pundits keep talking over each other.

I take a bite of the sandwich, watching the freelancers and Louis.

Thinking about how I need to get that phone.

Even if it kills me.

THIRTY-SEVEN

The sicario circled the block only once before he spotted Hayward's men.

They were parked along the curb in an SUV, the windows smoked just enough so at night it concealed its occupants but not enough that it would immediately raise the suspicion of any police officer that passed it.

He assumed there were at least two men stationed outside the hotel, which meant the two other freelancers were inside along with Hayward's right-hand man. He didn't know Hayward personally—had only met him the other day when he and his brother passed through the man's place—but he had heard enough about the man to know he prized his right-hand. Hayward probably didn't care much about the freelancers— they were simply hired guns—but he most certainly would miss his right-hand when this was all said and done.

But that was Hayward's fault. From what he understood, Hayward was advised to keep his right-hand behind, let the other men see this thing through, but Hayward was too worried the freelancers might somehow fuck it up—especially as President Cortez was coming in sooner than planned—so

Hayward sent his own eyes and ears to ensure the whole thing went smoothly.

He drove a stolen black Mercedes C-Class sedan, whose plates he'd swapped out with another black Mercedes C-Class sedan in the parking lot of the Hollywood Park Casino in Inglewood. The thing handled beautifully, and he thought maybe he would purchase one when he returned home, though he knew that level of luxury was too flashy for somebody in his line of work.

Maybe when he retired, then. Yes, he would purchase one when he retired.

He used the parking garage under the hotel and took the elevator to the lobby. He carried an overnight bag because that was to be expected for a businessman such as himself, though he wore only slacks and a dress shirt and jacket, no tie. A casual look for this late at night. Getting in late from a delayed flight, he would tell the clerk if asked.

The clerk didn't ask anything further than his name. Pablo Santander, the name on his credit card and ID said, though they were not his real name. The clerk entered the information into the computer, confirmed there was already a room booked, and handed him a keycard and asked if he'd like a porter to carry his bag.

He smiled and said, "I'm okay, thank you."

The clerked nodded and wished him a pleasant stay, and soon he was in the elevator headed to the seventh floor.

He found his room down the hallway, close to Room 736. That was where Hayward's men and the woman were right now. The room was booked two weeks ago, though Hayward's people managed to get in earlier than planned. The people he worked for managed to book his room on the same floor and in the same hallway. Across the hallway, to be exact, and one room away.

The room was nice enough for the price, but not anything

special. There were two beds, though he had no intention of sleeping. It was almost four o'clock now, and with Cortez arriving first thing in the morning, the job should be over quickly. He would be gone well before noon. He'd leave the keycard on the desk by the door and check out remotely. After he wiped down the room, of course. Even now, as he navigated the room, flicking on the lights, he made sure not to use his finger but the back of his hand.

He set his overnight bag on one of the beds, zipped it open, and dug under the clothes he packed as a decoy to the pistol buried beneath.

It was a Smith & Wesson M&P9 with a threaded barrel, what he'd come to decide was his favorite piece to use on a job like this. The magazine held seventeen nine-millimeter rounds with one in the chamber. More than enough to accomplish the job, plus take out the two men parked outside on the street.

He withdrew the suppressor from under the clothes and screwed it onto the barrel, then set the pistol on the bed next to the bag.

He grabbed a tissue from the bathroom and wrapped it around the TV remote to work the buttons. Soon he had the television on and was flipping through the channels as he settled back on the other bed.

He pulled out his cell phone and sent an encrypted text to his brother three thousand miles away, who had needed to hustle even faster to make it to Washington, D.C. in time.

In position. Go when ready.

THIRTY-EIGHT

At just after 5:00 a.m., Louis's phone vibrates on the desk. He grabs it as he stands from his chair and starts toward the bathroom, the phone to his ear.

I nearly shout at him.

"I have to pee."

He pauses, glances back at me with a frown.

"Hold it."

"Not sure I can. You want me to pee my pants?"

The phone to his ear, he makes a face, takes a deep breath.

Tweedledee and Tweedledum are still lounging on their respective beds. Tweedledum isn't on his cell phone anymore, but he has it on the bed beside him. Tweedledee's phone is still in his pocket.

Louis gestures at Tweedledee, whose bed is closer to me.

"Take care of her."

Louis doesn't wait for a response; he steps out into the hallway, murmuring into the phone.

Tweedledee grunts as he slides across the bed and stands up, facing me.

I push to my feet at the same time—and lurch forward, as if tripping over my own feet. Straight into Tweedledee.

Tweedledum is on his feet a second later, his Beretta in hand, the barrel aimed at my head.

Tweedledee pushes me away angrily—"What the fuck?"—and I stumble back and fall into the chair.

"I'm sorry! I just"—I hold up my zip-tied wrists—"I don't have much balance with my hands like this. Plus, I've been sitting for hours. My legs fell asleep."

Tweedledum keeps his gun trained on me while Tweedledee takes a step back. He glances at his counterpart, then at the door Louis disappeared through, and motions at me to stand up again.

I stand up.

Tweedledee reaches into his pants pocket—the right-hand side, fortunately—and pulls out a tactical knife, pops the blade. He motions with the knife toward the bathroom.

I move past him, conscious of Tweedledum tracking me with the Beretta. The bathroom door is closed, and I push it open and hit the switches inside the door, turning on the light and overhead fan.

Tweedledee says, "Toilet."

I pause, turn back around.

"Is that how you get your rocks off—watching a girl use the toilet?"

Tweedledee doesn't answer. For some reason, he doesn't get my sense of humor.

The lid is already up. I unbutton my jeans and push them and my underwear down as I sit on the cold toilet seat.

I stare back up at Tweedledee, ignoring Tweedledum who stands a couple feet behind him with his gun still aimed.

"Like what you see?"

He steps forward, holds up the knife. I hold out my hands,

and with one simple twist of his wrist the zip-tie snaps and falls to the floor.

As he shuts the door, he says, "One minute."

The moment the door closes, I reach for my jeans pocket, where I slipped Tweedledee's cell phone once I lifted it from him. Thankfully, the phone isn't locked. Of course it isn't. Why bother locking a phone that will be destroyed in a couple hours and doesn't contain any personal information?

I punch in Atticus's number, the same number I gave Erik the other day. I have to assume Erik didn't contact Atticus, and even if he did, it doesn't matter. Atticus needs to know I'm still alive. He needs to know what's happening, and how President Cortez is in danger. Most importantly, of course, he needs to know about my family.

"Thank you for calling Scout Dry Cleaners. Our normal business hours are Monday through Friday, seven a.m. to seven p.m., and on Saturdays eight a.m. to three p.m. We are closed Sundays."

A beep sounds, and that's when I hit the plunger to flush the toilet and start to whisper.

"It's Holly. My entire family is in danger. They need protection ASAP. I'm in L.A., and they want me to assassinate—"

The door handle turns, and at once I disconnect the call and shove the phone back into my pocket as I stand and start to pull up my underwear and jeans.

The door opens. Tweedledee stands there, the knife still in his hand, his face stoic.

"Minute's up."

"Can I at least wash my hands?"

He says it again, this time slowly.

"Minute's up."

He moves away as I step into the room. I head toward my chair in the corner when Louis returns.

Closing the door, he says, "We're still on schedule."

I'm almost to the chair when Tweedledee speaks, his voice low and menacing.

"You bitch."

I pause, glance back at him.

He says to Louis, "She took my fucking phone."

Before I can even argue my case, Louis grabs the fob from his pocket, and a firework explodes around my neck. I turn and fall back into the chair, my body jerking for the couple seconds it takes before Louis disengages the fob.

Tweedledee advances toward me, his face a storm of rage, the knife held up at his side.

"You fucking bitch."

I manage, "Wait—"

Louis zaps me with another firework, and I'm starting to wish I used the toilet, because if this keeps up much longer, I'm probably going to pee my pants.

With a shaking finger, I point at the floor.

"There!"

Tweedledee pauses long enough to spot his phone on the carpet, right beneath the bed. It's where I managed to kick it when Louis entered the room, granting me a second or two of distraction. I didn't have time to delete the call from the log, so if they check it, I'm screwed.

Louis disengages the fob, and I sit slumped in the chair, breathing heavily.

Tweedledum covers his counterpart with the Beretta as Tweedledee retrieves the phone from the carpet.

Tweedledee stares down at it for a beat, then shakes his head as he glances at the two men.

"Musta slipped from my pocket."

He tosses it on the bed and turns to the bag on the floor. He takes out a fresh zip-tie and crosses back over and tells me to hold out my wrists.

Once he's bound my wrists together, Tweedledee asks Louis, "How much longer before this shit's over?"

"Two more hours, give or take. Mr. Hayward will alert me once he gets notification. Then we can wrap this up and go home."

He pauses, and smiles at me.

"Well, except you."

He pulls the hollow point from his pocket, holds it up.

"You're going to stay here with this in your head."

THIRTY-NINE

Nova had positioned his car in a lot across the highway that faced the motel—about four hundred yards down from the park—and that was where he still was at almost nine o'clock that morning, his head tilted back on the seat, the windows down, listening to the morning traffic and trying not to fall asleep.

Besides the few times the motel door opened to let the same two freelancers out to smoke, nothing else happened. A housekeeper pushing her cart of towels and sheets had ignored the DO NOT DISTURB sign hanging on the doorknob. She knocked at the door, and one of the men answered, shook his head at her, and the housekeeper had continued on her way to the next room.

Despite the fact they believed all the men who posed a threat were in the motel room, James had returned to keep an eye on Holly's mom, just as Erik stayed in the neighborhood to keep an eye on Holly's sister and her family. Erik texted not too long ago to alert them that the sister's husband had left for work, but so far that was it.

Nova's phone buzzed with an incoming call from Atticus.

"Holly made contact."

He bolted upright in his seat.

"What? When?"

"Only a couple minutes ago. Her message was brief."

"Where is she?"

"Los Angeles, though I know that simply because she said as much. The message didn't last long enough for me to establish a location. The number appears to have come from a disposable. Nova, she confirmed what Erik said—her family is in danger."

Nova nodded, his gaze focused on the motel across the highway.

"I think we already came to that conclusion."

"That's not all. The people who took her want her to assassinate someone."

"Who?"

"I don't know. The message got cut off before she could say. But it's Los Angeles—it could be anybody. Although President Cortez of Mexico is flying in this morning for an event."

Nova remembered standing in a church in Colotlán and listening to Father Crisanto tell them about how the cartels had come for Alejandro Cortez because they wanted to punish his father. That had been right before narcos dragged the priest out into the street and murdered him.

Nova said, "Cortez is the target."

"How can you be so sure?"

"Call it gut instinct."

"I can't notify the authorities based on gut instinct, Nova. Besides, if President Cortez suddenly cancels his trip, the people holding Holly will probably kill her if Cortez is indeed the target."

"She's probably dead either way. The least we can do is make sure her family stays alive."

The motel door opened, and the same two freelancers

stepped out to light cigarettes. A moment later, a man appeared on the steps leading to the motel's second floor. He had dark hair and wore a dark suit. He climbed the steps casually, not looking like he was in any hurry.

Atticus said, "Nova, are you there?"

"Hold on a second."

Nova leaned forward in his seat. With all the toys James had supplied them, Nova didn't have a pair of binoculars.

The two smokers noticed the man coming their way and shifted their bodies in a naturally defensive position. They were no doubt carrying. One of the men even reached behind him but didn't pull out his gun.

The man in the suit held his hands to the side and smiled as he said something to the two men. The two men glanced at each other. The man in the suit said something else, and motioned with his head to the motel room. One of the men stepped toward the room and opened the door, spoke to somebody inside, and then another man appeared.

The man in the suit was now only a few steps away from the door. He still kept his hands held out at his sides. He glanced out at the parking lot, said something else, and the other men seemed to realize just how exposed they all were. The one who'd stepped out motioned the man in the suit inside. The man in the suit followed him into the room, and the two smokers flicked away their cigarettes before joining them.

As the motel door closed, Nova said, "Someone new showed up."

"Describe him."

"Dark hair and dark suit. That's all I could make out from this distance."

"Where is he now?"

"He just went into the room with the others."

Nova watched as the motel door opened again. The man in

the suit stepped out, this time a bit more cautiously, scanning the parking lot and second level to make sure nobody was watching. He had a pistol in his hand and was unscrewing the suppressor from the barrel as he closed the door and started back toward the stairs.

Nova said, "Shit."

He started the car but then immediately turned it off. He'd parked in a lot that gave him a great position to watch the motel but not a great position to reach the motel easily. That was because he hadn't foreseen any need to reach the motel.

Atticus spoke in his ear.

"What's wrong?"

"I think the new guy just took the rest of them out. Let me call you back."

Nova grabbed his gun off the passenger seat and jumped out of the car. He ran down the embankment toward the highway and paused once his feet hit the macadam. The morning traffic was congested but not moving too fast. He spotted an opening and darted out, sprinting across the highway, ignoring the blare of horns that followed in his wake, and then he was racing up the embankment on the other side.

The man in the suit was long gone. He'd appeared from around the side of the motel, so Nova wouldn't have been able to see what vehicle he drove even if he'd stayed.

Nova hurried across the parking lot and up the steps to the second floor. He kept the FNX-45 down at his side, concealing it the best he could. The last thing he needed was for somebody to spot the gun and call the police.

He hesitated outside the door. Tried listening for any sound inside, but the noise of the traffic was too loud to hear anything at all. He reached for the doorknob but didn't want to leave his prints. Besides, there was a chance the man in the suit hadn't killed all the men inside. There was a chance the man in the suit hadn't killed any of them.

Nova squared up to the door, raised his knee, and kicked at the spot just beneath the doorknob.

The cheap motel door gave way, and Nova entered with his pistol raised.

He stood motionless for a beat, and then lowered the gun.

All four men were dead. One was splayed out on the bed. Another was slumped at the table with several laptops open. The two smokers were on the floor. All of them had been shot three times each—twice in the chest, one in the head.

The man in the suit was clearly a pro.

Nova crossed over to the laptops. The video feeds coming through were from the cameras posted outside Holly's mom's and sister's places. Another one of the computers only had audio; the men had planted listening devices in the homes as well.

He stared at the screens for several seconds before he pulled out his phone and typed out texts for James and Erik.

A new player showed up and took out the men in the motel.

Dark hair and dark suit.

Be on the lookout—he's on his way to either of your locations.

FORTY

Ryan was in a hurry that morning, even more than he typically was, racing down to the kitchen with his shirt half undone while he used the electric razor to get the spots he missed. He offered up a quick excuse—"Forgot I had an early meeting"— grabbed a granola bar from the basket on the counter, kissed both boys on the head and his wife on the cheek, and then, bang, he was out the door.

The boys, sitting at the kitchen table, stared at the door for a couple seconds before diverting their attention back to their tablets.

This was how the summer would go, she realized. Stacey Holbrook wasn't going to offer to take her sons to the zoo every day. The boys may be out of school, but they wouldn't do much more than play video games or mess around on their tablets.

Well, not if she had anything to say about it.

"All right, who wants to take the first shower?"

Neither boy volunteered.

She cleared her throat, loud and overdramatic, and the boys rolled their eyes at her.

Max said, "Where are we going?"

Matthew said, "Yeah, where are we going?"

She crossed her arms meaningfully, furrowed her brow to try to make herself look stern.

"Who says we're going anywhere? Maybe we'll stay home and clean."

The boys looked stricken.

Matthew said, "Or ... we could not."

Max giggled and took the final swallow of his orange juice.

"Yeah, Mom, how about we go to the mall instead? Or the movies! The Rock has a new movie out, and Dad said he'd take us and that was *weeks* ago."

The truth was Ryan had wanted to take the boys to the movies—take all of them, Tina included, the whole happy family—but they simply couldn't afford it. Even the matinee tickets were expensive these days, and the boys would no doubt want snacks.

No, they ultimately decided, the money could be better spent elsewhere—like paying off one of their credit cards, or at the very least trying to get the balance down to a more respectable amount—but how does one explain such a thing to kids? They didn't understand credit card debt or interest rates or credit scores. All they understood was The Rock had a new movie out that their friends had seen but which they still hadn't.

Because Tina didn't want to start an argument, she said, "We'll see. Now, who's showering first?"

Both boys looked at one another, and shrugged simultaneously.

Max said, "Why don't you go first, Mom?"

She smiled and answered dryly.

"Why, aren't you the thoughtful son."

He beamed back at her but then immediately focused his attention on his tablet. So did Matthew.

She sighed.

"All right, you've forced my hand. We'll let fate decide who goes first. Rock, Paper, Scissors."

The boys groaned their annoyance, but they were grinning. They loved when decisions were made with the game.

Matthew and Max chimed in together—"Rock, Paper, Scissors, go!"—and Max ended up trumping Matthew's rock with his paper.

Matthew blurted, "Best out of three!"

Tina laughed and shook her head.

"Oh, no. Fate has spoken. Go get yourself a shower."

Matthew groaned again, only this time it wasn't in as much jest. He grabbed his tablet and started out of the kitchen.

Tina said, "Tablet stays behind."

"But—"

She cut him off.

"No buts, mister."

Max giggled and shouted, "Mister No Butts!"

After some more whining on Matthew's end, he finally gave up the tablet and sulked away. She would try to keep an ear out for the shower because there was a good chance Matthew would get distracted by the computer in his room. One thing that could be said about her boys, they were great procrastinators. They got that from Ryan's side of the family.

A half hour later, Matthew thundered down the steps, his hair not totally dry, and he immediately grabbed his tablet and wandered off into the living room.

Tina called out, "Max, your turn!"

Max, playing video games in the living room, shouted, "I don't need a shower!"

Tina closed her eyes, took a deep breath. Gave it a moment, and called out again.

"If you don't head upstairs in the next five seconds, I'll take every single video game in this house and throw them in the river."

An idle threat, maybe, but her tone was severe enough, and in three seconds Max was running up the steps.

She had just heard the shower start when the doorbell started ringing. Not once or twice but several times.

Ding ding ding ding ding.

Matthew, in the living room, called, "I'll get it!"

There was something about the incessant ringing, especially so early in the morning—in their neighborhood where soliciting was illegal—that caused a finger of dread to touch her spine.

She shouted, "Stay where you are!"

Matthew was already up, halfway to the door, but he sensed the urgency in his mother's voice enough to turn and head back to the living room.

The doorbell had quieted, and now there came a banging at the door—*bang bang bang bang bang*—and her first thought was that it was somebody crazy outside, some whacko who might go away if ignored long enough, but then just as quickly she worried that if nobody answered, the person might never go away.

She peered through the window in the side. A man stood on the doorstep, a tall black man in his mid-twenties, wearing khakis and a black T-shirt, a man Tina had never seen before. He pounded his fist against the door as he kept looking back over his shoulder.

Tina shouted, "We're not interested!"

The man paused, checked the street once more, then stepped back to address her.

"Please open the door. Your sister Holly sent me."

Her dread instantly snapped into panic. She knew she should ask this man more questions—how did he know Holly? where was she?—but before she knew it she unlocked the door and pulled it open, and that was when she saw the gun in the man's right hand, and her first thought was her sons, how all they wanted to do was see The Rock's new movie, and now this man was going to kill them.

But the man didn't raise the gun, didn't point it at her, and instead spoke in a calm, measured voice.

"You and your boys need to come with me right now."

She thought, How does he know about the boys?

But before she could voice the question, she heard the car coming their way, coming fast, coming *too* fast.

The man heard it, too. He turned his head to the street and the car coming their way. Not just down the street, but swerving *toward the house.*

The man lunged forward, pushing her back into the foyer, right as the car jumped the curb and tore over the lawn and crashed through the front door.

FORTY-ONE

"Mom? Mom!"

Matthew's voice, mixed somewhere in the crush of noise—pieces of the house falling around her, the car's engine ticking, blood thrumming in her ears—and the man was on top of her, shielding her with his body, and his voice was hot on her ear as he shouted.

"Get out of here!"

The next thing she knew the man rolled away, brought up his gun, and started shooting at the car. The driver attempted to open his door, but the car had smashed into the house too close to the wall, which meant the door wouldn't open far enough.

Tina didn't see what happened next because she scrambled to her feet and swung her focus toward Matthew standing in the living room entryway, frozen, his eyes wide, tablet held at his side, and she screamed at him—"Run!"—and at first it didn't look like he was going to move, stuck there as if hypnotized, but one of the bullets ricocheted into the wall only a few feet away from him, and like that he blinked and looked at her as Tina ran toward him, grabbed his hand, and yanked him deeper into the house.

A volley of gunfire erupted behind them, the man who pushed her inside shooting at the driver and the driver shooting back, and now Matthew was racing beside her, running awkwardly because she wouldn't let go of his hand, but that was okay, that was fine, she wouldn't let him go, would never let him go, and she saw the back door ahead of them, the morning light shining through it, and the backyard was there, the swing set and sandbox the boys never used anymore, but more importantly, there was escape, and she was so intent on getting the two of them out of there when she suddenly remembered Max.

She pivoted at the stairs, yanking Matthew with her, all at once regretting the decision—she should have let him go, pushed him forward toward the backyard, toward safety—but he was with her now, racing up the stairs too, and she could hear the shower still going in the bathroom, but she also heard Max's voice, calling out to her, shouting mommy mommy mommy!

"Where are you going?"

She thought it was Matthew's voice at first, though it was deeper than she remembered, much lower bass, and in her delirium she glanced down at him and saw he was looking back over his shoulder, and that was when she shifted her focus and saw the man on the first step, the gun at his side, his face awash in confusion.

Before she could respond, bits of plaster exploded around the man, and an instant later she heard more gunshots and kept running, pulling Matthew along, faintly aware that the man was firing back at the driver while he hurried up the stairs after them.

Max met them at the top of the steps, and he was soaked

and naked, having jumped straight out of the shower when he heard all the noise, and she let go of Matthew so she could pick Max up with both hands, just scooped him up like he was a toddler again, and his weight slowed her down but she didn't care and just kept running, straight for the master bedroom.

The man followed, walking backward up the steps, firing intermittently at the driver.

The bedroom overlooked the backyard, and one of the windows was right above the patio, and though the overhang was slanted she knew it would be possible for the boys to squeeze through the window, and yes, she knew they might get hurt in their fall to the grass below, but it wouldn't hurt like a bullet in the head would, and her thoughts were so jumbled she suddenly wondered what The Rock would do in a situation like this, how he would fight back against the bad guy, and she tried to open the window but it wouldn't budge, no matter how much she pushed and pulled, and it didn't occur to her until a few seconds later that it was locked and so she flicked off the locks and pushed open the window, fresh air blowing in on her face, Max now crying beside her, Matthew shouting something, and the bedroom door banging open as the man ran through.

He saw what she was doing, stared for a moment, then slammed the door shut and frantically scanned the bedroom for something to barricade the door with, and it was the dresser that was closest, the dresser Ryan's parents bought them when they moved into the house, and he shoved at the dresser, its legs tearing the carpet as it stubbornly moved closer and closer to the door, and she realized the dresser was the only thing that could save them, that could give them a few extra seconds, and so she ran over to help him, the little perfumes and candles on top of the dresser tipping over and falling to the floor.

The driver attempted to kick the door open right as they

put the dresser in place, and the driver started shooting at the door, bullets tearing through the dresser, and the window was directly across from the door, one of the bullets shattering the glass, and she knew that as long as the driver kept shooting there was no way they were going to escape through the window, no way at all.

The closet—that's where they needed to go, where they needed to hide, because it suddenly occurred to Tina that they weren't going to survive this, that the driver would manage to burst through the door and would kill them all, even the man she didn't know, the man who said her sister sent him.

She grabbed Max's arm and yanked him to the closet, flinging open the door and shoving him inside, and she shouted at Matthew to come too, Matthew who was now flat on the carpet, his hands on top of his head, trying to keep out the noise, and at first she didn't think Matthew heard her or if he did he wasn't going to listen, but then he jumped to his feet and raced to her, tears streaming down his face.

The closet was small, filled mostly with her clothes, some of Ryan's, and she backed into the farthest corner, her butt on the carpet, her back against the wall, and held both boys, all of them crying, while the driver out in the hallway kept shooting and kicking at the door.

The man stood in the closet doorway for a moment, stared down at them, and then stepped back out and closed the door, enveloping them in darkness.

"Mommy, Mommy, Mommy!"

She didn't know if it was Max or Matthew or both of them, sobbing into her, shouting it again and again, and she squeezed them tight, kissed both of their heads, telling them that it was okay, that everything was okay.

For a couple seconds there was silence, and then she heard the driver kick at the bedroom door again, a hard, solid kick, and she knew the door had opened wide enough for the driver to slip through.

The man fired at the driver but the driver fired back—she saw it all in her head, the men exchanging gunfire—until suddenly there was no longer a volley but only the sound of one gun firing bullets, and she saw the man get shot when she heard him shout something but his words were unintelligible, just gibberish, and besides, all she wanted to focus on now were her boys, both of them clinging to her as she kept kissing their heads.

The closet door opened.

The driver stepped inside.

Tina opened her eyes and saw him standing there, a tall Hispanic man dressed in slacks and a suit jacket. The man reloaded his gun as he stared down at them, his eyes dark and hard as he observed them in their final moments.

The man pulled back on the slide, began to raise the gun at them—and that was all Tina saw, her eyes now squeezed shut, holding the boys tighter than she'd ever held them before.

Two sudden gunshots—*boom boom*—and Tina jumped with each one, screaming, certain that both of her boys were now dead.

She opened her eyes and saw the man still standing in the doorway. He dropped to his knees, half his face gone, and stared at her with just the one eye before he fell over dead into several of her blouses.

The man—the man she had pictured shot and killed, the one her sister sent—must have done it. He was the one Tina expected to see, but the man who stepped forward was a big white man with a beard.

He had a gun in his hands, aimed at the driver, and once he was satisfied that the driver was dead, he looked at them cowering in the corner of the closet.

"Are you okay? Are you hurt?"

Tina didn't answer at first—she couldn't—but she ran her hands over both boys, searching for blood, and when she thankfully didn't find anything she shook her head at the man.

The gun now at his side, the man pulled out a cell phone and placed the phone to his ear.

"Family's secure. Target's down. And Erik—shit, we need an ambulance here ASAP!"

FORTY-TWO

Louis sets the backpack with the disassembled sniper rifle on the bed closest to the window, opens it up, and starts taking out the pieces.

I ask, "Can I do that?"

Tweedledee and Tweedledum have moved to separate corners, Berettas held at the ready. I might not have possession of the assembled rifle yet, but they aren't taking any chances.

Louis glances at the men for a beat, then shrugs.

"Be my guest."

I stand up from the chair and hold out my bound wrists. Louis motions at Tweedledee, and the freelancer slips his knife from his pocket as he approaches, slices apart the zip-ties, and then retreats to his corner.

Louis has the fob in his hand now, and motions at the bag.

"Get to it."

I begin picking out the pieces—the stock, bipod, barrel, suppression, everything—and put the Valkyrie together. The magazine is empty, so I don't insert it, and instead shoot a questioning glance at Louis.

He says, "Not yet."

The clock on the nightstand reads 7:32. Another half hour or so until President Cortez is scheduled to arrive at his hotel.

"Then when? Don't know about you, but I prefer not to have to scramble at the last minute."

He checks his watch. Does the math in his head, chews it over for a few seconds, then shifts his gaze back to me.

"Ten minutes."

I hold his stare, speak in a flat tone.

"I'm trembling with anticipation."

I return to the chair in the corner and stare out the window at the city street below. The sun has been up now for well over an hour, playing shadows off the tall buildings.

My mind, of course, drifts to my family and whether or not Atticus heard enough of my message to try to make sure they're safe. Then I start to wonder what if Atticus hadn't heard the message because Atticus has passed away, or something along those lines—something that caused him to get out of the business. Maybe the phone number still exists, but nobody monitors it anymore, not even James. In that case, my family is as good as dead. As am I.

So the real question is, what's going to happen to President Cortez?

He might die today, but it won't be because of me. Sure, I plan to go through the motions—hunker down in the chair with the Valkyrie propped up on the windowsill—but as soon as the man steps from his vehicle, I won't pull the trigger.

Well, that's not true. I may pull the trigger, but it won't be at his head. Maybe at the vehicle instead. At the windshield or the grille. If it's a fancy car, I'll try to take out the emblem that sits right on the hood.

Or ... maybe I won't do any of that. Maybe I'll simply refuse to pick up the rifle when the time comes. Let Louis zap me as much as he wants. Let Tweedledee and Twee-dledum threaten me with their guns. I'm not going to be walking out of this hotel room alive, so I might as well have some fun.

Then again …

What if Hayward is a man of his word, and he'll spare my family if I follow through with assassinating President Cortez? There's always the chance, isn't there? In that case, I would be crazy not to follow through.

Louis says, "Go ahead and load your weapon."

He pulls a single 6.5 Creedmoor cartridge from the backpack. The cartridge is wrapped in plastic. Smart. Keeps his fingerprints off the thing that will kill a country's sitting president and will maybe set off an international crisis.

"Just one round—you're joking, right?"

His expression remains predictably blank.

"Why? How many rounds does it take to kill a man?"

I don't answer.

"This isn't Fallujah. You aren't raining down cover fire. You're simply taking out one man with a headshot. You don't need more than one round."

He has a point, but I don't tell him that. Not my style to agree with douchebags.

"Fine."

I hold out my hand, but he tosses the cartridge on the bed beside the rifle. I lean over the bed to pick it up. Start to unwrap it. Go to load the bullet in the magazine but hold it up instead.

"Anybody want to kiss it for good luck?"

Nobody answers.

"Tough crowd."

I load the Creedmoor into the magazine, taking my time because I don't have anything else to do. I insert the magazine into the Valkyrie when Tweedledee's phone buzzes.

Tweedledee, holding his gun at the ready, glances down at his pocket.

Louis says, "Who knows your number?"

Tweedledee shakes his head.

"Besides the team, nobody."

Tweedledum keeps his gun aimed at my chest. He doesn't take his eyes off me when he speaks.

"Ignore it."

But it's a buzzing phone, and buzzing phones are hard to ignore. Keeping the Beretta trained on me with his one hand, Tweedledee slips the phone from his pocket with the other. Glances at the display on the front of the flip phone with a frown.

"Number doesn't look familiar."

Tweedledum says, "Ignore it."

Tweedledee looks conflicted. He knows he should listen to his counterpart, but he also wants to know who's calling.

In the end, curiosity gets the better of him.

He answers the phone.

"Hello?"

He listens for a couple seconds, and his frown deepens. Without a word, he closes the phone and drops it back into his pocket.

Louis says, "Well?"

"Wrong number."

"What makes you say that?"

"It was some guy from a dry cleaners. Said they'd found all my pieces and they're now safe and sound."

Louis doesn't like this at all.

"Let me see your phone."

Tweedledee says, "Why?"

"Let me see the fucking phone right now."

Louis's focus is on Tweedledee, and Tweedledee's focus is on Louis, which means the only person's focus still on me at the moment is Tweedledum.

Which is why I decide to kill him first.

As Tweedledee steps forward to hand his phone to Louis, I pull back the bolt to load the only round into the chamber.

Tweedledum shouts, "What the fuck are you doing?"

I smile at him, all nice and sweet.

"You missed your chance to kiss the bullet for good luck. Now it's pissed."

I swing the Valkyrie around, so it's aimed at his chest.

And pull the trigger.

FORTY-THREE

Due to the caliber and the close proximity, it's like Tweedle-dum's hit by a rocket—he flies back against the wall, instantly dead, his pistol falling from his hand.

I turn toward Louis and swing the Valkyrie at his face, and the suppressor clips his cheek as he tries to duck, the fob falling from his hand.

I pivot toward Tweedledee, jumping on the bed and springing at him as he raises his Beretta. He manages to fire off a round, which zings above my head, as I tackle him to the floor. The back of his head smacks against the wall, and his eyes cross momentarily. The gun is still in his hand, and I grab for it when lightning strikes and I jump back and hit the floor, shaking with all the electricity coursing my body.

I'm half-aware of Louis standing over me, the fob in his hand. Half aware that he has his cell phone to his ear, shouting, "I need you two up here, now!"

My focus right now is on Tweedledum, lying dead close by, and the Beretta that fell from his hand—the Beretta I'm right now trying to move toward, on my back, pushing myself across the carpet like a snail.

Louis's face looms over me, his eyes aflame with anger. He keeps his finger on the fob, pressed as hard as it will go, and he probably intends on holding the fob like that until the two other freelancers arrive.

"Stupid bitch. Stupid, stupid bitch."

He spits the words at me, then pauses long enough to glance over at Tweedledee.

"Get the fuck up."

Tweedledee moans in response.

Louis grunts another curse—"Fuck it"—and starts to lean down to grab Tweedledee's gun.

That's when, with the lightning still streaking through my body as I continue to crawl on the carpet, I stretch and lunge and feel the Beretta, just the grip with the tips of my fingers, so close but so far away.

Louis, realizing my intention, scrambles to grab Tweedledee's gun first—but by then I've managed to take possession of Tweedledum's Beretta, and I have the sight aimed at Louis, right at the spot between his eyes.

I pull the trigger.

His head snaps back. His body falls to the carpet. His finger releases the fob, and that constant lightning bolt racing through me fades away.

I start to stand when the door is kicked open. A Hispanic man rushes into the room, a suppressed pistol in hand. He instantly scans the room and searches out the most prominent threat. Takes him half a second to realize the threat is me.

He fires at me as I dive across the bed, firing back at him. One of my bullets clips him in the shoulder, but he barely reacts, his feet planted firmly on the floor, tracking me with his pistol. He shoots again as I fall to the floor between the beds. Flat on the carpet now, I aim at the man's feet beneath the bed.

Getting clipped in the shoulder may not have done much, but shattering his ankle is another story.

The man grunts in pain, tries to retreat into the hallway, but loses balance and falls to his knee. Before he can stand back up, I've already jumped to my feet and placed two bullets in his head.

I approach him slowly, this man I've never seen before, this man who I somehow know is a professional, the kind that works alone, not like the freelancers in this hotel room. Speaking of which ...

Tweedledee's still alive. The wall he's leaning against is wet with blood. He probably hit his head in the right spot that there's already brain damage and he'll eventually bleed out. It'd be cruel to keep him alive, and I don't consider myself a cruel person.

One bullet puts him out of his misery.

Taking a deep breath, I survey the room and make sure Louis and the two freelancers and the hitter are all down for good. Have to figure somebody on this floor has already called the front desk or even 911 directly, so time's wasting.

I grab Tweedledee's phone off the floor, shove it in my pocket. I search Louis for the key to the collar; put that in my pocket, too, along with the fob.

Tweedledum's Beretta is almost empty. I toss it aside as I bend to pick up Tweedledee's pistol and check the magazine. Fully loaded.

I peek out into the hallway. Someone has their door open down near the elevator. Nobody to be concerned about, just a random hotel guest, doing that stupid thing people do when they hear gunfire and so they want to poke their heads out like nobody will shoot at them too.

The elevator door opens. One of the freelancers steps out. He already has his gun in hand. He spots me down at the end of the hallway. The hotel guest's head disappears as he slams the door shut. The freelancer moves forward without even giving the guest a second's thought.

The door to the stairs is off to my right. Only a couple yards away.

I step out into the hallway and begin walking backward toward the stairwell door, firing at the freelancer.

The freelancer returns fire, and the wall by my head spits plaster.

A second later I reach the door and push into it with my back, and that's when I hear the frantic footsteps coming up and turn to see the second freelancer a half flight down. When he sees me, he raises his gun.

I step into the stairwell, let the door fall shut, and fire down at the freelancer. He has no cover and goes down in a second, the single gunshot echoing against the brick walls.

I don't move for a beat, trying to recalibrate, to catch my breath, knowing that right now there's the freelancer out in the hallway but also knowing there might be others.

Who sent the pro?

Five seconds pass. Ten seconds.

I keep the Beretta trained on the door, waiting for it to burst open. By now the freelancer has probably checked the hotel room, found all the dead bodies, and figured that his buddy is dead, too. Otherwise, his buddy would have called out to him. The freelancer might be standing on the other side of the door, debating what to do next.

After another five seconds, I decide I can't wait any longer. I start down the steps. Taking them at an angle, so my gun is aimed at the door. Stepping over the dead freelancer and continuing down.

Keeping the gun in hand, I dig the key from my pocket and I use my finger to feel for the tiny latch on the collar. Once I find it, I tear the collar from my neck but don't fling it aside. Instead, I stuff it in my back pocket, along with the key, and then pull out Tweedledee's phone.

I punch in Atticus's number and wait for the automated voice saying it's Scout Dry Cleaning.

"It's me. Call me back on this number."

Atticus calls back thirty seconds later, as I'm heading down to the second floor. By then an alarm has sounded, not the fire alarm but an emergency siren. The door on the second level opens. It's a man and woman and three kids, the kids shouting and their parents telling them to stay quiet.

I slip the Beretta in the waistband of my jeans. My T-shirt's not that baggy, and I hope nobody in their panic notices the slight bulge.

Atticus says, "Are you okay?"

"I'm fine. What about my family?"

"They're safe. Where are you?"

More people have filed into the stairwell. A few families but mostly business people wearing business clothes.

"We're evacuating the hotel right now."

Someone behind me says, "I heard there was a shooting."

Another person says, "I thought it was a fire."

One of the kids ahead of us, a little girl, starts screaming, "Are we going to die?"

In my ear, Atticus's calm voice says, "Have you eliminated all of your captors?"

Captors. That's one way of putting it.

"Almost."

"What does almost mean?"

"It means almost."

The alarm keeps going, echoing in the stairwell just like that single gunshot. We reach the first floor and pile into the lobby. The staff directs everybody to go outside. Police cars have already arrived, officers jumping out of the cars with their guns in hand.

Atticus says, "Holly?"

"Hold on."

The morning air feels good on my skin as we file outside. I scan the sidewalk and the street, searching for the freelancer. If he's made it out, I figure he'll try to disappear. That would be the smart thing to do.

Turns out the guy isn't smart.

He's standing across the street, on the fringe of a crowd that's started to grow, watching everybody exit the hotel.

I hurry over to one of the cops sliding a Kevlar vest over his head.

"Officer? That guy over there—the one across the street—I saw him inside with a gun!"

The freelancer seems surprised that I'm blatantly pointing him out.

The cop, already on high alert, snaps his focus to the crowd across the street.

"Who? Where?"

I point.

"There!"

The freelancer turns away and starts walking down the block, which is the last thing you want to do when somebody's pointing a police officer in your direction.

The cop doesn't say anything else to me. He starts running, shouting at another cop nearby, who also starts running. The freelancer, realizing he's been made, starts running, too.

I drift away from the crowd as more police cars arrive. A fire truck is headed down the street, blaring its horn. I head in the direction the two cops went. They've disappeared around a corner. I hear shouts, then gunfire. I pick up my pace, worried that the freelancer has taken out the cops, but when I turn the corner, prepared to grab the Beretta, both officers are still standing and the freelancer is on the ground. Dead.

I say into the phone, "Okay, I think that's all of them."

Atticus releases a breath, like he's been holding it this entire time.

"Where are you now?"

I check the street sign and tell him.

Atticus says, "I can make a call and have somebody pick you up in five minutes."

I keep walking down the street as two more police cars zoom past headed in the opposite direction.

"Not yet. This isn't quite over."

"What do you mean?"

"I was brought here to assassinate President Cortez."

Atticus releases another breath.

"Yes, I suspected it was him."

"He's supposed to arrive at a hotel a couple blocks away any minute now."

Hurrying down the sidewalk, I spot two crowds outside the hotel, one close to the entrance and one across the street. The one across the street has signboards and are chanting.

Protestors.

Atticus says, "I can make another call. Make sure he's alerted."

I pause.

"How many friends in high places do you have?"

"It depends. What are you thinking?"

I tell him. He's quiet for a moment, then sighs again.

"I'm not sure the plan is realistic."

"He has people inside his cabinet who are working against him. It's the only way Hayward and his people knew about the change in schedule."

"There are other ways they could have learned about the change in schedule."

"Call it a gut feeling, Atticus. Somebody close to him is dirty. There's only one way to sniff them out."

Atticus doesn't speak for another moment.

"I can make a call, but I can't make any promises. Besides,

what makes you think President Cortez will even give you the time of day?"

As I join the crowd outside the hotel entrance, I think about the night just outside La Miserias, in Fernando Sanchez Morales's mansion, stepping into the master bedroom to find Morales's wife and son cowering in the corner while the man known as the Devil stood over them.

"Trust me, Atticus. He'll want to hear what I have to say."

FORTY-FOUR

President Eduardo Cortez sat in the back of the armored SUV. He watched the tall buildings slide by outside the window and tried not to yawn.

He wasn't successful.

Imna Rodriguez, his closest aide and confidant, smirked at him.

"Try not to do that once we get there."

"Is that your professional advice?"

"It's what I get paid for."

Cortez smiled and shifted his focus out his window again. Their entourage consisted of two other armored SUVs—one leading them, one tailing them—as well as a handful of police cars. One of his bodyguards sat in the passenger seat up front, while his other security detail rode in the other vehicles. The middle seat in the SUV had been taken out and flipped around so it faced the rear back seat; Imna sat in this front seat facing him.

They'd left LAX a half hour ago and would be arriving at the hotel soon. And then, after a brief speech and a photo op with the state's governor, it would be back to the airport to continue on to Canada.

"Tell me again why we needed to squeeze this trip in?"

Imna was ten years his junior though she sometimes treated him like she was his mother. She adjusted her glasses as she frowned at him.

"It's good PR."

"For the governor, maybe. Not sure the President of the United States appreciates it."

Imna shrugged.

"You win some, you lose some."

Cortez yawned again. He couldn't help it.

Imna said, "Why are you so tired, anyway?"

"I haven't been able to sleep the past couple days."

"Why?"

"I don't know."

He was lying, of course. Cortez trusted Imna with practically everything—every little secret—but not the truth about his son … though he sometimes wondered if she knew, deep down inside, like a few of his other aides. Many of them had access to the same intelligence reports he did. While Alejandro was never publicly named as the one targeting cartel families—called El Diablo by the news media and the rest of the nation—many suspected it was his son. Only Cortez knew for sure. He knew that his son had been out there, still alive, hunting down the wives and children of the cartel families, and while he didn't approve of such means, he certainly hadn't gone out of his way to stop his son.

And then it was over. Almost a year ago this week. A skirmish outside a small town an hour south of Culiacán. A cartel head and his men murdered. While the cartel head's wife and son were unharmed—though he knew two people had intervened at the last second, a woman and man who took his son's body away. That was all they managed to get from the cartel head's wife. She had been so frightened she could barely describe them more than that.

The driver answered his cell phone, listened for a few seconds, then said they would be making a detour.

Imna asked, "What's going on?"

"There's an ongoing incident a couple blocks away from the hotel. The police want us to steer clear."

At the next intersection, the convoy made a right. Soon they were speeding down a side street, and Cortez leaned forward to look out the other window but couldn't see much except a fire truck headed in the opposite direction on another street, and then the convoy turned at the next intersection.

The driver said, "Almost there."

Imna sighed when she spotted the protestors. There looked to be fifty of them, maybe more. Along with a few news vans parked along the street and a few other police cars and a friendlier crowd gathered around the hotel's entrance.

Cortez smiled, always one to try to make the best out of a bad situation.

"Quite the welcoming party."

Imna eyed him hesitantly.

"Maybe we should have skipped this event, after all."

He shrugged and smiled again.

"We're already here. Canceling now would be rude."

"What would be rude is yawning in front of the governor. Try not to do that."

"I won't make any promises."

The SUV halted in front of the hotel. The bodyguard stepped out and waited for the security detail to move into position before he opened the back door. Shouts could be heard outside—the friendlier crowd near the hotel as well as boos and chants from the protestors across the street.

Cortez waited for Imna to exit first, as she always did, but she was now staring down at her cell phone.

He said, "Ready?"

She glanced up at him, her fingers tapping at the phone.

"I have to answer this email. I'll be right behind you."

He nodded and slid out of his seat and stepped outside. Both crowds became even louder, a raucous noise, and he thought it might be funny if he were to yawn right now, in front of everyone, but then he imagined the photos that would stream across the Internet and cable news and how Imna would be furious with him.

Cortez waved to the people near the entrance as he followed his security detail toward the open doors. He ignored the boos and chants across the street and some of the people on this side calling out his name—a skill he'd perfected over the years, just filter the noise from his mind and focus on the task at hand—and he only paused when a new name managed to push through all the rest, a name he'd been thinking about for the past couple days but one he didn't expect to hear this morning.

Somebody was shouting his son's name.

FORTY-FIVE

At first I'm not sure he hears me, what with everybody shouting and the crowd across the street chanting and booing, but then his stride starts to slow, and he turns my way, searching the crowd, until he spots me.

A woman steps out of the SUV, dressed in a pantsuit and glasses. She looks confused, like she isn't sure why President Cortez has stopped. His security detail looks just as confused. One of them steps close to him, whispers in his ear. President Cortez blinks, shakes his head, and looks like he's ready to keep moving forward into the hotel.

So I repeat the name, not shouting it like before but still saying it loudly and with force.

"Alejandro."

President Cortez pauses again. Stands there staring at me. I hold his gaze, aware of his security detail and the police all around me, and the Beretta digging into my back. There's a good chance I'll be thrown to the ground and arrested. But I've decided I have no choice but to take that chance.

The same bodyguard whispers again to President Cortez,

touches his arm to try to get him moving, but the older man waves him off.

President Cortez approaches me, slowly, still holding my gaze. When he's only a few feet away, I speak again, this time not as loud but still with enough force so he'll hear it over the crowd noise.

"I knew your son."

The man says nothing, studying my face.

"I was there that night."

His eyes go flat with understanding, but still he says nothing.

"I can tell you where to find him."

He's only a couple feet away now, his security detail hovering on both sides, ready to draw their weapons if need be. The crowd keeps shouting and chanting, but all of it has become background noise, a soft distant humming like a fly at a screen door.

I lean forward, slowly raise my hand and motion with a finger for him to come even closer.

He does, despite another warning from his security detail. The bodyguard who tried moving the president along has had enough. He tries to intervene, to step between me and the president, but Cortez holds up a hand, stopping him.

"It's okay."

"But, sir—"

"I said it's okay."

He's so close to me now, I could easily reach out and touch him. If I were indeed here to kill him, I could do it within a second. But I'm not here to kill him; I'm here to save him.

I speak into his ear, not a whisper but still loud enough so he can hear me over the noise.

"Somebody close to you wants you dead. They tried to force me to kill you."

President Cortez doesn't move for a long time, and then he tilts his head to speak into my ear.

"Did you kill him?"

Not looking at him, I nod.

"Did you bury him?"

I nod again.

"Will you tell me where you buried him?"

Another nod.

President Cortez is silent for another moment, then asks a final question.

"What do you need from me?"

I look up and see the security detail hovering, just feet away, as well as the aide still lingering back by the SUV. I lean forward again, this time my lips almost touching the man's ear.

"I need you to trust me."

FORTY-SIX

Imna Rodriguez was doing everything she could to remain calm. She had her cell phone out and was staring down at the screen as if reading an email or text message when in reality it was so she could focus her attention on something other than the fact President Cortez was supposed to be dead.

She was squeezing the phone so tightly she wouldn't be surprised if the thing cracked, and she had to take a moment to breathe, to try to center herself, and figure out what the fuck this girl was doing here.

Imna knew just as much as had been passed on to Oliver Hayward—the girl's name, her location in Alden, the fact she had once been a non-sanctioned assassin for the United States government, and that she was the one who killed Alejandro Cortez last year.

The cartels were certainly happy that Alejandro Cortez was no longer in play, but his father remained a thorn in their side. Which was why they'd wanted him dead for several years now. And which was why once they tracked down Holly Lin and then learned that President Cortez would be visiting California, everything seemed to fall into place.

By now Cortez should be dead on the sidewalk, blood pooling from his head wound, police going into overdrive to secure the scene and try to determine from which direction the bullet had come. One of the sicarios who passed through Hayward's only days ago would have been ready to take out the girl and the rest of Hayward's men, just like the sicario they sent to D.C. would have taken out the girl's family, as well as the men watching them.

No loose ends—that was the trick in a situation like this, the kind that was supposed to eliminate the head of state in another country, but something was wrong. She'd sensed it when their convoy made the detour to avoid the hotel with the fire trucks and police cars. The police were to swarm on the hotel eventually, but that was *after* the girl had taken out Cortez, not before.

Speaking of the girl, where did she go?

Imna realized President Cortez was moving again, heading into the hotel lobby, and she hurried to keep up with him, scanning the crowd as she went.

The girl was gone.

Sidling up next to Cortez, she asked, "What was that about?"

President Cortez shook his head. He looked pale. She couldn't begin to imagine what the girl said to him. Had she told him anything close to the truth, surely he would have had the security detail detain her, or have the police arrest her, or *something*. But none of that happened, and the girl was gone, and now they were in the lobby and a man in a gray suit approached them, some bigwig whose name Imna momentarily forgot, the man's shiny shoes echoing on the marble floor as he strode up to them with his hand extended.

"President Cortez, thank you for coming today."

The man spoke in Spanish, though it was clearly not his

first language, and Cortez smiled and responded in kind, and then Cortez asked where the closest restroom was located.

The man in the gray suit pointed down the hallway. Cortez thanked him and said he would be back soon. Before he could head in that direction, though, Imna touched his arm.

"Are you feeling okay?"

He forced a smile at her.

"Just a little lightheaded. I'll be right back."

Before he could take a step, she tried again.

"Who was the woman outside?"

Another forced smile.

"I'll be right back, Imna. Wait here."

She watched him depart, three bodyguards trailing him. The man in the gray suit turned to her and started speaking, again in that faltering Spanish. Part of her wanted to ask him who he was, but she knew she should already know his name, that it was her job to know such things, and before she knew it she cut him off with a curt smile.

"I need to make a phone call. Please give me one minute?"

The man smiled and nodded, and she stepped away, using the encrypted app on her phone.

Oliver Hayward answered after two rings, his tone wary.

"Why are you calling? Isn't it done yet?"

She wandered over to the corner of the lobby, by a table and some potted plants, and made sure nobody was nearby when she dropped her voice to a harsh whisper.

"No, it's not done. The girl's still alive."

This got Hayward's attention.

"What? No, that's impossible. That—"

She cut him off.

"We had a deal, and you fucked it up."

"I didn't fuck anything up. It's not my fault—"

"Cortez is still alive. And the girl just spoke with him outside the hotel."

Haywood didn't respond, thinking about it. He hadn't heard from any of his men, which had concerned him, but now hearing that both the girl and President Cortez were still alive, he began to panic.

Obviously, Hayward didn't know the two sicarios who passed through his place only days ago had been tasked with taking out his men. Imna had looked forward to telling him about it once Cortez was dead and she stepped away to cry in private—in an empty bathroom, perhaps, just herself and the cell phone and Oliver Hayward on the other end, at first happy that he had come through and then crestfallen once he learned about his men. She hadn't imagined he would be too angry—they were freelancers, from what Imna understood—but he would still feel betrayed. He should have known any trace to this hit would need to be eliminated; the cartels would want nobody left alive as witnesses, maybe not even Hayward himself despite the other service he provided.

Imna wanted to say something else, something to rub the salt in Hayward's fresh wounds, but that was when an alarm went off and strobes all around the lobby began flickering.

Hayward said, "What is that?"

Before she could answer, the man in the gray suit hurried over to her.

"Fire alarm, Ms. Rodriguez. We need to head outside."

She opened her mouth, not sure what to say but wanting to say something, when along with the blaring alarm and flashing strobes came a series of sudden gunshots somewhere in the hotel.

A woman in the lobby screamed.

Another person shouted, "What was that? *What was that?*"

In her ear, Hayward spoke again, asking what was wrong, but she disconnected the call and hurried past the man in the suit. The man called after her, telling her they needed to evacuate, but she ignored him and pushed past the people moving toward the exit, running in the direction she'd watched Cortez head only minutes ago.

A few police officers hurried past her, their guns drawn, and one of them tried to stop her from proceeding, but once she explained—shouted, really—that she was President Cortez's aide, he relented but told her to stay back.

Around the corner was a short hallway, and the emergency exit door at the end of the hallway stood open. One of the bodyguards was shouting at the police to hurry.

Imna followed them out to a side street and found one of the bodyguards still on the ground, though he was trying to pick himself up; blood ran down his face from his broken nose. The third bodyguard was standing but had his hands up. A gun lay at his feet; he was the one who fired it and wanted to make sure the police knew he was unarmed.

He pointed down the street.

"They went that way!"

Imna turned to the first bodyguard, the one holding the exit door open.

"What happened?"

The man's face was red and tight. He had one job, and he had failed to do it.

"Once the alarm sounded, President Cortez came out of the bathroom and ran for the door. The woman from outside —the one President Cortez was speaking to on the line—was waiting. She"—he paused, swallowed—"she attacked us. She grabbed him and put a gun to his head. They got into one of the SUVs. We fired after them, but—"

She turned away from him, wanting to scream out her frustrations.

One of the police officers had a radio to his ear. He turned to them, and shook his head.

"They're already on the freeway."

FORTY-SEVEN

This portion of the 110 has six lanes heading south, and I use all of them, swerving back and forth between cars as the speedometer ticks up to from 70 to 80 to 90.

I eye President Cortez in the rearview mirror, the man sitting in the back holding on to the "oh shit" bar.

"I suggest you put your seat belt on, Mr. President."

I spot flashing lights a quarter mile back, what may be two or four or six police cars. President Cortez notices me looking past him in the rearview mirror, and glances back through the rear window.

Turning back as he clips in his seat belt, he says, "What do you think they will do?"

"Nothing right now. They're just going to chase us. They won't intervene as long as they believe your life is in danger."

"Where are we going?"

The answer is *I'm not sure*, but that won't ease his worry. The fact is, everything had happened so fast—Cortez agreeing to trust me, me hurrying around to the side of the hotel where the SUVs were parked, giving Atticus the signal to remotely set off the hotel's fire alarm, and then waiting until Cortez and his bodyguards burst through the side door.

Now we were in one of those armored SUVs, a half-dozen police cars chasing us with more on the way, police helicopters no doubt headed in our direction, and the morning traffic on the 110 busy but not too congested, the speedometer now inching up to 95 mph.

I spot a sign for the 10 interchange, and keeping one hand on the steering wheel, I flip open Tweedledee's cell phone and dial Atticus.

He says, "Where are you now?"

"On the 110, almost to the 10. What's my timeline?"

"I'm still waiting to get confirmation from one of my contacts."

"Goddamn it, Atticus. We're running out of time."

"There's nothing I can do to pressure him. This is a big ask."

"Yeah, well, it's not like I can pull over to save us some time."

Atticus is quiet for a moment.

"Perhaps you can."

He tells me his idea, and directs me onto the 10 headed east. I cut off a bus as I take the turn, and soon we merge onto the 10.

Two helicopters are in the air, headed in our direction. At least one of them is a news chopper, and for the first time I'm thankful for the tinted windows.

I ask, "Have we made the news yet?"

Atticus tells me to wait a moment, then says, "Yes, they're already running the coverage. They don't appear to know President Cortez is with you. Once that happens, the coverage will go international."

"I don't have GPS on me. What's my route?"

Atticus relays the directions, and they're straightforward

enough that I disconnect and toss the phone onto the passenger seat.

President Cortez leans forward in his seat to look up at the helicopters in the sky.

"Are you sure this will work?"

Keeping both hands on the wheel, my foot pressed to the gas, still swerving from lane to lane, I decide to tell him the truth.

"No."

A couple minutes later we pass through the 405 interchange. Now there are a dozen police cars following us. The traffic becomes a bit more congested, and for the first time, I lift my foot off the gas. At the last second, I jerk the wheel and steer us over to the right lane to the next exit. We're going so fast it feels like the SUV comes up on two wheels as we take the turn. Going south on Bundy Drive now, there's a red light up ahead, but I tap the brakes, scan the traffic, and then breeze through it, nearly clipping the rear end of a pickup truck.

Swerving through more traffic, some of it oncoming, people leaning on their horns and shouting out windows. I make a hard turn onto Ocean Park Boulevard, the SUV almost fishtailing, and then ride the brake as I jerk the wheel once more, onto a side street, and press all my weight down on the gas pedal.

The SUV's needle ticks up, going from 60 to 65 to 70, and in the back President Cortez spots the fence ahead of us and shouts.

"Stop. Stop. Stop!"

We crash through the fence. I'm prepared for the airbag to deploy from the impact, but it doesn't. The SUV is large enough that we barrel through and continue out onto the airfield.

"Mr. President, welcome to the Santa Monica Airport."

FORTY-EIGHT

More news choppers fill the sky, three of them, as well as a police chopper. At least a dozen police cars have ringed the airfield. A few unmarked police cars, too. A few black SUVs. Two ambulances. Three fire trucks. The only thing they haven't sent yet is a tank, and I wouldn't be surprised if one's on its way.

Not even ten minutes have passed since we crashed through the gate, so that's a pretty impressive response time.

I eye President Cortez in the rearview mirror.

"That's a lot of people. You must be somebody important."

He doesn't smile at the joke. He stares out his window, watching all the flashing lights, his face tight.

"Where is he?"

He doesn't look at me when he asks the question, but that's okay. It's the question I've been expecting him to ask.

"All in due time."

"No"—his voice loud, his teeth gritted—"tell me now."

I keep watching him in the rearview mirror, waiting for him to shift his gaze to meet mine. When he does, I wait for a beat, and then nod.

"We buried him in a woods near the Chihuahua, Sonora border."

"Who do you mean by we?"

"An associate of mine was with me. He entered the country to help me stop your son. You have to understand, Mr. President, at the time I didn't know his story."

"How did you learn it?"

"Father Crisanto."

President Cortez shuts his eyes, takes a deep breath.

"I had heard Father Crisanto was murdered. Gunned down in the street in front of his church. How did you know to speak to him?"

"That's a long story. But the main thing is we tracked him down, and he told us about your son. About how the cartels wanted to hurt you, and so they targeted Alejandro and his family. Can I ask you a question?"

The man shuts his eyes again, and nods.

"When did you discover your son was the Devil?"

The Devil was what the news media had dubbed Alejandro Cortez. El Diablo. A serial killer who had targeted the wives and children of cartel bosses, abducted them, and burned them alive.

President Cortez looks out his window again. He doesn't speak for a long time, and then he tilts his face to meet my gaze again in the rearview mirror.

"Not for several months. I believed his body was among those found in the fire. My wife did, too. It … made it easier, having that closure. But then the murders started happening, to those women and children, and part of me began to suspect."

"How so?"

"At the time I believed nobody else could be so brazen. Not if they had anything to lose. And clearly by then my son had nothing to lose."

From the cluster of police cars, a man begins to approach. He wears a Kevlar vest with his badge hanging from a chain around his neck. He has his hands raised, holding a bullhorn in one of them.

"This must be the hostage negotiator."

I wait until the man is ten yards away—moving slowly, one cautious step at a time—before I lower my window a few inches. By now I figure a half-dozen snipers have set up all around the airfield, and I don't want to give them an easy shot.

"Take one more step, and I'll shoot him in the head!"

The negotiator freezes.

"Turn your sorry ass around and head back to your friends!"

The negotiator doesn't move. He's here to negotiate, and so far he hasn't had a chance to properly do his job.

Before the man can say something, I shout again.

"If you don't back away in the next five seconds, I'm going to blow his fucking brains out!"

The negotiator doesn't move at first, at least to my liking, so I start a countdown.

"Five!"

The negotiator takes a quick step back.

"Four!"

Another step.

"Three!"

Another step.

"Two and you better turn your ass around and get moving!"

The negotiator complies. He doesn't hurry, though, instead walks at a measured pace, probably to try to save face with his colleagues.

President Cortez shifts uncomfortably in his seat.

"How much longer?"

"I don't know. Hopefully my associate's contact comes through. If not …"

"Yes?"

"We're screwed."

The man doesn't answer, though he does smile, and stares out his window again. I watch him in the rearview mirror for another moment before I speak.

"Can I ask you a question?"

"Certainly."

"Why did you believe me?"

He thinks it over for a few seconds.

"I saw the truth in your eyes."

"What truth?"

"That you knew my son. That you were the one who … stopped him. It's been almost a year now. I have thought of him more often than usual the past couple days."

I watch him in the rearview mirror for another moment, then lean forward to check the SUV's glove box. I find a scrap of paper and a pen, and jot down several numbers. I pass it back to President Cortez.

He looks at the paper for a moment. Frowns at me.

"What is this?"

"GPS coordinates to where we buried your son. If something happens to me, I want to make sure I followed through with my end of the deal."

Without a word, he folds the paper and slips it into his jacket pocket.

"I need to know something, Mr. President."

He looks at me again.

"Go ahead."

"Besides the cartels, who benefits most in your government if you're assassinated?"

He thinks about it for a moment, then smiles.

"Quite a few people. I am not a popular man. My policies

have been hard on the cartels, and in turn, the cartels have stopped contributing their blood money to many of those corrupt in my government."

"Mexico doesn't have a vice president, does it?"

"No. If something were to happen to me, the *Secretario de Gobernación*, or Secretary of the Interior, would assume executive powers provisionally."

"Who's the current Secretary of the Interior?"

"A man named Felipe Abascal."

"Any bad blood between you and Felipe?"

"None I am aware of, but that doesn't mean there isn't any. Besides, he would not take over permanently. As I only have two more years in my term, Congress would select a substitute president by a majority of votes in a secret ballot. That person would be president until the end of the presidential term."

"So we know for a fact if you were assassinated, Felipe would take over, but it wouldn't be for long. Congress would need to elect somebody else."

"Yes."

"And that could be anybody."

President Cortez shrugs.

"I would not say just anybody, but there is no telling who may be elected."

"Would you say the majority of your Congress is corrupt? As in they would do whatever the cartels tell them to do?"

"I would like to think not, but I do not know for sure."

"Who was the woman that was with you when you arrived at the hotel?"

"My aide. She's been working for me for almost seven years."

"So you trust her."

"Yes."

"She goes with you everywhere."

"Yes."

"Knows your schedule."

"Yes."

He pauses, seeing where I'm going with this, and shakes his head.

"No. It … it cannot be her."

"Let me ask you this: when you arrive somewhere with your aide, who typically gets out of the vehicle first?"

He says nothing, staring out his window.

"I watched you motion for her to get out first. She didn't. Almost like she knew something bad was supposed to happen."

Still President Cortez says nothing.

"You understand why we're here, don't you? Somebody close to you has been feeding inside information to the people who wanted me to assassinate you. That person was providing up-to-the-minute intel. And that same person, if this goes as planned, will want to make sure I never get a chance to tell my story to the authorities. The last thing they want is for their plot to become known. Do you understand?"

He nods, his expression pained, the knowledge that he was betrayed too much to accept.

I ask, "What is your aide's name?"

"Imna Rodriguez."

I watch him in the rearview mirror.

"I hope I'm wrong about this."

He meets my stare again.

"So do I."

That's when Tweedledee's cell phone buzzes.

FORTY-NINE

The police had set up a perimeter around the airport of a couple blocks, mostly to keep the news media away. The security detail had driven her there once word reached them that that was where the woman had taken President Cortez, and she had to speak to several different police officers before they were allowed to drive through the barricade. Even then, more police cars were lined up outside the fence, making it difficult to see the SUV out on the airfield.

She stepped out of the SUV and was immediately met by an older black man with salt-and-pepper hair. He flashed his badge at her. FBI.

"Hello, Ms. Rodriguez. I'm Special Agent in Charge Bryan Rhodes. I understand you were with President Cortez before he was abducted."

She stared out at the airfield, trying to get a glimpse of the SUV. Above them, helicopters hovered in the sky.

"What is happening?"

"It appears we have a hostage situation."

"President Cortez is a guest in this country."

Forcing anger into her tone, the proper amount of outrage.

The man nodded, his face tight.

"I understand that, Ms. Rodriguez. And right now we're doing everything we can to ensure President Cortez's safety."

Her primary concern wasn't Cortez, of course. It was the woman. The woman who knew way too much. If somehow this ended without her being killed by the police, she would be arrested. Imna couldn't have that.

A radio on the agent's belt crackled, and a voice came through.

"Jones is approaching now."

Imna asked, "Who is Jones?"

The agent said, "He's the hostage negotiator."

She raised herself up on her tiptoes, like that would help her see over the barricade of police cars, but it didn't do much good. She could just glimpse a man walking toward the SUV on the airfield.

The voice came through the radio again.

"Driver's window coming down."

The agent unclipped his radio and spoke into it.

"How much?"

"Only a few inches. The target looks to be talking to the negotiator."

A moment of silence from the radio, the sound of the helicopters in the sky the only thing she could hear, and then the radio crackled again.

"Jones is falling back."

The agent said, "Repeat?"

"He's walking backward, returning to the cars."

The agent shook his head as he muttered under his breath.

"What the hell is going on?"

A few minutes passed in silence from the radio. Imna, growing impatient, tried seeing past the cars again, and she wondered how she was going to handle this, just how much power she could exert in this country—not to mention how much power the country would allow her to exert—when they heard the gunshots.

It sounded like distant firecrackers, almost lost under the noise of the helicopters, and immediately the radio crackled again.

"We have gunfire. I repeat: we have gunfire."

Her heart began thumping in her chest, a rush of adrenaline shooting through her, and she realized she needed to continue her act as the frantic, concerned aide.

"What happened? *What happened?*"

The agent ignored her, the radio to his mouth.

"Status?"

The radio crackled again.

"The driver's door is opening. And … a gun was just tossed out. Hands are up in the air, and … target is stepping out of the SUV. I repeat: target is stepping out of the SUV."

Imna was on her tiptoes again, straining to see, but a dozen agents were rushing out onto the airfield, their guns raised, and she couldn't see a thing.

The voice from the radio said, "Target is on her knees with her hands on her head. Officers approaching the SUV now."

Several seconds ticked by in silence from the radio, and Imna realized she was holding her breath. She knew if the news came that Cortez was dead, she would need to show tears, and she had been practicing the past week, forcing herself to think about her abuela, whom she had loved dearly, who had raised her most of her life and was shot dead in the street like she was nothing more than a crippled animal.

The radio crackled.

"They've secured the target. I repeat: they've secured the target. Now they're checking the SUV, and …"

Silence.

The agent said into his radio, "Status."

Another beat of silence, and then the radio crackled again.

"The hostage is dead."

FIFTY

She turned away at once, squeezed her eyes tight, and thought about her abuela. The tiny mole on her neck. The way she always smelled of flour and spices after she made dinner. The kiss she put on Imna's head every day before she left for school. And then, of course, the day Imna witnessed her gunned down in the street by those narcos.

Tears began to stream down her face, and she started shaking her head, muttering no no no under her breath.

Special Agent in Charge Bryan Rhodes was saying something into the radio, but his words were lost behind the sound of the helicopters. One of the security detail hurried over to her, placed a hand on her shoulder, tried to steer her back to the SUV, but she shook him off.

Wiping at her eyes, she turned to the agent.

"I want to see him. I want to see his body."

The agent hesitated, thinking about it. He shook his head.

"I'm sorry, Ms. Rodriguez, but not right now. We need to secure the scene."

"The president of my country was *murdered.*"

Putting all she had into the word, almost screaming it, but not wanting to overdo it at the same time.

The agent nodded solemnly.

"I understand that, Ms. Rodriguez, I do. But we have to go through protocol here. First, we secure the scene, and then—"

He pulled his cell phone from his pocket and checked who was calling him.

"I need to take this."

He turned away as he answered the phone, and Imna wiped at her eyes again. The security detail needed to see her reaction to this moment. Needed to remember it, so that they could later relay just how she had done everything in her power to respect President Cortez's memory and represent their beloved country.

The agent closed his phone and turned back to her.

"Sorry about that. Now, about what you were asking—"

She cut him off.

"What will happen to that woman?"

"Ms. Rodriguez—"

"She *murdered* him."

More tears fell down her face, but she purposefully didn't wipe them away. She wanted the man to see the tears.

The agent said, "The woman has already been taken into custody."

"Where will she go?"

"Right now she's not going anywhere. Apparently, she was involved in an incident out in Texas two days ago. Two U.S. Marshals were killed, so their office wants a piece of this, too. Trust me, this woman will get what's coming to her."

"She will be jailed, you mean."

"That's for the courts to determine."

"For murdering *our* president."

"Ms. Rodriguez, I know that—"

She cut him off again, speaking now between clenched teeth.

"I want to see her."

The agent frowned.

"I'm sorry?"

"I want to see this woman. I want to face the person who murdered our president. It is the least our country is owed."

The man said nothing at first, just stared at her. Imna kept the tears going. She doubted they would allow her to see the woman, but she needed to ask. It was what would be expected from her. She needed to be strong and brave for Mexico, and she needed to be the one to confront the person who killed their much-loved president.

Finally, the agent said, "Wait here. I need to make some calls."

She watched him step away, putting his phone to his ear, and she turned back to the security detail. She told them what happened, though she knew they had already figured it out. The few who were with President Cortez when he was taken from the hotel looked to be filled with shame. Good. They would forever carry the knowledge that they were responsible for what took place today.

The agent returned. He took her aside, and lowered his voice.

"I've been given the green light. You can meet with her, but only for a couple of minutes."

"Where is she?"

"They're holding her away in the security office here at the airport for the time being. If you'd like, I can drive you over there."

She nodded, wiping a few stray tears from her eyes for show, and followed the agent to his car.

FIFTY-ONE

The room is tiny—barely twenty square feet—with the walls bare and fluorescent lights buzzing in the ceiling. No windows. No two-way mirror. Not even a camera in the corner to monitor what's going on. Just a chair and me sitting on it, my hands behind my back, wrists bound by zip-ties.

When the door opens, an older man with gray hair looks in at me. He doesn't enter. He glances at somebody standing off to the side, nods once, and that's when she steps into view.

Imna Rodriguez.

She stares in at me for several seconds before stepping forward. The door closes behind her, and then it's only the two of us.

The woman scans the room, searching for a camera or wire or something that might record our conversation, and when she's satisfied there's nothing, she takes two more steps and leans forward so she's only a couple inches away.

She whispers, "Your family is dead."

I say nothing. She frowns.

"Do you think I am lying? Your entire family has been murdered."

Still I say nothing. Her eyes harden.

"The cartels sent a sicario to kill them. For what you did to Fernando Sanchez Morales. They demanded revenge."

I keep staring back at her. Silent.

Imna Rodriguez leans away, shakes her head.

"You created quite a mess. What happened to the men you were with?"

I ignore the question and ask one of my own.

"How much is the cartel paying you?"

Her eyes harden again.

"You do not know what you are talking about."

"The cartel has wanted Cortez eliminated for quite some time. That's why they went after his son and his family. Did you know I was the one who killed Alejandro?"

"Of course. That was why you were chosen."

I echo it: "Chosen."

"That is correct. It made the most sense for you to be the one who pulled the trigger."

"I was supposed to die back at the hotel, wasn't I?"

The woman nods.

"That is correct. You were not supposed to live so you could tell your story."

"But I am still alive."

She nods again, and her face darkens.

"That is why I am here."

She holds up her wrist, and the glass face of her watch glints in the fluorescents. She takes off the watch and opens the back, and she uses her fingernail to dig out a tiny white pill.

I say, "That's not aspirin, is it? Because I have the mother of all headaches right now."

She holds the pill up for me to see.

"It is not an aspirin, but it will take your headache away."

I look past the pill, stare into her face.

"What is that supposed to do—kill me?"

She nods.

I say, "Now why the fuck would I want to kill myself?"

"Again, you were not supposed to live so you could tell your story. That is why I am here now. To ensure your story ends."

I frown, tilt my head at her.

"No thanks, I'm good."

She says, "Your family is dead. You have no one to protect anymore."

I grin back at her.

"How does it taste, all the bullshit coming out of your mouth?"

She doesn't look amused.

"Take the pill."

I shake my head.

"Yeah, no thanks."

Her jaw tightens.

"I will not ask you again."

I close my eyes, issue a heavy breath.

"How about we work out a deal?"

"What deal?"

"You answer a question, and I'll take your stupid pill."

She doesn't answer, just keeps staring at me, so I take her silence as consent.

"Who is the cartel's choice for president?"

The question catches her off guard.

"It does not matter. You do not know the man."

I nod, like, *Duh, of course.*

"Yeah, you're right. But maybe he does."

That's when the door opens again, and President Cortez steps into the room. His dark eyes burn into Imna. He doesn't speak.

Imna moves at once—she is about the swallow the tiny white pill, but I spring up from the chair before the pill gets close to her mouth, the loose zip-ties around my wrists falling away, and I pluck the pill from her fingers and toss it in the corner of the room as I grab her arm with my other hand and shove her down into the chair.

Two FBI agents enter, and they quickly secure Imna Rodriguez. Not just her wrists, but her ankles as well, before they step back out into the hallway.

She glares up at President Cortez.

"You are a disgrace to our country."

I step between the two of them.

"Well, ain't you a peach?"

She doesn't acknowledge me, staring through me.

I smile down at her.

"Did you really think the FBI was going to let you see the person who just supposedly assassinated your president, let alone talk to her privately?"

She says nothing.

"In case you haven't noticed, I didn't kill President Cortez. And my family? I know they're alive because people I trust helped to keep them alive. The sicario you mentioned? He's dead. And you, well, I imagine you'll be returning to your country to spend the rest of your life in prison."

I glance back at President Cortez.

"Is that a safe assumption?"

He doesn't answer, staring through me at his aide.

I turn back to Imna.

"Now, I do have one more question for you, and I'd very much appreciate if you answered it. Where is Oliver Hayward's operation located?"

Her gaze refocuses back on me.

"I will tell you nothing."

I nod, slowly, holding her gaze.

"I'll be honest with you, Imna. I've had a rough couple of days, and I'm exhausted. This is the last place I want to be right now. So we can either do this the easy way or the hard way. My choice? We do it the easy way. Much less stressful, and nobody gets hurt."

She keeps glaring back at me, so I continue.

"President Cortez is certainly disappointed in you, but he knows you've had a hard life. I asked him about it while we were sitting out on the airfield. He told me about how your husband has cancer, and about your two children. About how the medical bills have been piling up. If the cartel is pressuring you in any way—such as threatening your kids—we can fix that. You're still going to have to answer for what you did, but we can make sure your husband and children are safe. If need be, we'll even get them out of the country. You may never see them again, but at least you'll know they're safe.

I pause a beat, letting that sink in.

"The hard way, on the other hand, is a bit different."

Imna Rodriguez says nothing.

I turn to President Cortez.

"If you don't mind, Mr. President, I'd like a couple minutes alone with your aide."

President Cortez stares down at Imna. The anger has faded from his eyes, replaced with disappointment. This is a woman he has known for several years, who he believed was a close confidant, somebody he could trust. I feel for the guy, because I've been betrayed by people close to me as well. One of them was my father.

"Mr. President."

He blinks, looks at me, nods quickly, and leaves the room.

Both of the FBI agents are still stationed out in the hallway. I step to the door and give them my brightest smile.

"You guys are probably wondering what's going on, right?"

Neither of them answers.

"There's no reason you should trust me other than the fact your superior probably received a call from his superior who probably received a call from his superior telling him to give me a lot of latitude with this prisoner. And so I guess what this all leads to is a simple request. Can one of you retrieve me a paperclip? Preferably a large one."

The guys aren't stupid—they know exactly the reason I'm asking for a paperclip—and it's clear from their faces they don't like the idea. The truth is, I don't like the idea either. But I stand there, staring back at them as I wait, and finally one of the agents walks away and soon returns with a shiny paperclip.

"Thanks, boys. Now hold tight. I shouldn't be too long."

I step back into the room to find Imna Rodriguez still glaring at me. I hold up the paperclip.

"Last chance."

She keeps glaring.

With a sigh, I close the door.

PART III

THE LOST BOY

FIFTY-TWO

Oliver Hayward cracked open another beer—his fifth or sixth or maybe it was his seventh, he'd lost track a couple of beers ago—and stared out at the darkness.

It was just past midnight. Hayward was typically in bed by now, but he couldn't sleep. How could he, after the major fuck-up that was today? Any sensible person would have packed his things and disappeared, but he couldn't do that, not with his whole operation and the kids and the women. He provided a valuable service to the cartels, and believed that despite today's failing, they still had a use for him.

"Do you know why I named this place Neverland?"

Hayward didn't wait for a reply, taking a long swallow from his bottle as he stared out into the darkness. He sat on a chair on the back porch overlooking the field; one of the guards could be seen, rifle slung over his shoulder, walking the perimeter.

"Growing up, my parents were not around much. My father was an important businessman, and when I say he worked all the time, I mean he worked *all* the time. I barely saw him. I saw my mother more often, but even then we didn't interact much. I don't think she ever wanted kids. She was too focused on her charity work to spend too much time with me. And so what was a boy my age supposed to do?"

Again, Hayward didn't wait for a reply.

"I read all types of books, including the entire Hardy Boys series. You ever read any of the Hardy Boys books?"

For the first time in several minutes, Hayward regarded Jose. The boy stood ramrod straight, his chin tilted up, his eyes closed. One of Hayward's empty beer bottles was balanced on the top of Jose's head, Hayward having told Jose that if the bottle fell and shattered then Jose would get a zap like he'd never gotten before.

Shaking his head, Hayward muttered, "Of course you never read any Hardy Boys books. You've probably never read a book. Do you even know how to read? Well, anyway, one of the books I read again and again was *Peter and Wendy*. Did you ever hear about Peter Pan?"

Jose didn't answer. Hayward fingered the fob in his left hand, considered giving the boy a quick zap just for the hell of it, but it felt good to talk like this, the alcohol having soothed his nerves, and he pushed on.

"Peter Pan was a boy who refused to grow up, and he had all these magical powers—he could fly, Jose!—and he had this fairy named Tinkerbell, and he was in charge of the Lost Boys. These Lost Boys had been taken away from their families when they were babies and brought to Neverland, and these boys, they were tough. And I … I sometimes thought of myself as a Lost Boy. My parents were extremely wealthy, and I never had to worry about anything, but still I saw myself as an outcast."

Hayward shook his head suddenly, as if to clear it, and realized with whom he had been sharing such private matters. He leaned forward and pointed the fob at Jose, his voice dipping into a whisper.

"I never told anybody about that before—not even my

therapists—and if you tell anyone, I am not only going to zap you, I will kill you myself."

Jose stood motionless with the empty bottle on his head, his eyes closed.

Hayward said, "Nod that you understand me."

The boy opened his eyes. Glanced at Hayward for a second but then quickly looked away.

"I'm not going to tell you again, Jose."

The boy knew what would happen once he nodded—the bottle would tip off his head, shatter on the ground—and he knew what would happen then. Jose had come to fear being zapped, which was good, Hayward thought. A boy should never be fearless. A fearless boy was a stupid boy. A dangerous boy.

When Jose didn't nod—when it became clear that he would refuse—Hayward pressed down on the fob.

The boy immediately jerked, and the empty bottle fell off his head.

But the bottle didn't shatter on the ground. Jose caught it inches before it hit, and he stood motionless, staring up at Hayward, who for an instant thought he saw defiance flicker in the boy's eyes, though maybe that was only his imagination or the alcohol or a combination of the two. Whatever the reason, Hayward didn't like it, not one bit, and he intended on zapping Jose until the boy passed out, but before he could press down on the fob again, Carla stepped outside.

"What are you still doing out here?"

Hayward looked at her, at first not sure what to say, and then smiled.

"Enjoying the nice evening."

"You should come to bed."

"I can't sleep."

"Take a pill."

"I don't want a pill."

"Everything will be okay, Oliver."

He shot to his feet so suddenly he stumbled, almost fell, and had to hold on to the railing to regain his balance.

"Everything will *not* be okay! Cortez is still alive. I failed. I failed the cartel."

Carla stared back at him with her typical unnerving calmness.

"If they wanted to kill you, they would have done it by now."

Hayward squeezed his eyes shut, shook his head. None of it made sense. He'd watched the TV for hours and listened to the reports about how President Cortez had been abducted and taken to an airport where they sat on the airstrip, police surrounding them, until gunshots were fired. For the first hour or so, the news reported that President Cortez was killed, but then news broke that he had actually survived, as well as that his longtime aide Imna Rodriguez had been taken into custody.

No word on Holly Lin. No word from Louis or any of his men.

He looked out at the dark field and the guard walking the perimeter. He put the beer to his lips, was about to take another long swallow, when suddenly the guard fell to the ground.

Hayward stared for a moment, then blinked, not sure he had seen what he just witnessed.

"Did you—"

Carla clamped her hand over his mouth, her eyes suddenly intense, and held a finger to her lips.

Hayward wasn't sure what was going on. He tried listening but couldn't concentrate, and then suddenly he heard gunfire somewhere out front, along with the sound of engines, and—

Was that the sound of a helicopter?

Hayward pulled away from her hand, whispered, "Is it the cartel?"

The intensity in Carla's eyes flared.

"No, you idiot. It's the feds."

She glanced down at Jose, then up at the shed sitting against the hill, and then at the armed dead guard out in the field.

"Grab the boy. We're getting the fuck out of here."

FIFTY-THREE

As two teams descend on the two side buildings, Nova and I follow the third team into the main building.

They breach the door and file inside, shouting out as they clear rooms, and then work their way up to the higher floors. So far word hasn't come that they've found Hayward or Carla yet, so Nova and I start up the steps after the team when the helicopter pilot's voice speaks in my earpiece.

"We've got movement heading toward the shed. Two adults, one carrying a child. One of the adults is armed with a rifle."

I pause on the steps, turn around to look at Nova.

"That has to be Hayward and Carla."

He says, "The child?"

"My money's on a kid named Jose."

I touch the button on my mike.

"As long as they have the kid, stand down. Nova and I are in pursuit."

We hurry back down the steps, then out the back through a screen door onto the porch. Beer bottles are scattered around a chair.

The helicopter hovers above the field, shining a spotlight on the shed.

The pilot says, "They just entered through the side door."

I roger that, and Nova and I sprint across the field. We slow as we near, pistols drawn. A soft light glows from the thin space under the door.

I step to the side, aim at the door, and nod at Nova. He kicks it open, and I rush in, finger on the trigger, scanning the inside.

Besides a riding lawnmower and other landscaping equipment, the place is empty.

Nova steps up beside me.

"Looks like that Rodriguez woman was telling you the truth about everything."

I nod and start toward the rear of the shed. We find the metal trapdoor in the floor easily enough.

Without a word, Nova moves to the side of the trapdoor and grabs the metal handle. He looks at me, and whispers.

"Ready?"

I whisper, "Not yet. In case anything happens to me, I want to be honest with you about something."

"What?"

"It's hard for me to say this. Maybe because we've known each other so long, and I consider you a close friend …"

I let it hang there for a second, and then smile.

"I'm not feeling the beard."

Nova nods, like that's exactly what he expected me to say.

"I'll take it under advisement, thanks. Ready?"

I nod, and aim my gun at the trapdoor.

Nova pulls open the door. I lean forward, ready to fire at any movement below.

Nothing.

Like the shed, the tunnel has a power source. There's light down there. Not bright light, but enough for somebody to see as they move underground from one country to the next. The metal ladder has ten rungs to the bottom.

I glance at Nova, and he lets the trapdoor fall all the way back, then hustles over to retrieve a small bag of fertilizer and drops it down the hatch. It lands with a heavy thud, but nothing happens.

I say, "Cover me."

I start down the ladder, using one hand to hold on to the rungs and the other hand to hold onto my gun, and then after four rungs, I drop to the ground in a crouch, immediately aiming down the tunnel. Still nothing.

I motion at Nova up top, and he starts to climb down. As he does, I marvel at the tunnel's craftsmanship. From top to bottom, the tunnel—at least this portion—is almost six feet tall. Strong wooden beams stand every couple of feet, surrounded by chicken wire to keep the earth from falling in. Small light bulbs are strung every five feet. From this angle, the tunnel moves straight for maybe fifty yards before it starts to curve.

Once Nova's made it down the ladder, we start moving forward. We move as quietly as we can, listening for footsteps farther ahead. Imna Rodriguez claimed the tunnel was about a half mile long. It's only after the first quarter mile, as the tunnel curves again, that we spot somebody standing farther ahead.

Jose.

He stands there, motionless, his face tilted down. He doesn't look up when he hears us approaching.

It's a trap—obviously it's a trap—but I'm unclear what the end game is here. Jose is their only hostage, from what the pilot told us. Without him, we have no reason not to shoot to kill.

The tunnel past him curves again. Hayward or Carla or maybe both of them are probably hiding right around the corner. Between the two, I imagine Carla is the one who will have the rifle. Hayward is a man who can't tell the difference between a hollow point and a full metal jacket.

When we're only ten feet away, Jose's body jerks. He cries out, and falls to the ground. He starts shaking, screaming, but neither Nova nor myself advance. Instead, as much as it pains us, we wait.

We don't wait long.

Carla steps around the corner, the rifle in her hands. She starts to raise it, to fire over Jose, but before she can, I quickly put a bead on her head and pull the trigger.

She falls in a heap.

Still, Jose continues to scream and writhe on the ground. Nova covers me as I hurry toward him. I pull the key I took from Louis from my pocket, hoping it'll unlock this collar like it unlocked mine. It does, and I tear the collar off Jose's neck and fling it aside. Even in the dim light, the bruised skin ringing the boy's neck is vivid. It looks like a hideous tattoo.

The boy's no longer screaming, and he's no longer writhing, but he is crying. I touch his arm, trying to calm him, but he flinches away on instinct. It's doubtful he's ever had any human contact that wasn't abusive.

"It's all right, Jose. You're safe now."

The collar, flung a couple feet away, vibrates with electricity. Then, all at once, the buzzing stops. Which means Hayward—and the fob he's been pressing all this time—is getting farther and farther away.

"Take him back."

Nova nods, and crouches down beside the boy as he looks up at me.

"Be careful."

"He's been drinking, Nova. Plus he doesn't have a gun. I think I'll be okay."

Nova grunts.

"Famous last words."

I frown at him.

"Still not feeling the beard."

He shoots me the bird.

I continue forward, stepping over Carla's dead body, and head deeper into the tunnel.

FIFTY-FOUR

I hustle through the tunnel, staying as quiet as I can, and soon hear unsteady footsteps ahead.

I shout, "Hayward!"

The footsteps pause for a beat, then start again, this time frantically. It sounds like Hayward stumbles, falls to the ground, picks himself up and keeps running.

I pick up my pace.

The tunnel curves once more, and then straightens out. I can see the end farther ahead, maybe seventy yards away. Like the entrance on the United States side, it dead-ends to a ladder. The trapdoor must be open, because bright light pours into the tunnel.

Oliver Hayward is maybe fifty yards away. With the light beyond him, he makes for an easy target. I could put him down with one simple squeeze of the trigger. But I don't. I let him hurry forward and scramble up the ladder.

By the time I climb up the ladder, Hayward hasn't gotten far. He stands motionless with his hands raised, a half-dozen federales aiming their guns at him. The moment my head pops up through the trapdoor, a few of the men shift their guns toward me, but an older man with a mustache tells them to ignore me, and they immediately aim again at Hayward.

This section of the tunnel opens up into a garage. Cinderblock walls, cheap roofing. An old car sits off to the side. The pungent smell of motor oil hangs in the air.

Hayward says, "Don't you know who I fucking am?"

None of the federales answer. The older man with the mustache approaches me. He holds out his hand, and speaks in English.

"I am Lieutenant Nicolás Pichardo. President Cortez ordered me and my men to be here tonight."

"Thank you, Lieutenant. Did President Cortez tell you anything else?"

"President Cortez simply ordered us to come here. He said he recently learned that there is a tunnel entrance in this garage. He had us arrest the people who own this garage, and told us to take anybody who comes through this tunnel into custody."

Hayward takes one look at me, and shouts, "Yes! Take me into custody!"

Lieutenant Pichardo ignores him.

"So far tonight nobody has come through the tunnel."

I nod, thank the man, and turn to Oliver Hayward.

He flinches away from me, shouts at the federales.

"What the fuck are you waiting for? Arrest me!"

Again, none of the men move.

I step up close to Hayward.

"President Cortez and I agreed you should be prosecuted on our side of the border. If you're prosecuted here, there's a good chance the cartel would orchestrate your escape. Or your murder."

Hayward looks past me, crazed, his eyes wide.

"Don't do anything stupid, Oliver. These men have been ordered not to kill you. Besides, I don't think you have it in you to do anything stupid. You know how I know? You're not a special person. I mean, you're the kind of person who imprisons and tortures women and children, but not the kind strong enough to attempt suicide by cop."

He glares at me.

"Fine. Take me back."

I smile at him, and shake my head.

"Not yet."

I reach into my back pocket, pull out the collar I had worn the past two days. I toss it on the ground at Hayward's feet.

"Put that on."

FIFTY-FIVE

Agents are waiting for us up in the shed. As soon as Oliver Hayward climbs out of the tunnel, they take him into custody. They put handcuffs on him, and when I offer them the fob, tell them that it works wonders, they don't look amused.

I follow them up to the main building. The helicopter has landed in the field. More cars and SUVs and ambulances have arrived.

Nova meets me in front of the main building. He's talking on a cell phone, and slips it into his pocket when he spots me.

"More kids here than we expected. They kept them in the other buildings. Crisis workers are headed here as we speak."

"Where's Jose?"

Nova nods at one of the ambulances.

"He's being treated."

I look at the one side building, then the other.

"Where are the babies?"

Nova points at one of the buildings, and immediately I start moving, almost unconsciously, my pace increasing to a jog. Three of the rooms on the first floor are packed with cribs. Almost all the babies are awake and crying. A few agents move from crib to crib, taking photographs, preserving what there is of the scene before the children are taken away.

I walk up to one of the agents, incensed.

"Who's taking care of these babies?"

The agent shakes his head.

"Nobody right now. They tell us people are on their way, but no idea how long that will take."

I move from crib to crib, searching for Star. I find her in the second room. She isn't crying like the other babies, but she doesn't look happy. She stares up at me, but I'm not sure she recognizes me.

I don't realize I'm reaching in to pick her up until a female agent steps up next to me.

"Do you know her?"

I look up, startled.

"What?"

I see the woman giving me a curious look, and shake my head.

"No, I don't. But take care of her, okay? Take care of all of them."

I don't wait for a reply. I walk past the woman and head back outside. Nova's waiting for me.

He says, "What was that about?"

I ignore the question.

"Thank you."

"For what?"

"For everything. For being there when I needed you. For saving my family."

"It wasn't just me. It was a team effort."

"I know. I need to thank Atticus and James, too. My family"—I pause, shake my head—"I guess I thought disappearing would somehow keep them safe. But they're not safe. They're never going to be safe, are they?"

Nova watches me for a beat, considering.

"Atticus and I actually talked about that."

"Talked about what?"

"Your family. A way to keep them safe."

"How?"

"WITSEC."

"Witness Protection? Be serious, Nova. What are they witnesses to other than what happened today?"

"Your father, for one."

I look at Nova but say nothing. Suddenly I can't speak.

"Your father is a rogue agent. An enemy of the state. That puts your family in danger. It's more than enough to put them in protective custody. Only Atticus says he doesn't have the pull to do that."

I wet my lips, manage to find my voice.

"Then who?"

"Our old boss."

I shake my head.

"Walter and I didn't part on good terms."

"That may be so, but it's still worth looking into. Otherwise, who knows when all this might happen again?"

I look away from him, not wanting to think about it. I'd heard how close the sicario the cartels sent had gotten to my sister and nephews.

Nova clears his throat.

"It wasn't just me and James in D.C. Somebody else was with us, too."

There's something about his tone I don't like.

"Who?"

"Erik Johnson."

At first I think I don't hear him right, but then once I realize that's what he said, my body tenses.

"What? How is that possible?"

"We ran into him in Alden. It's a long story, but he came out with us to D.C. because he wanted to help. And he did help, Holly. If it wasn't for him, your sister and nephews would be dead."

I look around the area, at the buildings and the cars and the agents, and all of it looks surreal, like it doesn't exist.

"What happened, Nova?"

"I didn't want to tell you anything before all of this was over. I knew it was better for you to be focused than to—"

I cut him off.

"Tell me what happened."

"He was shot three times. One of the bullets hit him near his spine. The surgeons have been working on him all day. Atticus called a couple minutes ago with an update. He's now in stable condition."

I don't know when it happens, exactly, but I turn away from Nova and start walking. He calls after me, saying my name, but I ignore him, and to Nova's credit, he lets me have my space. Doesn't follow me as I wander into the dark field. Moving as if in trance. Past the helicopter. Going farther and farther into the night. Until my foot kicks something on the ground. In the moonlight, I see it's a large soda bottle, filled with water. One of my targets from the other day.

I turn and look back at the place Oliver Hayward calls Neverland, at the lights and the vehicles and all the agents moving about, and I think about Erik. About how I allowed myself to get close to him, and how because of that he almost got himself killed. Just like almost everybody else I come in contact with, he's been marked by death.

I clench both hands into fists, place them over my mouth.

Fall to my knees.

Close my eyes.

And scream.

CODA

"Hello, Holly."

"Hello, Atticus."

"It's good to hear your voice when it's not during a crisis."

"Ditto."

"For what it's worth, I think you've made the right decision."

"I know."

"Some may say it's the only decision you could make under the circumstances."

"I know."

"It's not just your father who's put your family in danger. It appears the cartel would like them dead as well."

I say nothing to this. At least I had no power over my father's decision to go rogue. As for the cartel targeting my family, I started that ball rolling when I killed Javier Diaz.

Atticus says, "I know it may not seem like it now, but your family will eventually understand."

I touch the side of my face. It's where Tina slapped me earlier this morning. I was there when the agents gathered my family in the room and told them the truth about my father.

Not the exact truth—not about the covert stuff—but that he had faked his death, and that he was out there somewhere working with terrorists, and as long as he was out there, they were in danger.

Then the agents told my family about me. How I had been working with the government, too. How I had done something to piss off the cartel, and that the cartel now wanted to kill them as revenge.

I was standing in a side room when this happened, watching my family through a two-way mirror. Max was in Tina's lap, while Ryan sat close to her, his arm around her shoulders, Matthew beside him. I watched my mother in her seat, staring down at her lap. Completely stunned.

At one point Tina started shouting my name. Asking where I was. Why I wasn't there to face them. She handed Max off to Ryan as she shot her to feet, and she looked around the room, maybe for something to throw in anger, and that's when she noticed the mirror. She stormed over to the mirror, stared straight ahead. It wasn't quite close to me, but it was close enough.

"Are you in there, Holly? Are you there, you bitch?"

Ryan came over and walked her back to the group, trying to calm her down. The agents told them they would all be given new identities. That they would be provided with a new home, and jobs, and enough money to make sure they could get a fresh start.

I waited until the agents finished and they directed my family out into the hallway. I knew I should have stayed away, but I stepped out as they walked past. I saw my mother first. She made eye contact, but then quickly looked away.

Tina charged at me.

"What the fuck, Holly? *What the fuck?*"

One of the agents tried to hold her back, but he wasn't fast enough. Tina slapped me, just the one time. I didn't move, didn't react, and watched as my family was ushered down the hallway toward their new lives.

In my ears, Atticus clears his throat.

"Are you still there?"

"I'm here."

"Did you see Erik this morning?"

"Yes."

"Is he doing any better?"

I think about seeing Erik last night, and this morning. He was groggy last night due to the drugs, barely remembered my visit, but this morning he had been more alert.

I sat by his bed, tried to hold his hand, but he didn't seem to care. He just lay there, staring at the muted television, while the machines around his bed kept up their incessant beeping.

I whispered, "Thank you."

He didn't respond for the longest time, and when he did, he stared ahead at the TV.

"You don't have to be here."

I'd been shot before, had been beat up, one time stabbed, but never once had words hurt me so badly.

"I want to be here."

"No, you don't."

"Erik."

His face tensed, but still he wouldn't look at me.

"I'm a cripple now. Might have to use a wheelchair all my life. You really want to be with a cripple?"

This wasn't the Erik Johnson I knew. The Erik who told me about his childhood and how he ended up in Alden. The Erik who risked his life to save my sister and nephews.

This was a new Erik, one who would probably be here for a while. I couldn't blame this new Erik. I would resent me, too.

I reached out again, took his hand in mine, squeezed it.

"I want to be with you."

Now, standing on Independence Avenue, the Botanic

Garden behind me, I watch a black SUV pull up and stop at the curb.

"Atticus, I have to go."

"Goodbye, Holly. And good luck."

I close the phone and slip it into my pocket as I step forward and open the back door.

General Walter Hadden sits inside. He doesn't look at me.

I slide into the seat, close the door, and at once the SUV starts moving.

Walter doesn't speak at first. He has an iPad in his lap, and stares straight ahead out the windshield as the driver takes us past the National Mall. He looks much older than he did when I last saw him a year ago, like he's aged five years. I note he's not wearing his wedding ring.

I ask, "How's Marilyn and the kids?"

Walter looks at me for the first time.

"I would be lying if I said I thought I would ever see you again."

"That's sweet."

He frowns.

"Haven't missed your sarcasm, that's for sure."

I nod slowly, and take a breath.

"Can we start over? I want to thank you for what you did for my family."

"I simply made some phone calls. You're the one who agreed to come back to work for Uncle Sam."

Yes, I did agree. I had no choice. Not if I wanted to make sure my family was safe. Or get a chance to track down my father and confront him one last time.

"To be honest, I'm surprised you would have me back."

He shifts in his seat, stares out his window.

"Wasn't my first choice. But the truth is, something's recently come up and I could use an extra pair of eyes."

"You already have a mission for me?"

"Less than forty-eight hours ago, while you were having your fun out in L.A., an Air Force drone pilot stole some top-secret information and flew to Germany where we believe he planned to meet with a journalist."

"Why does this sound familiar?"

"Edward Snowden practically pulled the same stunt, only he initially went to Japan."

"So what happened?"

"A non-sanctioned team was sent in to bring him back."

"Your team?"

He cuts me a quick glance.

"I don't have a team anymore. This was a team you don't know."

"Okay, so what happened?"

"The team was ambushed. Three killed, but one managed to escape."

"The drone pilot killed them?"

Walter turns on the iPad, keeps his thumb on the home button to unlock it.

"No. It was a CIA asset who intervened before the team could take the pilot."

"How do you know it was a CIA asset?"

"Because she went dark a day before it happened. And we managed to catch her on video."

Walter pulls up a photograph, tilts the tablet so I can see. It's a black and white photograph, probably taken the day she entered the Agency. A young black woman with long hair.

"Her name is Alice Morgan. Thirty-three years old. Gradu-ated from MIT, was recruited into the Agency as an analyst five years ago."

"I thought you said she was an asset."

"She was."

"Since when does an analyst become an asset?"

"Apparently she had the skills required to make it happen. And she was good at her job, Holly. Very good."

"What happened to the drone pilot and journalist?"

"They've gone off the grid. As has Alice Morgan. That's where you come in. I need you to fly to Germany to meet with the remaining team member. Try to figure out what the fuck happened."

"I have one request."

"What?"

"I'd like Nova to work with me on this."

Walter makes a small smile, and glances out his window again.

"I like Nova. Always have. He's a good man. Trusted. I'd bring him back in a heartbeat, but not for this."

"Why?"

"He has a conflict."

"What conflict?"

Walter turns back to the iPad, taps the photo of Alice Morgan.

"She's his fiancée."

ABOUT THE AUTHOR

Robert Swartwood is the *USA Today* bestselling author of *The Serial Killer's Wife*, *No Shelter*, *Man of Wax*, and several other novels. He created the term "hint fiction" and is the editor of *Hint Fiction: An Anthology of Stories in 25 Words or Fewer*. He lives with his wife in Pennsylvania.

www.ingramcontent.com/pod-product-compliance
Lightning Source LLC
Chambersburg PA
CBHW021215250626
47155CB00008B/2818